The Affirmation of Eros:
Passion and Eternity in Friedrich Nietzsche's *The Gay Science*

Thomas Ryan

Table of Contents

Abstract	ii
Declaration	iv
Acknowledgements	vii
Abbreviations	ix
Introduction	1
1. Stoic Exercises: Cosmic Indifference	12
2. Epicurean Purgatives: Pleasure, Sensation, Irritation	40
3. Platonic Ascent: The Metaphysical Pathology	57
4. La Gaya Scienza: Nietzsche and the Passions	86
5. Diagnosing Eternity	113
6. Nietzsche's Eternity: A Voluptuous Art of Living	147
Conclusion	177
Bibliography	181

Acknowledgements

I could not have completed this thesis without the support of many throughout my candidature.

My supervisors have been an invaluable source of guidance and inspiration. I would like to thank Dr Michael Ure for his patience and good-humour, Prof. Keith Ansell-Pearson for his enthusiasm, and Dr Michael Janover, now retired, for his continued generosity. I would also like to thank my honours supervisor, Dr Aurelia Armstrong, for setting me on this path.

I am grateful to all those with whom I shared and discussed parts of this thesis. I am particularly thankful for Dr John Sellars' generous and insightful comments on chapter one, Dr Simon Scott's and Assoc. Prof. Alison Ross's astute questioning during various milestones, and Assoc. Prof. Matthew Sharpe's enlightening thoughts on the Hellenistic legacy.

I would additionally like to thank Peachy Vasquez for her assistance in successfully navigating the Monash bureaucracy.

Many post-graduate colleagues from Monash, Warwick, and other institutions have acted both as thoughtful interlocutors and generous friends. I would particularly like to express my gratitude for productive discussions on Nietzsche, the Hellenistic schools, and philosophy as therapy with Leah Carr, Bethany Parsons, and Federico Testa. It was a pleasure to join the Department of Philosophy at Warwick for an intellectually stimulating four terms. From Warwick I would particularly like to thank Dr Alfonso Anaya, Matt Godwin, Dr Dino Jakušić, and Dr Alex Tissandier. Upon returning to Monash I was heartened to enjoy many long research seminars (which invariably returned to Nietzsche) with Irene Dal Poz, Rob Moseley, and Andre Okawara.

Academic friends outside philosophy have provided me with indispensable advice and support over the last five years. In particular I would like to thank Dr Ben

Abraham, Ishan Chakrabarti, Dr John Edmond, Assoc. Prof. Ben Harris-Roxas, Ryan Jones, Navid Sabet, and radical staff and students at Warwick. I am grateful for encouragement and good-natured distraction from research from Heather Blacklock, Erin Cook, Sam Crisp, Léa Danilewsky, Andie Fox, Luke Mullins, Andrew Murray, Etueni Ngaluafe, and Ren Scurville.

Lastly I would like to thank my sister Rosie, my brother-in-law Chris, and my parents Michael and Jill for all their help making it through.

Dr Robyn Kath (Philosophy, University of Sydney) provided copy-editing services in the preparation of this thesis.

Abbreviations

Works by Friedrich Nietzsche

The following editions of Nietzsche's works are used in this thesis, unless otherwise noted. Arabic numerals refer to paragraph numbers within the cited work. Roman numerals refer to a work's major divisions. "P" refers to a preface and "F" to a foreword. References to other editions and to the translations of Nietzsche's essays that are only cited infrequently can be found in the main bibliography.

ASC	"Attempt at Self-Criticism." In *The Birth of Tragedy*, edited by Raymond Geuss and Ronald Speirs, translated by Ronald Speirs. Cambridge: Cambridge University Press, 1999.
HL	"On the Utility and Liability of History for Life." In *Unfashionable Observations*, translated with an afterword by Richard T. Gray. Stanford: Stanford University Press, 1995.
RWB	"Richard Wagner in Bayreuth." In *Unfashionable Observations*, translated with an afterword by Richard T. Gray. Stanford: Stanford University Press, 1995.
HH	*Human, All Too Human: A Book for free Spirits*. Vol. 1. Translated by R. J. Hollingdale. Cambridge: Cambridge University Press, 1996.
AOM	"Assorted Opinions and Maxims." In Vol. 2 of *Human, All Too Human*. Translated by R. J. Hollingdale. Cambridge: Cambridge University Press, 1996.
WS	"The Wanderer and His Shadow." In Vol. 2 of *Human, All Too Human*. Translated by R. J. Hollingdale. Cambridge: Cambridge University Press, 1996.

D	*Daybreak: Thoughts on the Prejudices of Morality*. Edited by Maudemarie Clark and Brian Leiter. Translated by R. J. Hollingdale. Cambridge: Cambridge University Press, 1997.
GS	*The Gay Science: With a Prelude in Rhymes and an Appendix of Songs*. Translated with commentary by Walter Kaufmann. New York: Vintage Books, 1974.
Z	*Thus Spoke Zarathustra: A Book for All and None*. Edited by Adrian Del Caro and Robert Pippin. Translated by Adrian Del Caro. Cambridge: Cambridge University Press: 2006.
BGE	*Beyond Good and Evil: Prelude to a Philosophy of the Future*. Translated with commentary by Walter Kaufmann. New York: Vintage Books, 1989.
GM	*On the Genealogy of Morality: A Polemic*. Translated, with Notes, by Maudemarie Clark and Alan J. Swensen. Indianapolis and Cambridge: Hackett Publishing Company, 1998.
TI	*Twilight of the Idols: or How to Philosophise with a Hammer*. Translated by R. J. Hollingdale. London and New York: Penguin Books, 1990.
A	*The Anti-Christ*. Edited by Aaron Ridley and Judith Norman. Translated By Judith Norman. Cambridge: Cambridge University Press, 2005.
EH	*Ecce Homo: How One Becomes What One is*. Translated by R. J. Hollingdale. London and New York: Penguin Classics, 1992.
KGW	*Nietzsche Werke: Kritische Gesamtausgabe*. Edited by Giorgio Colli and Mazzino Montinari. Berlin: Walter de Gruyter, 1967–78.
KSA	*Friedrich Nietzsche: Sämtliche Werke. Kritische Studienausgabe in 15 Einzelbänden*. Edited by Giorgio Colli and Mazzino Montinari. Berlin: Walter de Gruyter, 1980.

Works by Arthur Schopenhauer

The two volumes of *The World as Will and Representation* are cited by volume and section number.

WWR 1   *The World as Will and Representation.* Vol. 1. Translated and edited by Judith Norman, Alistair Welchman, and Christopher Janaway. Cambridge: Cambridge University Press, 2010.

WWR 2   *The World as Will and Representation.* Vol. 2. Translated by E. F. J. Payne. Indian Hills, Colorado: The Falcon's Wing, 1958.

Introduction

This thesis analyses Friedrich Nietzsche's (1844–1900) development of an art of living indebted to classical and Hellenistic philosophies in *The Gay Science*. Nietzsche's debt to the ancients revolves around their shared conception of philosophy as an "art of healing the soul".[1] The philosopher as therapist or physician is one who cares for the soul in the same way the medical doctor cares for the body. While the theme of the philosophical physician is a constant presence in Nietzsche's oeuvre, his most direct engagement with ancient therapies occurs throughout the 'free-spirit trilogy', which culminates in 1882's *The Gay Science*.[2] The ancient therapeutic tradition grants Nietzsche a standpoint from which he can await a "philosophical *physician* in the exceptional sense of that word".[3] Compared with his and our contemporaries, this orientation radically alters what is at stake in the practice of philosophy, in Nietzsche's words, not "'truth' but something else—let us say, health, future, growth, power, life".[4]

Interest in Nietzsche's therapeutic orientation has grown in recent years.[5] Scholars have investigated Nietzsche's precursors in the therapeutic tradition, especially from the Hellenistic period. Congruencies, contestations, and lines of influence between

---

[1] Cicero Tusc. 3.6.

[2] For an early indication of this interest see Nietzsche's 1873 unpublished plan for an essay, "The Philosopher as Cultural Physician," in *Philosophy and Truth: Selections from Nietzsche's Notebooks of the early 1870's*, ed. and trans. Daniel Breazeale (New Jersey and London: Humanities Press International, 1990), 69–76.

[3] GS P 2, emphasis in original.

[4] GS P 2.

[5] See Michael Ure, *Nietzsche's Therapy: Self-Cultivation in the Middle Works* (Lanham: Lexington Books, 2008) and Horst Hutter and Eli Friedland, eds., *Nietzsche's Therapeutic Teaching: For Individuals and Culture* (London: Bloomsbury, 2013).

Nietzsche and the Skeptics,[6] the Cynics,[7] the Epicureans,[8] and the Stoics[9] have been explored. The influence of the Stoics and Epicureans on Nietzsche has rightfully received the greater part of scholarly attention. Nietzsche suggests that these two schools are the "experimental laboratories" we should avail ourselves of in living our own lives.[10] In significant sections of *The Gay Science* Nietzsche evokes Stoicism[11] and Epicureanism[12] to either illustrate or give contrast to his own position.

Viewing Nietzsche through the lens of the Hellenistic schools also accords with a broader trend to reconsider the philosophical significance of this period. The work of Michel Foucault,[13] Pierre Hadot,[14] and Martha Nussbaum,[15] amongst others[16] has

---

[6] Jessica Berry, *Nietzsche and the Ancient Skeptical Tradition* (New York: Oxford University Press, 2011).

[7] R. Bracht Branham, "Nietzsche's Cynicism: Uppercase or lowercase?," in *Nietzsche and Antiquity: His Reaction and Response to the Classical Tradition*, ed. Paul Bishop (Rochester, NY: Camden House, 2004), 170–81.

[8] See Richard Bett, "Nietzsche, the Greeks, and Happiness (with Special Reference to Aristotle and Epicurus)," *Philosophical Topics* 33, no. 2 (2005): 45–70; Howard Caygill, "Under the Epicurean skies," *Angelaki* 11, no. 3 (2006): 107–15; Keith Ansell-Pearson, "Heroic-Idyllic Philosophizing: Nietzsche and the Epicurean Tradition," *Royal Institute of Philosophy Supplements* 74 (2014): 237–63; and Keith Ansell-Pearson, ed., "Nietzsche & Epicureanism," special issue, *The Agonist* 10, no. 2 (2017).

[9] See Martha C. Nussbaum, "Pity and Mercy: Nietzsche's Stoicism," in *Nietzsche, Genealogy, Morality*, ed. Richard Schacht (University of California Press, 1994), 139–67; R. O. Elveton, "Nietzsche's Stoicism: The Depths Are Inside," in *Nietzsche and Antiquity: His Reaction and Response to the Classical Tradition*, ed. Paul Bishop (Rochester, NY: Camden House, 2004), 192–204; Nuno Nabais, "Nietzsche and Stoicism," chap. 4 in *Nietzsche & the Metaphysics of the Tragic* (London: Continuum, 2006), 85–98; Thomas H. Brobjer, "Nietzsche's Reading of Epictetus," *Nietzsche-Studien* 32, no. 1 (2008): 429–52; Michael Ure, "Nietzsche's Free-Spirit Trilogy and Stoic Therapy," *Journal of Nietzsche Studies* 38 (2009): 60–84; Aurelia Armstrong, "The Passions, Power, and Practical Philosophy: Spinoza and Nietzsche Contra the Stoics," *Journal of Nietzsche Studies* 44, no. 1, (2013): 6–24; and Michael Ure, "Sublime Losers: Stoicism in Nineteenth Century German Philosophy," in *The Routledge Handbook of the Stoic Tradition*, ed. John Sellars (London: Routledge, 2015), 287–302.

[10] KSA 9:15[59].

[11] GS Prelude 34; GS 12; GS 99; GS 122; GS 305–6; GS 326.

[12] GS 45; GS 277; GS 306; GS 375.

[13] Michel Foucault, *The History of Sexuality*, vol. 3, *The Care of The Self* (New York: Pantheon Books, 1986); Michael Ure, "Senecan Moods: Foucault and Nietzsche on the Art of the Self," *Foucault Studies* 4 (2007): 19–52.

[14] Pierre Hadot, *What is Ancient Philosophy?*, trans. Michael Chase (Cambridge, MA: Belknap, 2004); Pierre Hadot, *Philosophy as a Way of Life: Spiritual Exercises from Socrates to Foucault*, trans. Michael Chase (Oxford: Blackwell, 1995).

[15] Martha Nussbaum, *The Therapy of Desire: Theory and Practice in Hellenistic Ethics* (Princeton: Princeton University Press, 1994).

[16] See Bethany Parsons and Andre Okawara, eds., "Self-Cultivation: Ancient and Modern," special issue, *Pli* (2016).

brought the ethical practices of the Hellenistic schools to wider philosophical attention. What these scholars draw from the Hellenistic sources is an approach to ethical deliberation centred on questions of the self, processes of self-formation, and the good life. This agent-centric approach provides an alternative to the narrow focus on right action of major ethical traditions. Nietzsche is a common reference point for those working on philosophies of self-formation. Consequently, a fuller elaboration of his contribution to the reception of the Hellenistic schools will advance not only the understanding of his philosophy, but this significant and growing strand of moral philosophy.

Notwithstanding the obvious importance of the Stoics and Epicureans to Nietzsche during his middle period, his ultimate rejection of the Hellenistic therapies and the terms of this rejection are relatively undeveloped. Why did Nietzsche turn away from the schools that at one point seemed to offer a viable way out of that "incautious and pampering spiritual diet, called romanticism"?[17] The claim of this thesis is that despite a common therapeutic orientation, we will not comprehend the depth and subtlety of Nietzsche's art of living unless we recognise his radical break with his forebears.

This thesis draws on the concept of eros to make sense of this reversal. It demonstrates that Nietzsche challenges Hellenistic therapies precisely for their exclusion of eros. Stoic *apatheia* and Epicurean *ataraxia* are two instances of the wider ancient understanding of happiness as tranquillity. They manifest the "desire for tranquillity" which, according to Nietzsche, motivated ancient philosophy more generally.[18] They hope to achieve tranquillity by eliminating (in the case of Stoicism) or diminishing (in the case of Epicureanism) our attachment to transient objects. Nietzsche claims that the ancient valorisation of tranquillity is symptomatic of an underlying cowardice in relation to the passions. But rather than cure this fear, the Hellenistic therapies offer merely palliative treatments which serve only to deepen their

---

[17] GS P 1.

[18] GS 110.

patients' malady.[19] Nietzsche hones in on the role of eternity in effecting these malignant or failed 'therapies': eternity promises the deliverance from transience.

Eros is not only the central concept of Nietzsche's criticism of the ancients. It is also plays a central role in the development of his own ethics of self-fashioning. Nietzsche's recuperation of eros allows him to investigate and experiment with forms of life that philosophers have hitherto either derided or ignored. *The Gay Science* is a pivotal moment in this development, because it is here that the role of eros and love in the good life becomes apparent. The passions, Nietzsche suggests, allow for a voluptuous enjoyment of life.

Nietzsche formalises his conditions for the affirmation of life in the doctrine of the eternal recurrence. Not only does the doctrine establish a passionately inflamed state of longing as Nietzsche's ideal. It directly challenges, and seeks to displace, the ancient ethics of eternity. While the ancient desire for eternity was premised on the denial of the passions, Nietzsche's craving for eternity entails affirming the intoxication of desire. By reading the renowned section 341 in the context of the pedagogy of eros Nietzsche puts forward in book four of *The Gay Science*, the thesis challenges and develops recent interpretations of this key doctrine,[20] namely the long-neglected 'cosmological' understanding,[21] and a particular development of the more popular 'practical' or 'existential' line of interpretation that I dub 'heroic'.[22] The existing literature does not sufficiently account for the central role of eros in the doctrine of the eternal recurrence. By connecting eros to the doctrine, the thesis better explains the importance of the eternal recurrence to Nietzsche's art of living.

---

[19] See Thomas Ryan and Michael Ure, "Nietzsche's Post-Classical Therapy," *Pli* 25 (2014): 91–110.

[20] See Lawrence J. Hatab, *Nietzsche's Life Sentence* (New York and London: Routledge, 2005), 115–25; Paul S. Loeb, "Eternal Recurrence," in *The Oxford Handbook of Nietzsche*, eds. Ken Gemes and John Richardson (Oxford: Oxford University Press, 2013), 645–71.

[21] Paul S. Loeb, *The Death of Nietzsche's Zarathustra* (Cambridge: Cambridge University Press, 2010), 11–31.

[22] Bernard Reginster, *The Affirmation of Life: Nietzsche on Overcoming Nihilism* (Cambridge, MA: Harvard University Press, 2006), 224–26.

By systematising Nietzsche's post-classical art of living, this thesis lays the necessary groundwork for further questions about Nietzsche's philosophical project. The most pressing such question concerns the viability of the passion for knowledge in sustaining a post-classical philosophy or, in other words, whether Nietzsche successfully rescues the philosophical drive for truth from its nihilistic impasse. Does *The Gay Science* present an alternative to the 'moraline' unconditional will to truth?[23] Nietzsche himself asks "To what extent can truth endure incorporation? That is the question; that is the experiment".[24] The achievement of this thesis is to give coherence to Nietzsche's diagnoses of past philosophies as forms of sickness, alongside the centrality of eternity, both to these diagnoses and to the prospects of devising a viable therapy.

Chapter one contextualises Nietzsche's affirmative, post-classical art of living through his shifting evaluation and ultimate rejection of Stoicism across the works of his middle period (1878–1882). Recent scholarship has explored Nietzsche's meta-philosophical debt to the Stoics incurred in his therapeutic conception of philosophy.[25] While I refer to Nietzsche's diagnosis of indifference as a symptom of a Stoic temperament, my primary concern in this thesis is with the substantive issue of the role of the passions in the good life. On this substantive issue, the apparent similarity between the cosmic perspective of the Stoic sage and the Nietzschean intoxication with the world belies a deeper incompatibility between the two ethical projects.

This chapter analyses Nietzsche's volte-face on Stoic indifference, from apparent endorsement in *Human, All Too Human* to sustained attack in *The Gay Science*. The charge in the later work is that the Stoic disposition evacuates the world of value. The

---

[23] On Nietzsche's tortured reflections on the will to truth, see Maudemarie Clark, *Nietzsche on Truth and Philosophy* (Cambridge: Cambridge University Press, 1990); Bernard Williams, *Truth and Truthfulness* (Princeton: Princeton University Press, 2002), 12–19; and Christopher Janaway, "The Gay Science," in *The Oxford Handbook of Nietzsche*, eds. Ken Gemes and John Richardson (Oxford: Oxford University Press, 2013), 267–69. See also Nietzsche's claim in A 6 that he makes a *"moraline-free"* (emphasis in original) judgement on humanity.

[24] GS 110.

[25] See Ure, *Nietzsche's Therapy*; Hutter and Friedland, *Nietzsche's Therapeutic Teaching*; Marta Faustino, review of *Kulturkritik et philosophie thérapeutique chez le jeune Nietzsche*, by Martine Béland, *Journal of Nietzsche Studies* 47, no. 3 (2016): 488–92.

tranquillity granted by Stoic indifference turns on the opposition between the *pathê* and universal reason. The Stoic aspiration to embody universal reason implies the destruction of the passions. While Nietzsche inherits Schopenhauer's criticism of the Stoics as hypocritically driven by pride, he deepens its force by rejecting the tranquillity of the sage as monotonous. The Stoic aspires to expand the boundaries of the self by eliminating the passions; Nietzsche's ethical ideal pursues the same goal by incorporating an ever more comprehensive and diverse panoply of affects.

In *The Gay Science*, Nietzsche unfavourably compares the Stoic's hard and insensitive temperament with the Epicurean's "subtle irritability" [*feine Reizbarkeit*].[26] Whereas the Stoic denies the pleasures and pains of the world, taking pride in his capacity to heroically endure the accidents of existence, the Epicurean admits of these pleasures and pains and, due to his sensitive disposition, selects his surrounds carefully to suit. Nietzsche's rejection of Stoic rationalism leads him to an engagement with Epicurus' school.

Chapter two examines Nietzsche's sympathetic, yet ultimately critical, assessment of the Epicureans. Nietzsche turns to Epicureanism over Stoicism because the Epicureans' sensitivity to accident is a necessary condition for the good life. Nietzsche finds a "subtle irritability" preferable to Stoic insensitivity because it allows for a deeper and richer attachment to the world: the Epicurean has the means to escape Stoic monotony.[27]

In the second volume of *Human, All Too Human*, Nietzsche praises Epicureanism as an antidote to metaphysical anxiety and speculation. It is Epicurus' "wonderful insight" that "to quieten the heart it is absolutely not necessary to have solved the ultimate and outermost theoretical questions".[28] He expresses sympathy for the modest happiness of Epicurus who needs only "a little garden, figs, little cheeses and in addition three or

---

[26] GS 306.

[27] GS 306.

[28] WS 7.

four good friends".[29] By the time of *The Gay Science*, however, Nietzsche departs from and criticises Epicurus' modest happiness. Epicureans cope with their irritable temperament by fleeing to the garden. More precisely, Nietzsche argues that Epicurean *therapeia* consists of purgative exercises that aim at protecting its patient from transience. In *The Gay Science* he rejects Epicurus' negative hedonism as a coping strategy born of weakness. He reverses Epicurus' recommendation to flee into the garden, counselling "build your cities on the slopes of Vesuvius!" and "live dangerously!"[30] While the Epicureans possess the temperament to forge an intense attachment to life, Nietzsche claims, they lack the audacity to pursue an adventurous, experimental art of living. By the end of his middle period, Nietzsche sees Epicurean voluptuousness as too modest. In contrast, he encourages "thirsty life and drunkenness of life"[31] and an "insatiable lust for possession and spoils".[32] Thus *The Gay Science* augurs the return of Dionysus in the post-Zarathustran works. Chapter two systematises Nietzsche's qualified praise and ultimate rejection of the Epicurean philosophical therapy.

Throughout *The Gay Science*, Nietzsche uses Stoicism and Epicureanism to articulate his own anti-Hellenistic art of living. Where Stoicism withdraws and Epicureanism contracts one's sensitivity to transience, Nietzsche considers the expansion, in both scope and intensity, of one's entanglement with transient objects as a necessary condition of a sufficiently strong attachment to life. This demand implies a recuperation of eros: one must not just endure life, one must love it.[33]

Chapter three approaches Nietzsche's anti-Hellenistic recuperation of eros through his relationship with Plato. The chapter focuses on Plato's pedagogy of eros in *The*

---

[29] WS 192.

[30] GS 283, emphasis in original.

[31] GS 278.

[32] GS 292.

[33] GS 276; GS 326; GS 334; GS 341.

Symposium, wherein tranquillity is guaranteed by love of the ever-present and unchanging form of the good. Plato's philosophical lover escapes the vulnerability of human erotic aspiration to the transient nature of its object by means of the ascent to metaphysics.

Nietzsche considers Schopenhauerian resignation as the logical and historical culmination of Platonism. Plato and Schopenhauer's accounts of desire are connected by their shared belief that the transcendence of desire is the only condition of its satisfaction. Schopenhauer combines this belief with the disenchanting knowledge that such transcendence is an illusion. Schopenhauer's disbelief in transcendence leads to his advocacy for the "denial and abandonment of all willing" and thereby "a passage into empty *nothingness*".[34]

For Nietzsche, an empty nothingness is the horizon of possibility for the Platonic–Schopenhauerian account of desire. Our inherited Platonism fails as an art of living because it cannot sustain an attachment to life. He names this failure of desire nihilism. To overcome nihilism, then, he requires a rejuvenated account of desire and the passions *not* tied to the possibility of transcendence.

Chapter four investigates Nietzsche's rejuvenated account of the passions in *The Gay Science*. The genealogy of the *Leidenschaften* shows the importance of the Augustinian case against the Stoics and the post-Augustinian secular love poetry of the Provençal troubadours for the conceptual history of the passions. Nietzsche's allusion to the troubadours in the first volume of *The Gay Science* is made explicit in its second volume, which he subtitles "*la gaya scienza*". Only by following both the conceptual history of the passions and Nietzsche's shifting evaluation of the passions across the middle period can we make sense of Nietzsche's self-conscious allusions to the troubadours he claims invented passionate love.[35]

---

[34] WWR 1.71.

[35] BGE 230.

The second part of the chapter traces the development of Nietzsche's account of the passions, from *Human, All Too Human* to *The Gay Science*, where the passions are a necessary condition of the good life. This development is illustrated with reference to the prefaces Nietzsche writes for his earlier works in 1886. In these prefaces, Nietzsche claims that each work is one rung on "a long ladder upon whose rungs we ourselves have sat and climbed".[36] Nietzsche's ascent arrives at a happiness premised upon the flourishing of the passions.

Chapter five tightens the focus of Nietzsche's break with the ancients to the role of eternity in consoling for the fear of death. Nietzsche contests the characterisations of eternity present in the main ethical traditions of antiquity because, he argues, these characterisations express pathological judgments about the value of existence. In Platonism, the eternal is conceived as unchanging, perfect, and immune to the passage of time. In Stoicism, the eternal appears as the dynamic, but lawful and rational procession of nature. In Epicureanism, eternity figures in the infinite descent of dead atoms through void, as the painlessness before birth and after death to which the philosopher aspires. Nietzsche holds that these figures' veneration of the unchanging, the rational, and the painless entails a concomitant contempt for transient particulars and the natural lives these transient particulars comprise.

Nietzsche shows how in each tradition we find a refraction of a common fear of transience. His diagnosis in each particular case exposes an acute awareness of and hostility to transient existence. The diagnoses of classical figurations of eternity as *kronophobic* poses the question of how Nietzsche's affirmation ethics coheres with his renovated conception of eternity, the eternal recurrence.[37] Plato and Nietzsche agree that the passions put eternity at stake. How does Nietzsche's conception of the passions allow him to avoid the enervating eternities of the ancients?

---

[36] HH P 7.

[37] Bernd Magnus coins the term *kronophobic* to endorse Nietzsche's diagnoses of traditional understandings of eternity as symptomatic of a fear of transience. See "Nietzsche's Eternalistic Counter-Myth," *The Review of Metaphysics* 26, no. 4 (1973): 604–16.

Chapter six answers the question posed in chapter five by linking Nietzsche's voluptuous art of living with the doctrine of the eternal recurrence. Nietzsche elaborates his position in relation to the Hellenistic schools. In particular, he attacks the Hellenistic aspiration to live a complete life in a single moment. This aspiration, Nietzsche claims, is a symptom of old age. I consider Nietzsche's opposition between youthfulness and senescence in his 'untimely' essay *On the Utility and Liability of History for Life*. In that work Nietzsche was concerned with the debilitating effects of an overgrown historical sense, seeking refuge from history in youthful naïvety. In *The Gay Science*, his rejuvenated account of the passions allows for a more sophisticated pedagogy of eros. Love, he claims, has to be learned.[38] Rather than blind folly, Nietzsche expounds a sensitivity and exposure to transience as necessary for a sufficiently intense attachment to life.

Against both classical philosophical therapies and contemporary interpretations of Nietzsche, I show how his voluptuous art of living implies an intoxication with and enjoyment of desire. The centrality of eros to the good life sheds light on the doctrine of the eternal recurrence. One longs for the eternal recurrence of life if and only if one has learned to love oneself in Nietzsche's sense of the intoxication of unquenchable desire. This reading develops the 'practical' interpretation of the doctrine of the eternal recurrence as pertaining to the character of the affirmation of life, rather than the 'theoretical' claim that life is eternally recurrent. It challenges 'practical' interpretations that hold that the affirmation of the eternal recurrence heralds the cancelation of desire. On the contrary, the doctrine implies the enjoyment and intensification of the desire for nothing but one's life repeated into eternity. This passionately inflamed state of longing is Nietzsche's image of health, not just for himself ("what is it to us that Herr Nietzsche has become well again?") but for humanity.[39]

---

[38] GS 334.

[39] GS P 2.

This thesis develops our understanding of Nietzsche's art of living, first by showing how he formulates it as an explicit challenge to ancient philosophies and *therapeia*, which he comes to conceive as illnesses, and second by clarifying and systematising the significance of his recuperation of eros as a necessary condition of affirmation. Nietzsche's ethics of affirmation requires the affirmation of and by eros.

1. Stoic Exercises: Cosmic Indifference

Writing on Nietzsche's engagement with Stoicism, Martha Nussbaum argues that the Stoic practice of indifference to external goods is a kind of self-protection that expresses a fear of the world and all of its contingencies.[1] Far from his claims to strength and peace of mind, the Stoic "looks like a fearful person, a person who is determined to seal himself off from risk, even at the cost of loss of love and value".[2] Nietzsche makes a similar claim about Stoicism in *The Gay Science*. The Stoic, here, exchanges a life of external pain and pleasure for one of internal virtue, because the life beholden to external commitments is plagued by pain and burden.[3] Nietzsche questions this exchange and the pessimism it contains regarding external goods: "We are *not so badly off* that we have to be as badly off as Stoics".[4]

Nevertheless, an earlier Nietzsche strongly endorses the Stoic temperament. Discussing how one responds to the terrible knowledge that value falsifies the world,[5] Nietzsche praises those "firm, mild and at bottom cheerful soul[s]" who live in accordance with nature and who forgo "much, indeed almost everything upon which other men place value".[6] These souls achieve a simpler and emotionally cleaner life

---

[1] This modern view of Stoicism follows Hegel's influential account in his lectures on the Philosophy of History. Under the chaotic political conditions of the Roman empire "the whole state of things urged [individuals] to yield themselves to fate, and to strive for a perfect indifference to life – an indifference which they sought either in freedom of thought [Stoicism] or in directly sensuous enjoyment [Epicureanism]". These two Hellenistic schools, with Skepticism, served this goal by "rendering the soul absolutely indifferent to everything the real world had to offer". (Georg Wilhelm Friedrich Hegel, *The Philosophy of History*, trans. John Sibree [Mineola, NY: Dover, 1956], 317–18). For further discussion of Hegel's reception of Stoicism see John Sellars, "Marcus Aurelius in Contemporary Philosophy," in *A Companion to Marcus Aurelius*, ed. Marcel van Ackeren (Chichester, UK and Malden, MA: Wiley-Blackwell, 2012), 532–44 and Michael Ure, "Stoicism in Nineteenth-Century German Philosophy," in *The Routledge Handbook of the Stoic Tradition*, ed. John Sellars (Routledge, 2015), 287–302.

[2] Martha C. Nussbaum, "Pity and Mercy: Nietzsche's Stoicism," in *Nietzsche, Genealogy, Morality*, ed. Richard Schacht (University of California Press, 1994), 160.

[3] Epictetus defends this exchange in the Encheiridion 13; 25.

[4] GS 326, emphasis in original.

[5] That "every belief in the value and dignity of life rests on false thinking" (HH 33).

[6] HH 34.

through the purifying pursuit of knowledge, as the Stoic achieves a tranquil state of mind through communion with universal reason.

Nietzsche explains his shifting assessment of the Stoic temperament between 1878's *Human, All Too Human* and 1882's *The Gay Science* in his preface to the latter's second edition. This book marks the convalescence from a period of "determined self-limitation to what was bitter, harsh, and hurtful to know" during which his pain was overcome only by a "tyranny of pride" not to suffer the nauseous consequences of pain.[7] He credits his recovery to a cheerfulness that allows him the "attraction of everything problematic", the chance for adventure, and a love of life like that for someone who "causes doubts in us".[8] Already in 1881's *Dawn*, Nietzsche considers his engagement with Stoicism in this manner. Wracked by physical sickness, Nietzsche requires above all a defence "against all pessimism".[9] Such is provided by a pride which holds the thoughtless comforts of the healthy—"the noblest and most beloved of the illusions in which he himself formerly indulged"—in contempt.[10] Nietzsche uses this pride, and the bitter contempt which accompanies it, as a counterweight against his intense physical pain: as an "*advocate* of *life* in the face of [the] tyrant [of pain]".[11] Despite its role in combatting sickness, this pride remains a consequence and condition thereof. At the crack of convalescence, when pride is no longer required to combat physical pain, it appears to Nietzsche as "vain and foolish", as a dominating influence that he will seek to fend off.

If Nietzsche rebukes Stoicism as itself a condition of sickness, it is not so obvious what work his new notion of cheerfulness—"what above all is needed"[12]—does in distancing his new health from Stoicism. To this end, this chapter sets out the Stoic

---

[7] GS P1.
[8] GS P3.
[9] D 114.
[10] D 114.
[11] D 114, emphasis in original.
[12] GS P4.

cheerfulness that Nietzsche endorses in *Human, All Too Human*, and seeks to explain how he comes to regard this cheerfulness as insufficient for human flourishing in *The Gay Science* and beyond.

In this chapter I investigate Stoicism as a philosophical therapy and Nietzsche's debt to this approach. I begin with an examination of the chief Stoic teaching, to live according to nature, according to the early Greek Stoic Chrysippus (c. 282–206 BCE). I lay out the attendant doctrine of indifference to external goods, noting the modern objections of Schopenhauer and Nietzsche. I follow the debate over nature and indifference to the later Roman Stoics, in particular Seneca (c. 1 BCE–65 CE), Epictetus (c. 55–135 CE), and Marcus Aurelius (121–180 CE). I find three intertwined currents of thought regarding the Stoic ideal: of moderation, of asceticism, and of cosmic consent. After teasing out the congruities and tensions between these three notions, I situate Nietzsche in relation to these Stoic ideals, especially in relation to the cosmos, a site of philosophical reflection.

In what follows my purpose is two-fold. First I would like to elaborate an account of Stoicism with sufficient fidelity to explain its influence on Nietzsche. This is necessary to grasp both his explicit praise of Stoicism in *Human, All Too Human*, and his continuing implicit reference to the conceptual tools of Stoicism through *Dawn* and *The Gay Science*. The second motive behind this chapter is to understand the terms of Nietzsche's explicit rejection of Stoicism in *Dawn* and *The Gay Science*. For this end what is required is an account of how Nietzsche conceptualised Stoicism in the early 1880s. Notwithstanding his previous classical scholarship, Nietzsche increasingly identifies Stoicism with a philosophical disposition, expressed in but not confined to, the school's doctrines. His criticisms take on the form of a diagnosis of the pathologies of this disposition rather than a direct confrontation with Stoic doctrine. In both aspects, the aim of this chapter is to lay the groundwork for Nietzsche's ethics of affirmation in *The Gay Science*, which will be elaborated in the following chapters.

Life according to nature

Diogenes Laertius tells us that the founder of the Stoic school, Zeno (c. 333–261 BCE), was the first to recommend the life lived "in agreement with nature".[13] Stobaeus, to the contrary, says that Zeno only taught to live harmoniously with oneself, that is, "in accordance with one concordant reason".[14] Stobaeus leaves the Stoic concern for nature to Zeno's successors: first Cleanthes (c. 331–232 BCE), who taught to live in harmony with nature as a whole, and then Chrysippus, who taught to live in harmony with the "experience of what happens by nature".[15] In either case, it was not until Chrysippus (the third Stoic leader) that Stoic doctrine was collected and systematised to the extent that the orthodoxy of the life lived according to nature could be established.[16] Before him, there was a diversity of opinions amongst Zeno's students as to the proper end of life;[17] with him the question was settled.

Chrysippus' highly systematised account of the end has a dual character. If Zeno's teaching was of internal consistency, and Cleanthes' was of consistency with the cosmos as a whole, Chrysippus marries both conceptions together in his recommendation that one live according to "both universal nature and more particularly the nature of man".[18] This dual imperative is only possible because of the connection the Stoics draw between the individual's nature and the nature of the whole, namely that one regulative principle, reason, pervades both the whole cosmos and each individual. The law of the cosmos is human rationality writ large. Indeed, the position

---

[13] DL 7.87.

[14] Stobaeus 2.75,11–76,8 = LS 63B.

[15] Stobaeus 2.75,11–76,8 = LS 63B.

[16] John Sellars, *Stoicism* (Chesham: Acumen, 2006), 8.

[17] Besides Cleanthes, two other students of Zeno and putative Stoics, Herillus and Dionysius, declared the goal of life to be, respectively, knowledge and pleasure. (DL 7.166–67.)

[18] DL 7.89.

that human nature is an intrinsic part of cosmic nature is one of Stoicism's enduring tenets.[19]

The Stoics hold that the central concern of human nature is self-preservation. This is an instance of their more general claim that all individuals (human and otherwise) naturally seek to maintain their own constitution. This concern is given to the individual by cosmic nature, through a process encompassed by the Stoic term *oikeiôsis*. The term describes the manner in which nature disposes the individual towards its own constitution. Because the individual is well-disposed or endeared to itself by nature,[20] acting on this disposition is at once to act according to one's own nature and according to nature as a whole. Because plants, animals, and humans differ in their constitution, they will differ in the kind of life which nature prescribes, but the underlying principle—the maintenance of this constitution—is the same.

The theory of *oikeiôsis* contrasts sharply with the claim of other Hellenistic schools that pleasure is a human's first and natural impulse. But more than a simple counter-argument, the theory serves as the basis of Stoic ethics. Ethics begins, for the Stoics, with the observation that amongst the animals, nature has bestowed reason on humans alone.[21] Nature regulates plants through appropriate vegetative processes. Animals, which have been additionally granted impulse and sensation, live according to nature by following these faculties. In humans, "vegetative" processes like digestion as well as impulse and sensation are still operative, but to these reason has been added. While the constitution of non-human animals is tended to by impulse, humans are characteristically rational and hence require maintenance of their rational constitution: their soul.

---

[19] Brad Inwood and Pierluigi Donini, "Stoic Ethics," in *The Cambridge History of Hellenistic Philosophy*, (Cambridge: Cambridge University Press, 1999), 676.

[20] *Oikeiôsis* is reportedly a difficult term to translate. Pembroke uses "well-disposed" (S. G. Pembroke, "Oikeiôsis," in *Problems in Stoicism*, ed. A. A. Long [London and Atlantic Highlands: The Athlone Press, 1971], 116), while Hicks uses "endeared" (DL 7.85), and Inwood and Donini use "affiliation" (Inwood and Donini, "Stoic Ethics," 677).

[21] DL 7.86.

According to the Stoics, value resides in those objects which aid in the preservation of the rational soul. What falls within the Stoic's ethical concern is what pertains to the rational soul: correct and incorrect judgements. Nevertheless the Stoic, as a rational animal, remains an animal, and external goods may nurture or harm her constitution at a pre-rational, pre-ethical level. Since food, shelter, and other external goods neither aid nor harm the preservation of the rational soul, they do not fall within the Stoic's ethical concern. In this sense, it is appropriate to human nature to value health, family, and social relations, if only ever "under reserve" or "if Fate permits".[22]

> Those objects of one's primary impulses such as food or health or wealth, although apparently beneficial to every human being, do not contribute to the preservation of a rational being *qua* rational being. They only contribute to its survival *qua* animal.[23]

Acting under reserve, the Stoic insulates herself from disappointment should such external goods (which it is appropriate to take and enjoy) prove to be out of reach.[24] The Stoics nominate external objects, which neither aid nor harm one's rational soul, as indifferents.

Indifference in theory

The Stoic indifference to external goods is conditioned by an awareness of vulnerability in the external world. Our lives are inexorably subject to the procession of fate and external causes, no matter what our individual desires and aversions may be. A desire for external goods will be either fulfilled or frustrated, but according to the Stoics which outcome eventuates is not under our control. To judge an external object as a good or an evil is, therefore, to give one's happiness as a hostage to fate. The only route to "happiness", according to the Stoics, is through that which is under our control: "the

---

[22] Pierre Hadot, *What is Ancient Philosophy?* (Cambridge, MA: Belknap Press, 2004), 134.

[23] John Sellars, *The Art of Living: The Stoics on the Nature and Function of Philosophy* (Aldershot: Ashgate, 2003), 58.

[24] Richard Sorabji, *Emotions and Peace of Mind: From Stoic Agitation to Christian Temptation* (Oxford: Oxford University Press, 2000), 54.

will to do good and to act in conformity with reason".[25] Thus Epictetus, for whom Nietzsche developed an admiration during the period of *Human, All Too Human*'s publication,[26] counsels that we should cultivate an indifference towards what is not under our control, since it cannot contribute to our virtue. This condition prohibits the sacrifice of one's virtue for bodily pleasure or physical health,[27] or the impassioned pursuit of the social goods of reputation, property and office, since the attainment of these goods does not fall exclusively under our own control. The Stoic will, rather, treat these external goods as a matter of indifference, and will not judge their attainment or loss as a good or an evil. This does not, as we have seen, preclude the Stoic from holding preferences amongst the indifferents; for instance she may prefer health to sickness, as long as she is not misled into the belief that such preferences contribute to her virtue.

The Stoic who holds preferences between indifferents is in an uncomfortable position. She is committed to distinguishing between, for example, a feast and a plain loaf of bread, even though she denies there is any difference in value between the two. There would appear to be no basis, if the Stoic account of value is correct, for preferring one over the other. The Stoics overcome this difficulty by appealing to the distinction between an individual's rational constitution (the real grounds of virtue) and animal constitution (the grounds of mere preferences). The Stoic may *prefer* one indifferent to another, so long as she does not incorrectly judge it a good.

The Stoic term for the appropriate pursuit of preferred indifferents, according to reason and without mistaking an indifferent for a good, is *eklogé* (selection). Epictetus quotes Chrysippus' defence of the selection of preferred indifferents under reserve:

---

[25] Hadot, *What is Ancient Philosophy?*, 127.

[26] Thomas H. Brobjer, "Nietzsche's Reading of Epictetus," *Nietzsche-Studien* 32 (2008): 430.

[27] The contrast between Epictetus, for whom "disease is an impediment to the body, but not to the moral purpose" (Ench. 9) and Nietzsche, for whom philosophy *is* the transposition of states of health and disease "into the most spiritual form and distance" (GS P3) is here striking.

> "As long as the consequences are not clear to me, I cleave ever to what is better adapted to secure those things that are in accordance with nature; for God himself has created me with the faculty of choosing things [*eklektikón*]. But if I knew that it was fated (in the order of things) for me to be sick, I would even move towards it."[28]

The division between goods and preferred indifferents rests on the independence of one's virtue from one's bodily conditions. This distinction does not rest on a dualism between mind and body, since the Stoic's materialism extends to the mind's bodily nature.[29]

For the Stoics, virtue consists in the state in which the harmful emotions, the *pathê*, are eliminated. The emotions are precisely those cognitions through which we misapprehend nature: they are mistaken judgements. This understanding of emotions allows the Stoic to undergo various bodily and mental disturbances with her virtue, and hence *apatheia*, intact. *Pathos*, for Seneca, "does not consist in being moved by the impressions that are presented to the mind, but in surrendering to these and following up such a chance prompting".[30] These "first movements" [*propatheia*] include physical movements, such as the buckling of one's knees before danger, as well as "bites and little contractions of the mind".[31] Such movements are involuntary, and only become emotions if one assents to their occurrence as appropriate, an independent volition.

Nietzsche agrees with the Stoic counsel, to subject one's primary inclinations and aversions to the strictures of "our reason and our experience".[32] He claims that these feelings originate in often false, disguised, and inherited judgements that one ought to replace with one's own. Yet he is unwilling to grant the stronger Stoic claim that one's capacity for judgement is independent of the feelings brought about by one's bodily and mental constitution. In *The Gay Science* he cautions that certain diets produce

---

[28] Epict Diss. 2.6.9–10.

[29] Friedrich Albert Lange, *The History of Materialism* (London: Routledge & K Paul, 2010), 97. While Lange's *History of Materialism* was influential for Nietzsche's account of the Hellenistic schools, we can find a contemporary and competing account of Stoicism's psychophysical holism in Christopher Gill, *The Structured Self in Hellenistic and Roman Thought* (Oxford: Oxford University Press, 2006).

[30] Sen. De Ira 2.3.1–2.

[31] Sorabji, *Emotion and Peace of Mind*, 67.

[32] D 35.

"ways of thinking and feeling that have narcotic effects".[33] In his later *Ecce Homo*, Nietzsche argues that nourishment, location, and climate, "little things which according to the traditional judgement are matters of indifference", are constitutive of one's virtue. Here Nietzsche denies the independence of conscious thought from bodily and mental conditions on which the Stoic division between goods and preferred indifferents depends, and thus the security of the happiness achieved solely through intellectual virtue.[34]

Schopenhauer attacks not only the security of Stoic happiness, but its possibility. Schopenhauer claims that Stoic happiness, the blissful life free from emotional disturbance, is unattainable, even for "those purely rational types", practical philosophers.[35] This is because, on his account, "the blissful life" contains an inner contradiction. According to Schopenhauer, life on earth is a "narrow, paltry, and ephemeral" experience and a "state or condition of suffering".[36] One can find deliverance from suffering in "a better existence" only by means of "moral effort, sever renunciation, and the denial of our own self".[37] The blessedness which the Stoics strive for, then, is not achievable within the constraints of earthly life: life and suffering are inextricably linked and the quest for perfect tranquillity is inevitably frustrated. Schopenhauer thinks that this contradiction is exposed by the approbation the Stoics give suicide. Seneca sanctions the wise man to "quickly take leave of life and cease being a trouble to himself" should "the utmost pinch of need arrive".[38] This advice is of a kind with the more famous Cynic dictum that "we must procure either understanding

---

[33] GS 145.

[34] In a hopeful section at the opening of *The Gay Science*, he ventures to ask whether our reason and experience under the banner of science might be brought to bear on "all that has given colour to existence" (*GS* 7). We can understand Nietzsche as wishing to extend and develop the Stoic program of the rational analysis of values.

[35] WWR 1.16.

[36] WWR 2.48.

[37] WWR 2.48.

[38] Sen. Ep. 17.9.

or a rope [for hanging ourselves]".[39] That is, the progression of our practical reason will either grant us tranquillity or indicate that death is preferable to the continued tribulations of life. But Stoicism professes to cure us of these tribulations, that nothing in life correctly understood is an evil, and that therefore, nothing should compel us to suicide. Stoicism is supposed to lead to a blissful life but instead "philosophises away" life or, if this proves too great a task, recommends its cessation. Suicide remains a tonic of last resort for the Stoic, and this reveals that Stoicism is more sedative than curative regarding life's ills. In some situations suicide may be (as the Stoics argue) a virtuous action, but it is never a happy one.

At the time of *Human, All Too Human*, Nietzsche praises the Stoic attitude to suicide. In *HH* 80 he singles out the "bravest Roman patriots" as adopting a "natural, obvious" response to the decline of their powers.[40] Against this "victory for reason" he sets a "mania for prolonging our lives" even in conditions of distress "when lacking the strength to come closer to the real goal of life".[41] Nietzsche rejects the anxious longing of those who are "enamoured of life".[42] In subsequent chapters we will see that Nietzsche reverses his rejection of a passionate attachment to life, but even now we can detect a break with Stoicism. The "real goal of life" for a thinker or artist is, according to section 209 of the same work, to infuse one's works with a "better self". Again, we will interrogate the connection between the love of life and Nietzsche's project of the self in subsequent chapters.[43]

Epictetus puts little stock in the task of choosing between preferred and non-preferred indifferents. Instead, he claims that we ought to devote our attention to the

---

[39] Plu. De Stoic. 14 in WWR 1.16.

[40] HH 80.

[41] HH 80.

[42] HH 80.

[43] HH 209.

only thing that is genuinely good, the fashioning and maintenance of a virtuous soul, in accordance with its rational nature.

Of primary importance in this fashioning is to jettison the false judgements by which we conventionally value external goods and in doing so guard ourselves against the passions that originate in these false judgements. Transience is in the nature of all external objects, and so we should not be disturbed if something we are fond of is destroyed. Epictetus counsels that we recognise and affirm this nature, to prepare ourselves for the inevitable passing of all things.

> If you are fond a jug, say, "I am fond of a jug"; for when it is broken you will not be disturbed.[44]

Purifying oneself of false judgements is a task of constant self-discipline. Epictetus directs the Stoic who experiences something outside his control to turn to what is under his control—his own faculties—in order to respond. In particular, Epictetus refers to the *hêgemonikon* or commanding faculty, "the thing which utilises everything else, submits everything else to the test, selects, and rejects".[45] The *hêgemonikon* comprises the faculties of impression, impulse and assent. As has been shown, of these, humans share impression and impulse with other animals. It is the capacity for rational assent, the ability "to weigh and evaluate [one's] representations"[46] and respond appropriately, that is distinctively human. Standing between one's impressions and impulses, the faculty of assent is "that part of the mind that engages in conscious decision-making processes".[47] Assent is "a distinctive kind of causal contribution that a rational agent (and only a rational agent) can make to the production of an action",[48] and it is in this sense that the Stoic's response to an event is under his own control.

---

[44] Ench. 3.

[45] Epict. Diss. 4.7.

[46] Gretchen Reydams-Schils, *The Roman Stoics: Self, Responsibility, and Affection* (Chicago and London: The University of Chicago Press, 2005), 26.

[47] Sellars, *Stoicism*, 105.

[48] Donald Rutherford, "Freedom as a Philosophical Ideal: Nietzsche and His Antecedents," *Inquiry* 54, no. 5 (2011): 515.

Epictetus's counsel is to exercise the faculty of assent, such that the Stoic's commanding faculty operates according to reason and nature. The faculty of assent is an ineliminable part of human action. When one fails to act in accordance with nature, it is not the case that one's assent is bypassed, but that one assents to an incorrect judgement of either impressions (by ascribing value to a jug of which one is fond, for example) or impulses (by reacting with anger or some other emotion). The later Roman Stoics were increasingly concerned with the faculty of assent as the locus of psychological self-control.[49] Through the use of spiritual exercises which work upon assent, the Stoic habituates himself to the proper use of the faculty such that his "external impressions will not run away from [him]".[50] The harm of the passions is precisely that they run away from us, escaping our control.

While the Stoic practicing the withdrawal from external goods implied by *apatheai* ("freedom from passion") does forgo their attendant pleasures—since these are dependent on false judgements of their worth—the Stoic does not forgo all emotional impulse. On the contrary, just as the passions are dependent on false judgements, the Stoic *eupatheiai* ("good emotions") are emotional impulses dependent on correct judgement. While the Stoic avoids laughter at obscenity, in the theatre, or as a result of intoxication (since all three are beyond his control), his indifference to external goods does not preclude him from a serene cheerfulness and even laughter at the "near-universality of human folly and delusion".[51] Epictetus provides an example of this serene cheerfulness, when he shows how a Stoic might respond to the threat of physical violence.[52] Because the Stoic is secure in the knowledge that his body is nothing to him, and that only he controls his moral purpose, he can mock someone who attempts

---

[49] Reydams-Schils, *The Roman Stoics*, 26.

[50] Ench. 10.

[51] Stephen Halliwell, *Greek Laughter: A Study of Cultural Psychology from Homer to Early Christianity* (Cambridge: Cambridge University Press, 2008), 304.

[52] Epict Diss. 1.1.22–25.

coercion: "My leg you will fetter, but my moral purpose not even Zeus himself has power to overcome".[53]

As a result the passions, which the Stoics counsel against, should not be identified with emotional impulse *in toto*, but rather the condition which obtains when these impulses overstep their "proper and natural proportion"[54] and continue "disobedient to the dictates of reason".[55] Chrysippus likens an excessive emotional impulse to the momentum an athlete picks up running: he cannot "stop or change [direction] whenever he wants to".[56] The track sprinter who overshoots the finish line exceeds the measured distance of the race, just as the impassioned individual goes beyond the measure of reason. Chrysippus warns against this excess.

Chrysippus returns to the athletic metaphor in his pathology of the passions:

> The passions are called ailments not just in virtue of their judging each of these [external] things to be good, but also with regard to their running towards them in excess of what is natural.[57]

Here Chrysippus expresses a moderate approval of, or at least indifference towards, the opinion that external possessions are a good, as long as this opinion is kept within the bounds of reason. The indifferents falls within these bounds since, as long as one participates in virtue, one's moral goodness is neither helped nor harmed by choices between indifferents, as long as the Stoic is not misled into incorrectly appraising an indifferent as a moral good. Chrysippus's contention is that, while they do not contribute to our virtue, there are natural activities, for instance social participation and raising a family, which can be undertaken in moderation.

---

[53] Epict Diss. 1.1.22–25.

[54] Chrysippus in Galen, "On Hippocrates' and Plato's doctrines," 4.2.14 = LS 65J.5.

[55] Stobaeus 2.88,8 = LS 65A.1.

[56] Chrysippus in Galen, "On Hippocrates' and Plato's doctrines," 4.2.15-18 = LS 65J.6-9.

[57] Chrysippus in Galen, "On Hippocrates' and Plato's doctrines," 4.5.21 = LS 65L.1.

Hypocrisy

Schopenhauer charges with hypocrisy the Stoic who possesses and enjoys supposed indifferents while denying their value. According to the doctrine of indifferents, a Stoic may take part in a luxurious Roman banquet, all the while protesting that the fine food and wine are merely preferred indifferents, and not real goods. Schopenhauer claims that the Stoic who behaves in this manner is simply self-deluding in "boldly asserting that they gained nothing whatever from the whole feast".[58] Schopenhauer argues that Stoicism should be understood as a theoretical translation of the practical spirit of Cynicism, that "life in its simplest and most naked form, with the hardships that naturally belong to it, is the most tolerable, and is therefore to be chosen".[59] The Stoics accept the Cynic's claim that desirous and passionate attachments cause more suffering than the possession of the desired object can assuage. Rather than renouncing the enjoyment of external objects, the Stoic is satisfied in the conviction that this renunciation is possible, if demanded by fate. By this theoretical move, in which everything is "reduced [...] to a mental process", Schopenhauer concludes that the Stoics have "sophisticated themselves into all the amenities of life".[60]

The theory of indifferents grants the Stoic latitude in everyday life, so long as she holds the correct convictions, to indulge in available luxuries. Schopenhauer's claim is that this marks a divergence between Stoic theory and lived experience. This divergence is illustrative of the tripartite structure of Stoicism detected by Sellars. According to Sellars, Stoic philosophy aims at a "distinctively rational way of life" (*bíos*), underpinned by rational discourse (*logos*) and achieved through the use of philosophical exercise and training (*áskēsis*).[61] Since *áskēsis* constitutes the means through which philosophical ideas are translated into philosophical actions, the

---

[58] WWR 2.16.
[59] WWR 2.16.
[60] WWR 2.16.
[61] Sellars, *The Art of Living*, 7.

manner in which Stoic exercises treat indifferents will shed light on what Schopenhauer claims is a failure of Stoicism. Marcus Aurelius counsels, in an exercise aimed at purifying the soul's concern for earthy indifferents, as follows:

> Observe the courses of the stars as if revolving with them and reflect upon the continuous changes of the elements into one another; for impressions such as these are for cleansing the filth of earth-bound life.[62]

Epictetus, too, recommends as the "only way" to freedom from the emotions, "to despise the things which are not in our power".[63] Yet, if things outside of one's control and the goings-on of earth-bound life are indifferents, the Stoic lacks the grounds to despise them, or decry their filth, since these dispositions imply strongly negative valuations. The incongruity in this case is the reverse of that which Schopenhauer identified. Whereas the Stoic's actions, according to Schopenhauer, betray the positive regard in which they hold external goods, Stoic exercises suggest an equally inappropriate negative regard, given their supposed indifference. The contemptuous attitude towards externals that Marcus Aurelius and Epictetus recommend one adopts solves the practical problem Schopenhauer identifies in that it counteracts the growth of desires for luxuries to which one might become accustomed. Yet it achieves this at the cost of multiplying Stoicism's theoretical difficulties. The Stoic who adopts this attitude of contempt for externals tacitly admits that self-mastery is a struggle between drives, in this case one's appetite, fed by regular gratification, and the pride in self-control that is threatened by appetite.

While Chrysippus tolerates the judgement of externals as welcome (within the bounds of reason), in the later Seneca, these bounds have tightened almost entirely. Seneca has it that the passions, since they are in essence irrational, cannot be brought under the control of reason. In contrast to the measured emotional response which Chrysippus sanctions, for Seneca "if reason prevails, the passions will not even get a

---

[62] Marcus Aurelius 7.47.

[63] Ench. 19.

start".[64] Seneca argues that the position that we ought to control rather than eliminate the passions is "misleading and useless", and "to be regarded just as the declaration that we ought to be 'moderately' insane, or 'moderately' ill".[65]

The banquet table of life

Seneca finds cheerfulness in obedience to God, counselling only the defiant endurance of chance events.[66] Epictetus instructs similarly, that we steel ourselves against the impositions of chance by despising the things that are not under our control, in order that we not desire them.[67] One exercises control over oneself, against the passions, through attuning one's judgements with that of the universal rational ordering of the universe. Seneca's cheerfulness thus depends on the Stoic division between the internal rational faculties, which fall under our control, and the hostile external world, which does not, and will indeed thwart our pursuit of *eudaimonia*.

Epictetus is aware of the tension between the rational moderation of and the ascetic withdrawal from the valuing of external goods, and exhibits this tension in a parable that one ought to live as one behaves at a banquet.[68] He speaks approvingly of two kinds of banqueters: the first, like Chrysippus, samples politely and values what fate brings, not desiring a dish outside of her grasp and not detaining a dish when the time comes to pass it on; the second, like Seneca, not only controls her desire for distant dishes and goods, but maintains this indifference when the good is within grasp, in fact despising it as an external, and therefore of no real value. A striking example of the second kind of banqueter is Zeno, the founder of Stoicism, who reportedly "declined most invitations to dinner".[69]

---

[64] Sen. Ep. 85.9.

[65] Sen. Ep. 85.9.

[66] Sen. Ep. 16.5.

[67] Ench. 19.

[68] Ench. 15.

[69] DL 7.1.

The banqueter who refrains from partaking in external goods is wedded to the Stoic division between the self and a hostile external world. Under this division, the task of the Stoic is to heroically endure the world's impositions, while perfecting his (internal) virtue. Simplicius, in his Neoplatonic commentary on the *Enchiridion*, reads Epictetus as presenting a progression towards the banqueter who "transcends the realm of generation"[70] and, in despising external things, joins in the governance of the universe "without being subordinated within it".[71]

Both banqueters remain tied to an appraisal of themselves and the world from an individual perspective. The first partakes in the polite satisfaction and moderation of personal desires, ready to digest whatever fate happens to bring. The second engages in a disdainful asceticism in which moral perfection is achieved by abstention from worldly proceedings and is rewarded by a share in the proud and divinely detached rule of the world.

However, a more or less ascetic individualism committed to the sharp distinction between the self and the external world does not exhaust the Stoic ethical project. Diogenes Laertius describes the Stoic *telos* as a life lived "in accordance with our own human nature as well as that of the universe".[72] Sellars finds in Epictetus, and more explicitly in Marcus Aurelius, a strain of Stoic thought that emphasises this double aspect of life 'according to nature' in broadening the human perspective to that of the universe.[73] Marcus writes:

> Of the life of man, his time is a point, his substance flowing, his perception faint, the constitution of his whole body decaying, his soul a spinning wheel, his fortune hard to predict, and his fame doubtful; that is to say, all the things of the body are a river, the things of the soul dream and delusion, life is a war and a journey in a foreign land, and afterwards oblivion.[74]

---

[70] Simplicius 53,8–54,5.

[71] Simplicius 53,8–54,5.

[72] DL 7.88.

[73] John Sellars, "The Point of View of the Cosmos: Deleuze, Romanticism, Stoicism," *Pli* 8 (1999): 12.

[74] Marcus Aurelius 2.17.

Marcus here takes on the perspective of the river of existence, drawing on Heraclitus. On the scale of this perspective, the particular details of an individual's life—his fame, his fortune, and his political power—shrink to a point that will soon return to oblivion, being "taken up into the [...] life-giving principle of the cosmos".[75] The Stoic who has adopted the point of view of the cosmos can properly appreciate the indifference of nature to the speck of their own life within the immensity of all other existence. Sellars terms this strain of Stoic thought, which practices a loving consent to our place in the whole, "cosmic Stoicism", in contrast to the "human Stoicism" of "heroic endurance or patient fortitude" exemplified by Epictetus and Seneca.[76]

Adopting an impersonal cosmic perspective "will free one from the emotional turmoil that goes with"[77] the limited first-person point of view. The cosmic perspective is not the transcendental point of view of Simplicius' Neoplatonic reading of Epictetus, which escapes the "realm of generation". Instead, the Stoic attains the cosmic perspective by identifying with this very realm, or with the generative principle that the Stoics variously call nature, reason, and God. This identification allows him to cheerfully affirm the proceedings of nature as expressing God's will. External events are no longer interpreted as hostile and chance impositions from the world, but as an ineliminable part of rational fatefulness. This view is not confined to the later Roman Stoics. The Greek Cleanthes' *Hymn to Zeus* praises Zeus for "[making] the uneven even and [putting] into order the disorderly": "For you have thus joined everything into one, the good with the bad, that there comes to be one ever-existing rational order for everything".[78] Throughout the development of Stoicism there exists a strain of thought that anchors indifference to externals in the practice of communion with the rational cosmos.

---

[75] Marcus Aurelius 6.24.

[76] John Sellars, "An Ethics of the Event: Deleuze's Stoicism," *Angelaki* 11, no. 3 (2006): 164.

[77] Sellars, *The Art of Living*, 154.

[78] Cleanth. Hymn 18–21.

Whither Nietzsche?

Nietzsche's deep affinity for Stoicism has been widely acknowledged. Nietzsche adopts both the form of Stoic philosophy as *"eine Kunst des Lebens"*,[79] and many of its substantive commitments: its rejection of pity, its affirmation of fate, and its fundamental aspiration to live (in some sense) with nature. By "nature", the Stoics refer to that teleological divinity which endears individuals to themselves through *oikeiôsis*, and the consequent drive to self-preservation which underlies the Stoics' broader ethical theory. Pity is rejected as a species of distress, to suffer which harms an individual's rational constitution. According to Epictetus, pity is assent to another's judgement that she is affected by external evils. But this judgement is necessarily mistaken, since externals are a matter of indifference. Epictetus suggests that one sympathise "as far as words go", but not "in the centre of [one's] being".[80] The divine providence which endears us to ourselves additionally ensures that fate proceeds according to reason. By adopting the perspective of this providence (nature itself), the Stoic comes to understand the rational place of all things within the whole, and thus not only endures, but lovingly affirms her own fate. These substantive Stoic positions are grounded in a teleological understanding of nature—that nature has endeared us to ourselves and that the art of living is synonymous with obedience to nature.

Yet no part of Stoicism receives more explicit condemnation from Nietzsche as the Stoic understanding of nature, and in particular their contention that individuals are disposed by nature towards self-preservation. Whereas in *The Gay Science* Nietzsche's treatment of Stoicism is primarily concerned with the Stoic temperament, in *Beyond Good and Evil* he turns to the Stoic theory of nature.

> "According to nature" you want to *live*? O you noble Stoics, what deceptive words these are! Imagine a being like nature, wasteful beyond measure, indifferent beyond measure, without purposes and consideration, without mercy and justice, fertile and desolate and

---

[79] "An art of living" (R. O. Elveton, "Nietzsche's Stoicism: The Depths Are Inside," in *Nietzsche and Antiquity: His Reaction and Response to the Classical Tradition*, ed. Paul Bishop [Rochester, NY: Camden House, 2004], 192).

[80] Ench. 16.

uncertain at the same time; imagine indifference itself as a power—how *could* you live according to this indifference?[81]

Whereas for the Stoics, "it was not likely that nature [...] should leave the creature she has made without either estrangement from or affection for its own constitution",[82] for Nietzsche—indebted to Schopenhauer's anti-teleological view of the world—nature is precisely so indifferent to our individual affairs. He argues that it is only anthropomorphic projection that allows the Stoic to think of nature as prescribing the Stoic way of life. In this projection the Stoics are unremarkable:

> But this is an ancient, eternal story: what formerly happened with the Stoics still happens today, too, as soon as any philosophy begins to believe in itself. It always creates the world in its own image; it cannot do otherwise. Philosophy is this tyrannical drive itself, the most spiritual will to power, to the "creation of the world," to the *causa prima*.[83]

The reason that Nietzsche specifically remarks upon the Stoics is not their anthropomorphism, but their denial thereof. Instead of living *according to* nature as they pretend, the Stoics have read nature *according to* Stoicism. That is, they have believed in Stoicism as an underlying principle of nature, all the while pretending to perceive nature free from anthropomorphic projection. It is this self-deception which Nietzsche attacks. Indeed, according to Nietzsche, *all* previous philosophies have believed in themselves, and in doing so, tyrannised the world. This immediately raises a number of questions regarding the status of Nietzsche's own philosophy. Does Nietzsche 'believe' in his own philosophy? If so, is his criticism of Stoicism merely a lament on the way to repeating the same mistake in his translation of "man back into nature"?[84] If not, how does Nietzsche avoid following the Stoics into self-deception? The role played by poetry, music, and artistic creation in *The Gay Science* will go some way towards allaying this concern, as we will see in the second half of this thesis.

---

[81] BGE 9.

[82] DL 7.85.

[83] BGE 9.

[84] BGE 230.

At the very least, the Stoics claim to find empirical confirmation of the theory of *oikeiôsis* in so-called 'cradle arguments'.[85] The self-concern of infants in the cradle testifies, so they say, that nature is the source of this self-concern. The theory of *oikeiôsis* is not *just* an a priori claim, although as Brunschwig notes this is how Chrysippus is reported to justify it.[86] But if *oikeiôsis* is deployed to explain observable phenomena, it is open to refutation on empirical grounds. Nietzsche makes this point when he subjects the instinct of self-preservation to criticism as an explanatory principle.[87] That the explanatory power of the instinct of self-preservation has previously been championed by philosophical dogmatism is no reason in itself to reject it. Nietzsche makes the same argument regarding the soul in the previous aphorism. While the "soul atomism" of Christianity "ought to be expelled from science", this does not require the expulsion of any and all soul-hypotheses.[88] Rather, such hypotheses ought to be granted "citizen's rights in science", that is, subjected to scientific analysis and accepted or rejected accordingly. The same is true regarding the instinctual behaviour of organic individuals. While in the case of the soul Nietzsche simply proffers a number of hypotheses, in the case of instinctual behaviour he is more confident of having found the correct account, against the principle of self-preservation in both Stoicism (as dogma) and Darwinism (as scientific theory).

> A living thing seeks above all to *discharge* its strength—life itself is *will to power*; self-preservation is only one of the indirect and most frequent *results*.[89]

He finds self-preservation a superfluous principle: it is explained by the notion that organic things seek to exercise their power, not only to conserve it. The desire of prior philosophers to restrict the biological instinct to self-preservation is, according to

---

[85] Jacques Brunschwig, "The Cradle Argument in Epicureanism and Stoicism," in *The Norms of Nature*, eds. Malcolm Schofield and Gisela Striker (Cambridge: Cambridge University Press, 1986).

[86] Brunschwig, "The Cradle Argument in Epicureanism and Stoicism", 129.

[87] BGE 13.

[88] BGE 12.

[89] BGE 13.

Nietzsche, symptomatic of conditions of distress.[90] Such philosophers *require* all their strength for self-preservation, and thus the projection of their own temperament which comes to stand for "nature" bears the mark of this need.

For the Stoics, nature (or God) directs the expression of an individual's power inwards, towards the maintenance of its own constitution; for Nietzsche such expression is free of such theological constraint. Thus, while the broad aim of Nietzsche's philosophy accords with that of the Stoics', in that both strive to foster and perfect the expression of one's power, their contents diverge sharply.

Both the Stoics and Nietzsche seek a cheerfulness purified by the pursuit of knowledge.[91] For both, feelings and emotional states correspond to judgements and evaluations, and the purification of feelings is to be achieved through cool, rational reflection.[92] But whereas the Stoics believe this coolness gives rise to a tranquil indifference to the outside world, according to Nietzsche a great character "possesses [feeling] to the highest degree" and thus *values* to the highest degree. Such a character is able to *control* feelings without their removal.

For both Nietzsche and the Stoics, a condition of knowledge is the capacity to transcend the limited point of view of the individual. "[T]he eye of knowledge" allows Nietzsche's sage to no longer "experience the stars as something 'above'"[93] in much the same way as Marcus Aurelius sees the earth as "in its entirety [...] merely a point in space".[94] But for Nietzsche, again, it is not the elimination of feelings which aids in the

---

[90] GS 349.

[91] GS 343.

[92] In D 35, Nietzsche warns against trusting one's feelings above "the gods which are in *us*: our reason and our experience". A later note entitled "*Should one follow one's feelings?*" similarly recommends their habitual sifting by reason (Friedrich Nietzsche, *The Will to Power*, trans. Walter Kaufmann and R. J. Hollingdale [New York: Vintage Books, 1968], section 928).

[93] BGE 71.

[94] Marcus Aurelius 4.3.

venture for knowledge, but the development and control of a more comprehensive and diverse panoply of feelings.[95]

For both Nietzsche and the Stoics, the means of the pursuit of knowledge is broadening of the individual's intellectual perspective to encompass existence on a grander, cosmic scale. Adopting this cosmic perspective is instrumental in the Stoic achievement of indifference, or devaluation, just as as it is in Nietzsche's revaluation. Yet the rationally ordered cosmos to which the Stoics appeal as a ground for this transcendental perspective is unavailable to Nietzsche. Without the God's-eye view of the Stoic, it remains to be seen how Nietzsche ascends to a supra-individual perspective. Nietzsche rejects indifference and the Stoic cosmos, but remains indebted to Stoic thought on both accounts.

Value

The well-being of the Stoic sage is impervious to the world's apparent evils. The sage correctly judges that such external objects threaten him with no real harm. By judging objects according to their natural value, the sage frees herself from the harm of the passions and achieves tranquillity. As we have seen, Nietzsche understands the Stoic view of nature as a projection of the Stoic temperament. The case of "natural value" is no different:

> Whatever has *value* in our world now does not have value in itself, according to its nature—nature is always value-less, but has been *given* value at some time, as a present—and it was *we* who gave and bestowed it.[96]

Nietzsche makes the striking claim that indifference has been bestowed upon external objects as a consequence of a Stoic desire for as little pain as possible.[97] On Nietzsche's telling, Stoic doctrine is a rationalisation of the Stoic temperament. In effect, he accuses the Stoics of a kind of meta-philosophical negative hedonism, because

---

[95] GM III 12.

[96] GS 301, emphasis in original.

[97] GS 12.

they supposedly give up the capacity for pleasure in return for avoiding pain.[98] In this, according to Nietzsche, the Stoics implicitly agree that pleasure and pain are intimately related such that large or small quantities of one necessarily imply the same of the other. By dulling their sensitivity to both pleasure and pain, the Stoics ensure that knowledge of the (therefore) indifferent external world contributes to the sage's tranquillity.

Nietzsche is concerned with finding a criterion of value distinct from 'nature', at least insofar as we consider this as the world purified of anthropomorphisms. He claims to find an alternative measure under the heading of 'life'. While all values serve the demands of a certain *kind* of life,[99] Nietzsche wishes to judge values on the basis of the extent to which they *promote and preserve* life.[100] By 'life', Nietzsche refers to the instinctive drive to discharge one's strength which he believes to have established as essential to explain the behaviour of living things. As far as the Stoic directs his energies exclusively towards the maintenance (preservation) of his rational soul and treats the external world with indifference, he is, according to Nietzsche, leading an impoverished life. The operative distinction is, we might say, between a Stoic will-to-live (*oikeiôsis*) and Nietzsche's will-to-power. This is why Nietzsche describes the Stoics as petrified[101] and statuesque.[102]

Stoicism's petrification is due to the Stoic's minimisation of both pleasure and pain. The clear implication is that Nietzsche would rather as much pain as possible, in order to open the possibility for "new galaxies of joy".[103] The means to cultivating both pleasure and pain, according to Nietzsche, is science. In *The Gay Science*, Nietzsche

---

[98] On this supposed negative hedonism, see Thomas Ryan and Michael Ure, "Nietzsche's Post-Classical Therapy," *Pli* 25 (2014): 91–110.

[99] BGE 3.

[100] BGE 4.

[101] GS 326.

[102] GS 12.

[103] GS 12.

closely aligns joy with pleasure or voluptuousness [*Wollust*], in sharp contrast with Stoicism, and indicating a radicalised Epicurean sensitivity to the world.

Correct judgements concerning the value of objects comprise the central goal of Stoic therapy. Thus for the Stoic, truth will always help us on our way towards happiness and consequently is of supreme utility. For Nietzsche the situation is less fortuitous. His claim, repeated consistently throughout his corpus, is that belief in "unities which do not exist",[104] "basic errors of all sentient existence",[105] and "the constant falsification of the world by means of numbers",[106] may well prove a necessary condition of life. The progress of science in these areas, to the extent that it displaces belief in these necessary falsehoods, is deleterious to our happiness: for Nietzsche there is a tragic conflict between science and life, between truth and value. He asks, "to what extent can truth endure incorporation? That is the question; that is the experiment".[107]

Cosmic therapy

In 1881 Nietzsche conceives of the Hellenistic schools as "experimental laboratories"[108] for the development of practical wisdom. The results of these experiments rightly "belong to us", in that we are entitled to practice Stoic, as well as Epicurean, techniques of living according to our own needs. In particular, Nietzsche reports that he has learnt from Stoicism to ask, in the midst of storm and strife, "What does it matter?".[109] That Nietzsche believes we can help ourselves to Stoic practices without a commitment to the broader Stoic system perhaps explains his continued use of Stoic exercises after his shift away from Stoicism itself in the early 1880s.

---

[104] HH 19.
[105] GS 110.
[106] BGE 4.
[107] GS 110.
[108] KSA 9:15[59].
[109] KSA 9:15[59].

Marcus Aurelius' technique of ascending to the point of view of the cosmos is one exercise that Nietzsche adopts as his own. In section 380 of *The Gay Science,* Nietzsche describes how one might confront the question of the value of morality. One must "rise, climb, or fly" to a height outside of morality:

> One has to be *very light* to drive one's will to knowledge into such a distance and, as it were, beyond one's time, to create for oneself eyes to survey millennia and, moreover, clear skies in these eyes.[110]

The eyes which Nietzsche creates to survey millennia of moral history allow him to transcend the limited first-person view of the individual. Unlike Marcus, however, Nietzsche has no ready-made cosmic perspective or God's-eye view to which he can aspire. Both Nietzsche and Marcus reject any conception of the self as separated from or opposed to the world.[111] However, Nietzsche's new cheerfulness, as propounded in book five of *The Gay Science* (published with the second edition in 1887), is predicated not on an identification with the cosmic God, but on the "greatest recent event—that 'God is dead.'".[112] The therapeutic success of adopting a cosmic point of view on the world hinges upon the Stoic conception of the cosmos and its capacity to ground correct judgements regarding nature. In the absence of the regulative cosmic power of God, Nietzsche attempts to expand his perspective beyond the narrow individual point of view. This may still carry a sedative effect in that it exposes the folly in our conventional first person valuations, but it cannot guarantee happiness in the same way as it does for the Stoics. Indeed, given Nietzsche's claim in the preface to *The Gay Science* that life has "become a problem",[113] it is not at all obvious that bringing more perspectives to bear on our condition will not harm our tranquillity and cause us distress. Nietzsche seeks a solution to this problem in a daring, adventurous

---

[110] GS 380.

[111] Elveton, "Nietzsche's Stoicism: The Depths Are Inside," 195.

[112] GS 343.

[113] GS P 4.

engagement with the world,[114] and as far as he goes along these lines he leaves Stoicism behind.

Marcus Aurelius uses the cosmic perspective to quiet the soul and diminish the perceived importance of worldly affairs: "the earth as a whole is but a point in the universe".[115] Nietzsche draws precisely the opposite conclusion from adopting the point of view of the cosmos:

> Whoever looks into himself as into vast space and carries galaxies in himself, also knows how irregular all galaxies are; they lead into the chaos and labyrinth of existence.[116]

Rather than indifference towards the infinitesimally small, Nietzsche deduces a cosmic grandness and profundity from the cosmic perspective. The cosmic perspective grants Nietzsche a "dance floor for divine accident":[117] the cosmic platform gives Zarathustra's life a profundity opposed to the lives of the last human beings who "[make] everything small".[118] Nietzsche does not seek the cosmic perspective to remind himself of his own smallness, but to shade life with cosmic grandeur and in doing so revalue life within the natural world.

By 1882 Nietzsche saw the Stoic need to ground happiness in universal reason as indicative of an impoverished and unpredictable life. The Stoic's exchange, by which she forgoes worldly pleasures in order to avoid worldly pains, is defensible only in a world so hostile, dangerous, and painful as to make worldly engagements unbearable. But, according to Nietzsche, such an exchange exaggerates the pain and misfortune in the world and ignores the profusion of worldly palliatives and pleasures.[119] Nietzsche's rejection of Stoic rationalism leads him to an engagement with that other great Hellenistic school, Epicureanism. In *The Gay Science* Nietzsche expresses a preference

---

[114] GS 343.

[115] Marcus Aurelius 8.21.

[116] GS 322.

[117] Z 3 "Before Sunrise".

[118] Z 1 "Zarathustra's Prologue" 5.

[119] GS 326.

for the Epicureans' sensitivity to the world over Stoic indifference.[120] The next chapter examines the terms of this preference as well as Nietzsche's ultimate assessment of Epicurus as "essentially" Romantic.[121]

---

[120] GS 306.

[121] GS 370.

2. Epicurean Purgatives: Pleasure, Sensation, Irritation

Where Nietzsche baulks at the Stoic's ambitious and speculative cosmology, he finds common ground with the Epicureans' caution regarding ultimate convictions. The Stoics and Epicureans concur in holding a form of divinity as the sage's highest aspiration, but while the Stoics conceive of the divine as the rational procession of the whole of nature, the Epicureans celebrate the divine as a serene independence from human concerns. The gods, according to Epicurus (c. 341–270 BCE), exist in a state of perfect bliss, separated from our world and indifferent with human affairs. They incarnate the Epicurean ideal of freedom from pain and fear, in strict opposition to the interventionist gods of Greek myth, and the providential God of the Stoics.[1] The Epicurean sage, although she aspires to divinity, achieves this precisely by shucking off her concern for the actions, particularly the wrath, of particular divine beings. Consequently, Epicurean philosophy aims at dispelling fears which groundlessly impinge on human happiness.

Nietzsche echoes the Epicurean sentiment that one should neither fear the gods' wrath nor be seduced by the notion of their "personal providence".[2] It is Epicurus' "wonderful insight," according to Nietzsche, that "to quieten the heart it is absolutely not necessary to have solved the ultimate and outermost theoretical questions".[3] And 'to quieten the heart' is exactly the task which Epicurus sets for philosophy: for him, the blessed [*makarios*] life is one that is free from pain and fear and his counsel is that we direct every effort to ridding ourselves of these evils.

Epicurus singles out two fears as particularly harmful to human happiness: fear of the gods and fear of death. Both of these fears arise from "a certain irrational

---

[1] And, as Nietzsche notes in GS 277, the concerned Christian god.
[2] GS 277.
[3] WS 7.

perversity"[4]—belief in the opinions of the multitude regarding the gods and regarding death. Thus the task of Epicurean philosophy is to reform the minds of individuals affected by these erroneous beliefs, and in doing so free them from the harm wrought by irrational fears. In this sense Epicureanism adopts the ancient medical model of philosophy aimed at treating the soul. The Roman Epicurean Lucretius (c. 99–55 BCE) describes his poem *De Rerum Natura* in these terms, as using the sweetness of poetry to deliver his Epicurean balm, in the same way as, when physicians administer a bitter medicine, "they first touch the rims about the cups with the sweet yellow fluid of honey".[5]

In this chapter I present Epicureanism as a philosophical therapy. I consider three aspects of the Epicurean therapy: its doctrinal commitments, the exercises that the Epicurean student and sage employ, and the limits on possible experience set by the Epicurean temperament. As I will show, the effect of each of these is to limit the exposure of the Epicurean to the pains of existence through a diminution of her passionate engagements with, and activity within, the world. I conclude with an analysis of *ataraxia*, the Epicurean ideal, and consider Nietzsche's criticism of this. As in chapter one, my goal is to understand both the influence of Epicureanism on Nietzsche as well as his conception and use of "Epicureanism" in the middle period. To begin, I introduce the principal goal of philosophy according to Epicurus: to allay both the fear of the gods and the fear of death.

Physics against fear of the gods

Motivated by the task of alleviating the fear of the gods, Epicurus and his followers propound a physical theory that is strictly materialist, offering natural explanations of cosmological and meteorological phenomena that were hitherto blamed on the gods.[6]

---

[4] DL 10.81.

[5] Lucr. 1.921–950.

[6] Liba Taub, "Cosmology and Meteorology," in *The Cambridge Companion to Epicureanism*, ed. James Warren (Cambridge: Cambridge University Press, 2009), 124.

The therapeutic motive of natural enquiry is made explicit in Epicurus' letter to Pythocles:

> In the first place, remember that, like everything else, knowledge of celestial phenomena, whether taken along with other things or in isolation, has no other end in view than peace of mind and firm conviction.[7]

Epicurus explains one such meteorological phenomenon, thunder, which was mythically ascribed to Zeus,[8] through no less than four distinct natural hypotheses.[9] Lucretius, following his forebear, lists ten.[10] The goal of Epicurean meteorology is not to arrive at a single definitive account of phenomena, but to assuage human fear of the gods. Epicurus warns against the kind of enquiry that would narrow down the range of natural explanations since in it "there is nothing [...] that contributes to our happiness".[11]

The Epicureans do not purport to give a definitive account of meteorological phenomena, as this is unnecessary for and in some cases destructive towards, their therapeutic purpose. It is unnecessary, since the attainment of *ataraxia* depends only on the rejection of divine explanations and the consequent removal of fear of the gods. It is sometimes destructive, since the possession only a single hypothesis lends itself to dogmatic fixation. In *The Wanderer and his Shadow*, Nietzsche approves of this Epicurean strategy. With only a single account of a particular phenomenon, he observes, we risk overstepping the limits of our capacity to know distant and obscure events. We are in danger of falling into the "superstitious trap" of dogmatism,[12] or becoming embroiled in "a laborious pondering over a single hypothesis which, being

---

[7] DL 10.85.

[8] Homer describes the fear which thunder caused, as an instrument of Zeus' will, both mortals and other gods (Il. 21.190–199).

[9] DL 10.100.

[10] Lucr. 6.96–159.

[11] DL 10.79.

[12] Taub, "Cosmology and meteorology," 111.

the only one visible, is a hundredfold overrated".[13] Epicurean meteorological explanations, Nietzsche notes, sanction the consolation that "things may be thus but they may also be otherwise".[14] This consolation is won at the cost of not looking *too deeply* into nature. Anything more than a possible explanation of natural phenomena is superfluous to Epicurean physics—"the stimulus to enquiry ceases once [freedom from fear and anxiety] is attained".[15]

For Epicurus, then, the ethical impulse circumscribes the purview of science. The Neo-Kantian Lange, whose *History of Materialism* was a formative influence on Nietzsche,[16] finds such a science "childishly inadequate" compared to "true scientific enquiry".[17] Indeed, the Epicurean does not wish to perform the rigorous analysis of natural events which gives Lange's modern science a rich and complex understanding of the world. Since they restrict natural enquiry to narrow boundaries, the Epicureans are only able to account for a narrow range of natural phenomena and human experience. The Epicureans understanding of life is necessarily limited in comparison with one informed by more thorough scientific enquiry.

Nietzsche follows Lange's criticism of the unscientific modesty of Epicurean physics, stating that "Epicurus denied the possibility of knowledge, in order to retain moral (or hedonistic) values as the highest values".[18] And yet, Nietzsche does not oppose Epicurean explanations to a true science, absolved of ethical commitments. Instead, he detects a competing ethical root at the base of modern scientific enquiry. The starting point for the scientific attitude, according to Nietzsche, is the unconditional will to

---

[13] WS 7.

[14] WS 7.

[15] Frederick Albert Lange, *The History of Materialism* (London: Routledge & K Paul, 2010), 1:103.

[16] Thomas H. Brobjer, *Nietzsche's Philosophical Context* (Urbana and Chicago: University of Illinois Press, 2008), 32–36.

[17] Lange, *The History of Materialism*, 1:106.

[18] Friedrich Nietzsche, *The Will to Power*, trans. Walter Kaufmann and R. J. Hollingdale (New York: Vintage Books, 1968), section 578.

truth—to hold truth above all other values.¹⁹ But this will to truth, the unconditional rejection of deception, is ambiguous in its motivation. It could grow either from the desire not *to be* deceived or from a desire will not *to* deceive. In the first sense, science would be justified so long as it harms us to be deceived—"One does not want to be deceived because one assumes that it is harmful, dangerous, calamitous to be deceived".²⁰ But for Nietzsche it is, at the start of scientific enquiry, an open question whether deception is always so harmful, dangerous, and calamitous. Precisely because science values truth above utilitarian concerns and because science pursues truth even at the cost of human happiness (and indeed, at any cost), Nietzsche concludes that science cannot grow out of the prudential desire not to be deceived. The only alternative, he claims, is the will against deception in the second sense, a desire not to deceive: a *moral* demand to tell the truth unconditionally.

Thus, according to Nietzsche, both the Epicureans' natural enquiry *and* modern science are grounded in *moral* demands. While Lange criticises the inadequacy of Epicurean natural enquiry because it aims at happiness—in the form of negative hedonism—rather than truth, Nietzsche claims that modern science is similarly grounded in a moral dictum, namely the unconditional will to truth. In book four of *The Gay Science*, he celebrates his own compulsion to physics²¹ as a result of a competing ethical position, his commitment to the virtue of *Redlichkeit*—honesty or probity.²² Nietzsche's mention of *Redlichkeit* comes at the conclusion of a diatribe against "moral chatter", and so presumably he finds reason to distinguish it from the moral truthfulness of modern science. Yet by the time of book five's publication in 1887, Nietzsche is more self-conscious, conceding that:

---

¹⁹ GS 344.

²⁰ GS 344.

²¹ Nietzsche speaks of physics in the ancient sense of the study of *phusis* or nature, rather than the more restrictive modern discipline.

²² GS 335. The translation of *Redlichkeit* is contentious. In common German the word is approximated by 'honesty' or 'probity', however for Nietzsche the word takes on a technical meaning in the middle period, not captured by a single-word translation.

> [E]ven we seekers after knowledge today, we godless anti-metaphysicians still take our fire, too, from the flame lit by a faith that is thousands of years old, that Christian faith which was also the faith of Plato, that God is the truth, that truth is divine.[23]

Here Nietzsche admits that *Redlichkeit* has it genesis in the unconditional will to truth. Having rejected the latter's metaphysical foundation, Nietzsche acknowledges that *Redlichkeit*, like science is now "*in need of* a justification".[24] The admission does not force Nietzsche to reject *Redlichkeit* wholesale, but demands Nietzsche give an alternative, non-metaphysical account of the value of truth.

If Nietzsche rejects the *unconditional* will to truth, and he surely does, this opens a space for deception, mendacity, and "the most unscrupulous *polytropoi*" on the side of which "the great sweep of life has actually always shown itself to be".[25] It also raises the prospect that some form of the will to truth may remain as a conditional value in Nietzsche's thought, as suggested by the new table of cardinal virtues he draws in section 556 of *Dawn*, where Nietzsche reserves *Redlichkeit* for oneself and one's friends. In subsequent chapters we will see how Nietzsche's passion for knowledge grounds a commitment to *Redlichkeit*.

The after-death

Besides the fear of the gods, which the Epicureans remove by means of their modest physical enquiry, the other great fear which Epicurus identifies as fundamentally injurious to tranquillity is the fear of death. In particular, Epicurus argues against the position—common in ancient cults and subsequently adopted by the Christian tradition—that one ought to fear death because of the harms one might suffer in the afterlife. He achieves this by conceiving of the soul as part of the material and mortal body.[26] Upon death, according to the Epicureans, the soul simply disintegrates into its

---

[23] GS 344.

[24] GM III 24, emphasis in original. Nietzsche adds parenthetically "which is not to say that there is one".

[25] GS 344, a reference to Odysseus' virtuosity in deception.

[26] Christopher Gill, "Psychology," in *The Cambridge Companion to Epicureanism*, ed. James Warren (Cambridge: Cambridge University Press, 2009), 126.

constitutive atoms, in opposition to the immortal soul according to Plato and to Christianity. Epicurus claims that this account of the soul rules out the possibility of harm after death, since after death one can suffer neither pain nor distress. This argument is put in both his *Letter to Menoeceus* and second amongst his *Principle Doctrines*:

> Accustom thyself to believe that death is nothing to us, for good and evil imply sentience, and death is the privation of all sentience; therefore a right understanding that death is nothing to us makes the mortality of life enjoyable, not by adding to life an illimitable time, but by taking *away the yearning after immortality.*[27]
>
> Death is nothing to us; for the body, when it has been resolved into its elements, has no feeling, and that which has no feeling is nothing to us.[28]

The Epicurean claim that definitive death—death as the permanent dissolution of the material soul—precludes all harm associated with death remains contentious.[29] Modern commentators agree, however, that definitive death successfully dispels one species of the fear of death: the fear of punishment in hell. Death is "the cessation of one's existence, the first moment of a state of nonbeing, which is *beyond harm or gain*".[30]

Nietzsche calls the reemergence of the idea of definitive death, after Christianity had expunged it as an Epicurean doctrine, an "unspeakable benefit" and Epicurus' triumph —that "the 'after-death' no longer concerns us".[31] Yet again, the Epicureans narrow the scope of human concern and yet again, as Nietzsche notes, "we have grown poorer by *one* interest" from following the Epicureans.[32]

Nietzsche can celebrate the freedom from the fear of punishment in hell without acceding to the stronger Epicurean claim that death precludes all harm or the

---

[27] DL 10.124–25, emphasis added.

[28] PD 2.

[29] See Thomas Nagel, "Death," *Noûs* 4, no. 1 (1970): 73–80 and Joel Feinberg, "Harm to Others," in *The Metaphysics of Death*, ed. John Martin Fischer (Stanford: Stanford University Press, 1984) for two representative, contrary accounts, both attributing harm to the deprivation which death causes.

[30] Feinberg, "Harm to Others," 171, emphasis added.

[31] D 72.

[32] D 72.

Epicurean account of death as the permanent dissolution of a material soul. Indeed, Nietzsche rejects this simple materialist account of death, frequently referring to his own posthumous status[33] and claiming in relation to the writing of *Thus Spoke Zarathustra* that "one pays dearly for being immortal: one has to die several times while alive".[34] We will consider Nietzsche's discussion of death in subsequent chapters, particularly in relation to a Wagnerian *Liebestod* in chapter four, and the classical fear of death in chapter five.

The Epicurean compromise

In response to both the fear of the gods and the fear of death, the Epicureans' philosophical doctrines involve them in a compromise. Their means of removing unhealthy concerns are, in both cases, a narrowing of perspective. Nietzsche claims that it produces a poorer life as a result. The Epicureans give up all but the barest pleasures in return for a life of as little pain and suffering as possible. For Nietzsche, this is a constitutional demand:

> The Epicurean selects the situation, the persons, and even the events that suit his extremely irritable, intellectual constitution; he gives up all others, which means almost everything, because they would be too strong and heavy for him to digest.[35]

Both the Epicureans and the Stoics aim for a life free from disturbance. The Stoic achieves this through insensitivity to events in the outside world. On the other hand, the Epicurean avoids situations which would upset her delicate sensitivities. The Epicurean settles for "a garden, figs, little cheeses, and three or four good friends".[36] We might note at the point that Epicureanism admits of *some* worldly attachments and

---

[33] GS 365; TI "Maxims" 15.

[34] EH "Books" Z 5.

[35] GS 306.

[36] WS 172.

hence *some* degree of an attachment to life.³⁷ As we will see, in *The Gay Science*, Nietzsche is unsatisfied by the depth and intensity of the Epicurean attachment to life.

In *The Gay Science 306*, where Nietzsche distinguishes between the Epicurean and Stoic temperaments, he suggests that "those whose work is of the spirit"³⁸ will profit from an Epicurean disposition. The "hard Stoic skin with porcupine spines" is necessary only for those who find themselves in volatile social conditions.³⁹ In other situations, where a Stoic insensitivity is not *required*, Nietzsche claims that "subtle irritability" [*feine Reizbarkeit*] is essential to spiritual work and to those who spin "*a long thread*".⁴⁰

The preceding aphorism sheds light on Nietzsche's meaning. Moralists who preach self-control above all else afflict their followers with an aversion to "natural stirrings and inclinations," to "any instinct or free wingbeat," because these involuntary impulses seem to threaten such control.⁴¹ By turning himself "into a castle," the one who strives after self-control cuts himself off "from the most beautiful fortuities of his soul," as well as "all further *instruction*".⁴² In his quest for self-control, he turns away from any productive relationship he might otherwise have with the outside world —"one must be able to lose oneself occasionally if one wants to learn something from things different from oneself".⁴³

The one who turns himself into a castle in *GS 305* is undoubtedly the Stoic of *GS 306*: the former seeks to wrest control of himself from the accidental and the exterior;

---

³⁷ See James I. Porter, "Epicurean Attachments: Life, Pleasure, Beauty, Friendship and Piety," *Cronache Ercolanesi* 33 (2003): 205–27.

³⁸ GS 306.

³⁹ GS 306.

⁴⁰ GS 306, emphasis in original. Nietzsche repeats the idea of spinning a long thread from a letter to Erwin Rohde, March 22 1873. There, in discussing his and Rohde's ambitions for the future, he writes: "our lives must spin themselves out long enough to make sure that many of our wishes become deeds". Nietzsche employs the motif of the thread of life weaved by the Fates in Greek myth. If the Fates spin us a long thread, we will benefit from "Epicurean arrangements".

⁴¹ GS 305.

⁴² GS 305.

⁴³ GS 305.

the aim of the latter is to become "ultimately indifferent to whatever the accidents of existence might pour into [his stomach]".[44] Why might such a temperament be incapable of spinning a long thread? When Nietzsche returned to preface *The Gay Science* in 1887, he described philosophy itself as an "art of transfiguration".[45] Philosophers, according to Nietzsche, constantly transpose their lives—including their pains and "everything that wounds [them]"—into the most spiritual form.[46] The long thread is the result of this process of spiritualisation, which takes philosophers' lives as raw material. The Stoic suffers an impoverished life, according to Nietzsche, because he is insensitive to the wealth of accidents and externals which punctuate his life and thus cannot incorporate them into spiritual work.[47] The Stoic who swallows stones in *GS 306* is, in this sense, similar to the Christian in *D 70*, who accepts "*any food*" and digests "opposites like pebbles".[48] While this digestive versatility constitutes an admirable display of the church's power, it nevertheless exposes an "astonishing crudeness" in its insensitivity to that which is consumed.[49] Both the Stoic and Christian who swallow stones recall modern man in *HL 4*, who has become so enamoured with his historical sense that he "drags around with him a huge quantity of indigestible stones of knowledge".[50] At issue in all three cases is a deficiency in the individual's *plastic power*:

> the capacity to develop out of oneself in one's own way, to transform and incorporate into oneself what is past and foreign, to heal wounds, to replace what has been lost, to recreate broken moulds.[51]

---

[44] GS 306.

[45] GS P 3.

[46] GS P 3.

[47] This criticism foreshadows Nietzsche's claim in *BGE 9* that the Stoics see nature wrongly, namely "according to the Stoa" and "only after [the Stoic] image".

[48] D 70.

[49] D 70.

[50] HL 4.

[51] HL 1.

Nietzsche's conclusion in *GS 306* is that, while the Stoic might swallow stones and be present for the accidents of existence, both will pass through him as matters of indifference—they will not affect him and they will not provide for his spiritual nourishment.

The Epicurean, in comparison with the Stoic, retains a sensitivity to the accidents of life and for this very reason, tries to *avoid* such accidents. The thread that she spins depends on the tending of her natural stirrings and inclinations, and the careful arrangement of externals. The Epicurean sensitivity *to* the world is necessary for any engagement *with* the world. But because the Epicurean mollifies her sensitivity by sheltering from the accidents of existence, she does not achieve the kind of attachment that Nietzsche is seeking.

> A strong and well-formed human digests his experiences (deeds, misdeeds included) as he digests his meals, even when he has hard bites to swallow.[52]

In *The Wanderer and His Shadow* 172, as well as *The Gay Science* 45, Nietzsche emphasises the smallness and the modesty of the Epicurean life. That the Epicureans' needs are met by such small pleasures, and that their sensitivity is so finely attuned to the smallest of wants, explains why Nietzsche calls their irritability *subtle* [*feine*]. This smallness of life also explains why Nietzsche breaks with the Epicureans. Although their sensitivity ensures that they digest and incorporate the accidents of existence, their weak stomachs prevent them from embracing a wide and diverse range of experiences. This smallness and narrowing of perspective is reflected not only in the Epicurean doctrines, but also in their purgative philosophical exercises.

---

[52] GM III 16.

Philosophical purgatives

Epicurean practical philosophy is primarily purgative.[53] Epicurus identifies the sole good, pleasure, with "the absence of pain in the body and of trouble in the soul,"[54] and so the attainment of pleasure is more properly the removal of pain and anxiety. Epicurus distinguishes two kinds of pleasure: dynamic pleasures that consist in the movement between need and satisfaction (or between sickness and health) and static pleasure that consists in the blissful state which results when one is free and secure from pain altogether. The latter of these constitutes *ataraxia* (freedom from disturbance), the prime Epicurean goal. This freedom from disturbance is modelled by the Epicurean gods, whose divine indifference to worldly concerns frees them from the fears and anxieties which plague human existence.

This tranquillity is a fragile condition. In contrast to the Stoic, who finds happiness solely in moral virtue and thus gives no hostage to the external world, Epicurus admits some needs as necessary if we are to be happy, to be rid of disease and, more fundamentally, to live.[55] These needs are natural and easy to satisfy, yet, if left untended, will imperil the Epicurean's happiness. Even ensconced in her garden, the Epicurean's need for food, shelter, and sociality are satisfied, but not extinguished. Indeed, the Epicurean's neediness and what Nietzsche calls their "subtle irritability"[56] are what drive them into the garden. Epicurus' happiness at quieting his unnecessary desires and carefully tending to those that remain is "the happiness of eyes that have seen the sea of existence become calm, and now they can never weary of the surface and of the many hues of this tender, shuddering skin of the sea".[57] The tender

---

[53] Voula Tsouna, "Epicurean therapeutic strategies," in *The Cambridge Companion to Epicureanism*, ed. James Warren (Cambridge: Cambridge University Press, 2009), 249.

[54] DL 10.131.

[55] DL 10.128.

[56] GS 306.

[57] GS 45.

shuddering of Epicurus' existence testifies to the vulnerability of his tranquillity. As a consequence, the Epicurean way of life requires constant maintenance: a perpetual tending to natural desires (and concomitant dynamic pleasure) which makes possible the tranquil happiness (and static pleasure) of *ataraxia*. Nietzsche suggests something similar in *The Gay Science* 288: that a "great mood incarnate" would involve "a continual ascent as on stairs and at the same time a sense of resting on clouds". The Epicurean is involved in the continual care for her natural desires and, inasmuch as she achieves *ataraxia*, transcends these desires to participate in divine indifference.

The joy of existence

Despite the purgative nature of Epicurean philosophical practice, the Epicureans maintain that such exercises give access to positive experience of happiness or joy. In the Proem to the second book of *De Rerum Natura*, Lucretius describes the serene sanctuaries afforded him by the study of philosophy. In particular, he employs the metaphor of spectating a shipwreck. The philosopher, secure on dry land, gazes upon the tribulations of others as the sea tosses them to and fro. Knowledge, bequeathed to him by Epicurus, secures Lucretius from harm and thus grants him the highest happiness:

> But nothing is more delightful than to possess lofty sanctuaries serene, well fortified by the teachings of the wise, whence you may look down upon others and behold them all astray[58]

Lucretius is careful to distinguish between two kinds of joy granted by gazing upon the suffering of others. The first, what we might call the experience of *Schadenfreude*, he explicitly denies. He claims that it is not the suffering of others that is delightful in itself, but rather that the suffering of others reveals what ills he has secured himself from. Knowledge, for Lucretius, affords the philosopher a position of comparative security removed from the suffering of the unenlightened multitude.

---

[58] Lucr 2.7–10.

He depicts the philosopher as overlooking the sea of existence. Epicurean knowledge removes the philosopher from the shuddering surface of troubled waters and the unrelenting threat of suffering. The philosopher stands securely atop solid and rocky cliffs at shore, while out to sea the multitude is embroiled in shipwreck. Thus Lucretius conceives of philosophy's principle benefit as displacement from the passions: not only spatial separation but psychological detachment. His static [*katastematic*] pleasure is the satisfaction of observing the trials and tribulations of others, to which, as philosopher, he is not subject.

When Nietzsche, in *GS 45*, claims that he has understood Epicurus as no one has previously and evokes the image of the shuddering sea of existence, placing Epicurus atop the cliff with no shipwreck in sight, we can understand this in the context of Lucretius' use of the metaphor of the shuddering sea. In claiming a novel insight into Epicurus, Nietzsche questions the authority of Epicurus' most famous student. Nietzsche's heterodox reading of Epicurus ends with the observation that "never before has voluptuousness [*Wollust*] been so modest".[59] Whereas for Lucretius, philosophy guarantees freedom from suffering, Nietzsche paints Epicurus as "a man who was suffering continually".[60] In Nietzsche's portrait, Epicurus' happiness is not grounded in a comparison with the hapless non-philosopher, but the 'shuddering sea' of existence itself—the ever-present threat of new and returning pains. Nietzsche's point in highlighting the modesty of Epicurus is two-fold. Firstly, he rejects Lucretius' presumptive immodesty or pretension to secure impassivity: the Epicurean is sensitive to the accidents of existence as much as the non-philosopher. As we have seen, this fine-grained sensitivity *characterises* Epicureanism for Nietzsche. Secondly, Nietzsche claims that the state of calm which constitutes the Epicurean ideal could only be invented by someone experiencing Epicurus' continual suffering. Epicurean *ataraxia* belongs to the broader Hellenistic ideal of tranquillity—of "stillness, mildness, patience, medicine,

---

[59] GS 45.
[60] GS 45.

balm in some sense"⁶¹—which trades away the value of the passions in return for a calm and quiet life. Epicurus' notion of happiness betrays a modest appreciation for the passions, inasmuch as he maintains a passionate sensitivity, but Nietzsche desires more.

Nietzsche returns to the metaphor of seafaring and shipwreck repeatedly in *The Gay Science*. In *GS 124*, Nietzsche alludes to the recently announced (in *GS 108*) death of God, after which "we have left the land and have embarked […] there is no longer any 'land'".⁶² Nietzsche again denies the possibility of the secure Lucretian standpoint and mocks those who "feel homesick for the land as if it had offered you more *freedom*".⁶³ As Blumenberg shows, Nietzsche pushes this metaphor further, through the experience of a shipwreck "in which the artificial vehicle of self-deception and self-assurance was long since smashed to pieces"⁶⁴ and then to newly discovered dry land:

> Terra firma is not the position of the spectator, but rather that of the man rescued from shipwreck; its firmness is experienced wholly out of the sense of the unlikelihood that such a thing should be attainable at all.⁶⁵

Nietzsche begins 1887's book five of *The Gay Science* with a section titled "the meaning of our cheerfulness [*Heiterkeit*]"—that after the news of the death of God, "at long last our ships may venture out again, venture out to face any danger" of which presumably the most likely is shipwreck.⁶⁶ In Nietzsche's use of the metaphor of seafaring and shipwreck, and his counterposition of his own ideal to the tranquil spectatorship of Epicurus, we see that an essential component of Nietzsche's philosophical therapy is an appreciation of, an engagement with, and even an adventure through the passions.

---

[61] GS P 2.

[62] GS 124.

[63] GS 124, emphasis in original.

[64] Hans Blumenberg, *Shipwreck with Spectator: Paradigm of a Metaphor for Existence* (Cambridge, MA: MIT Press, 1997), 20.

[65] Blumenberg, *Shipwreck with Spectator*, 21–22.

[66] GS 343.

The "spiritual joyfulness" that finds pleasure in existence is an attractive sentiment for Nietzsche.[67] Epicurus' practical philosophy aims at a happiness that is free from metaphysical commitments or concerns over ultimate convictions, and for this reason Nietzsche admits he looks like an Epicurean.[68] Yet Epicurus has little time for adventure or the world outside his garden. Rather, he is concerned only with relieving his own pain, a concern Nietzsche diagnoses as appropriate only for "a man who was continually suffering".[69] The needs served by Epicureanism come, not from a superfluity of life, which Nietzsche's cheerfulness in the 1880s celebrates, but from its impoverishment, seeking "rest, stillness, calm seas, [and] redemption from" himself.[70] His needs, both bodily and of the mind, are modest, satisfied by little cheeses and deliverance from fear.

In section 349 of *Assorted Opinions and Maxims* we find another evocative, literary depiction of the Epicurean temperament, described as the "freezing point of the will":[71]

> "Finally, one day, it arrives, the hour that will envelop you in a golden cloud free from pain: where your soul takes pleasure in its own fatigue and, happy in a playing patiently with its own patience, is like the waves of a lake that lap at the shore on a calm summer day in the reflect glow of a brightly coloured evening sky, lap again, and then grow still—without end, without purpose, without being sated, without need—wholly at peace, while rejoicing in change, wholly absorbed in the ebb and flow to the pulse of nature"[72]

Nietzsche indicates that this tranquil pleasure of the afternoon is "the feeling and language of all invalids".[73] The Epicurean enjoyment of repose, rather than granting lasting happiness, eventually gives way to boredom. He concludes that this boredom, dissatisfaction with restfulness, is the prospect of a "thawing breeze for the frozen

---

[67] Keith Ansell-Pearson, "True to the Earth: Nietzsche's Epicurean Care of Self and World," in *Nietzsche's Therapeutic Teaching*, eds. Horst Hutter and Eli Friedland (London: Bloomsbury, 2013), 102.

[68] GS 375.

[69] GS 45.

[70] GS 370.

[71] AOM 349.

[72] AOM 349.

[73] AOM 349.

will".[74] He conceives of his own boredom with Stoic and Epicurean therapies a sign of coming convalescence.

Nietzsche considers the emergence of a immodest, voluptuous cheerfulness in his work as synonymous with his return to health.[75] In the coming chapters I make sense of this anti-Hellenistic stance through the lens of a recuperation of eros. This requires, in chapter three, a consideration of Nietzsche's relationship to Plato through a reading of *The Symposium*.

---

[74] AOM 349.

[75] GS P 1.

3. Platonic Ascent: The Metaphysical Pathology

Both the Stoics and Epicureans practice a philosophy of caution against the passions.[1] Stoic *apatheia* and Epicurean *ataraxia* are instances of the tranquillity celebrated by all the Hellenistic schools in the period Nietzsche dubs the "afternoon of antiquity".[2] Nietzsche makes clear, as I have shown in the two preceding chapters, that this ideal is not his own. Rather than the diminution of the passions, Nietzsche envisions their proliferation and intensification in order to open up "new galaxies of joy".[3] In this chapter I set the scene for Nietzsche's anti-Hellenistic recuperation of the passions through an examination of passionate love as it appears in Plato's *Symposium*.

If Nietzsche in *The Gay Science* laments what he sees as the timidity of the schools of late antiquity, it may be suggested that his recuperation of the passions marks a return to the birth of philosophy. And if Nietzsche conceives the philosopher as a practitioner of eros, this places him in close company with Plato, who in the *Symposium* depicts love as proper task of the philosopher.[4] Nevertheless, the most appropriate object of philosophical love according to Plato is the stable and eternal form of the good. Plato's love leads the philosopher into the metaphysical realm, and if Nietzsche is to adopt Plato's erotic orientation, he must find a way to avoid following Plato into metaphysics.

In this chapter I explicate Plato's treatment of love in the *Symposium*. I elucidate Plato's concept of philosophy as the highest form of love and Socrates as an example of the best kind of lover. I connect the Platonic account of desire with Schopenhauer, before explaining how Schopenhauer's rejection of transcendence leads to him to

---

[1] In BGE 198 Nietzsche suggests *all* prior *eudaimonistic* moralities offer just recipes against the passions and their danger.

[2] GS 45.

[3] GS 12.

[4] The *Symposium* was, during his time at Schulpforta, Nietzsche's favourite work from Plato, and "one of his favourite ancient texts". Thomas Brobjer, *Nietzsche's Philosophical Context: An Intellectual Biography* (Urbana: University of Illinois Press, 2008), 45.

resignation. On Schopenhauer's account, eros necessarily fails to find satisfaction. Nietzsche considers Schopenhauerian pessimism the historical culmination and logical extension of Platonism. Noting the consequent necessary failure of the Platonic erotic pedagogy, Nietzsche attempts an anti-Platonic, anti-Schopenhauerian renovation of eros and the passions, which I will consider in chapter four.

In chapter four, I argue that Nietzsche is aware of the danger posed by Platonic idealism, and draws on the Provençal concept of *gaia scienza* and the supposed "invention" of a passionate, secular notion of love in order to arrest a slide to metaphysics.[5] Contrary to the wretched state of the impassioned lover depicted in the *Symposium* redeemed only by transcending the mortal realm, the love of the troubadours "encouraged self-sufficiency among human beings".[6] The title of Nietzsche's *Gay Science* recalls both the art of the troubadours, and the more modern, scientific, demands of intellectual probity—Nietzsche's *Redlichkeit*—which compels him to naturalism. Nietzsche's science owes much to, but exceeds, the naturalism of modern science. While modern science aspires to describe the world "objectively", free from the distortions and falsifications of perspective, Nietzsche's *gay* science is centrally concerned with the problem of value. It portends the question "whether science can furnish goals of action".[7] The task which Nietzsche sets the gay science is to cultivate passionate attachments to worldly objects through careful attention.[8] His naturalistic disposition enables him to read value in the world without becoming deceived into Platonic idealism; his philosophical ascent is not an escape from nature, but a return.[9]

Nietzsche thus situates himself between the Stoics, who oppose and subordinate the passions to reason, and Plato, whose passionate devotion to the form of the good

---

[5] BGE 260.

[6] Irving Singer, *The Nature of Love*, vol. 2, *Courtly and Romantic* (Cambridge and London: MIT Press, 2009), 51.

[7] GS 7.

[8] GS 334.

[9] TI "Expeditions" 48.

culminates in a flight from the world. He attempts a theory of value which denies that objects are "beautiful, attractive, and desirable" in themselves, but nevertheless sustains passionate attachment to such objects. I argue that the resulting account gives Nietzsche a collection of techniques for cultivating and training the passions in accordance with the promotion of human flourishing. As Nietzsche concludes in *GS 334*, "love, too, has to be learned".[10]

On graduating from boarding school in 1864, Nietzsche named the *Symposium* as his favourite ancient text.[11] The same year he had written an essay on the work titled *"On the relationship of Alcibiades' speech to the other speeches in Plato's Symposium"* and around 1875 would write in a note that "Socrates, simply to confess it, stands so near to me, that I almost always fight a battle with him".[12] In *The Gay Science*, Nietzsche conceives of philosophy as a species of love and in particular as the highest form of love. Plato too conceives philosophy as the treatment of eros, and nowhere is this made more explicit than in the figure of Socrates in the *Symposium*. But if Nietzsche and Plato share the orientation of philosophy towards the treatment and perfection of eros, this similarity also explains their bitter rivalry as to how eros should be philosophically trained. As Cooper notes, "Nietzsche seeks to take on Plato—and seeks to *rival* Plato by following Plato's way in the pursuit of a decidedly non-Platonic end".[13] Cooper's claim is that Nietzsche proposes the will to power as a unifying account of human striving and, like Plato with eros, purports to have hit upon "the 'thing' in which it finds fullest satisfaction".[14] But whereas Plato finds the highest expression of eros in metaphysical contemplation, Nietzsche spurns metaphysics. According to Cooper, the 'thing' in which the will to power finds its fullest satisfaction

---

[10] GS 334.

[11] Brobjer, *Nietzsche's Philosophical Context*, 45.

[12] KGW IV 6[3].

[13] Laurence D. Cooper, *Eros in Plato, Rousseau, and Nietzsche: The politics of infinity* (University Park, Pennsylvania: Pennsylvania State University Press, 2008), 11, emphasis in original.

[14] Cooper, *Eros in Plato, Rousseau and Nietzsche*, 12.

is the eternal recurrence of all things. The end point of Nietzsche's philosophical treatment of desire is that one "*crave[s] nothing more fervently*" than the recurrence of the very same life.[15]

What follows is a consideration of the *Symposium* to the extent necessary to illuminate Nietzsche's rejection of Plato's metaphysics of love and his concurrent adoption of a therapeutic model of philosophy. While incomplete, this reading is sufficient to explain Nietzsche's objection to the metaphysical therapy of eros.

Framing the Symposium

The *Symposium* opens with Apollodorus, a follower of Socrates, responding to an unnamed questioner. Apollodorus's friend has asked for an account of a party hosted by the tragic poet Agathon, involving Socrates and Alcibiades, where the three and others gave speeches on the topic of love. It turns out that Apollodorus is well prepared to give such an account, having recently recounted the party's speeches to Glaucon (who also appears as an interlocutor in the *Republic*). This framing illuminates how Plato's audience would have read the seven speeches that make up the bulk of the dialogue. That Alcibiades is included amongst the speakers on love is surprising, since he joins the party only after the other speeches have concluded. He enters, drunk, with a band of revellers. Rather than speaking in praise of love, Alcibiades professes to "speak the truth" in praise of Socrates.[16] Alcibiades is a "manifest lover", according to Cooper, in that rather than simply offering a speech *about* love, he "unambiguously demonstrate[s] or *act[s]* upon it before our eyes".[17] The "truth" which Alcibiades

---

[15] GS 341.

[16] Symp. 214e.

[17] Cooper also counts Apollodorus, Aristodemus, and, equivocally, Socrates as "manifest lovers". Apollodorus and Aristodemus both, like Alcibiades, love Socrates. Apollodorus' love of Socrates (and philosophy) cures him of his "most miserable" prior state (Symp. 173a). Aristodemus, who attends the party but doesn't speak, was Socrates' most devoted admirer when the party was held, on Apollodorus' account (Symp. 173b). Socrates speech is similarly an enactment of love but differs from the other three manifest lovers' contributions since it is also a speech *about* love and because he enacts a love of wisdom rather than the passionate love of another person. (Cooper, *Eros in Plato, Rousseau, and Nietzsche*, 110)

speaks and enacts is the lover who is afflicted by his passions. The twenty-year-old Nietzsche of 1864 concurs: the figure of Alcibiades in the *Symposium* "illustrate[s] the effect of love for beauty on the actual life of men".[18] His arrival heralds "the turning point of the artistic drama and philosophy toward reality".[19] Alcibiades represents the actual afflicted lover and with him the task of the *Symposium*—to treat the unruly passions—becomes most clear.

Socrates and Agathon give the final two speeches before Alcibiades' entrance. They receive the highest applause, with only the comic poet Aristophanes objecting after Socrates concludes. The contest between their accounts—love of the beautiful and love of the good—is, according to Strauss, "the great theme of the *Symposium*".[20] But not only do Agathon and Socrates present contrasting accounts of love, they represent two factions of Athenian society. While the speech of Socrates is the centrepiece of the dialogue, the preceding five speeches give voice to "the mythic and traditional conceptions [of love] prevalent in Greek society"—they lay the foundation upon which Socrates builds and to which he reacts.[21] And, although perhaps "all Platonic wisdom"[22] resides in the definition that "love is desire for the perpetual possession of the good",[23] the accounts of desire and of the good which unfolds through the first five speeches are essential for grasping Plato's final position. One of Plato's primary concerns, here as elsewhere, is to distinguish philosophy from existing cultural traditions in the Athenian *polis*, and furthermore to establish its supremacy. Socrates represents the insurgent philosophical tradition. Agathon, on the other hand, stands for tragic poetry, philosophy's strongest opponent. The role of Socrates' speech in the

---

[18] Friedrich Nietzsche, "On the Relationship of Alcibiades' Speech to the Other Speeches in Plato's Symposium," *Graduate Faculty Philosophy Journal* 15, no. 2 (1991), 4.

[19] Nietzsche, "On the Relationship of Alcibiades' Speech to the Other Speeches in Plato's Symposium," 5.

[20] Leo Strauss, *Leo Strauss On Plato's Symposium* (Chicago: University of Chicago Press, 2001), 28.

[21] Irving Singer, *The Nature of Love*, vol. 1, *Plato to Luther* (Cambridge and London: MIT Press, 2009), 50.

[22] Singer, *The Nature of Love*, 1.53.

[23] Symp. 206b.

Symposium, is to establish philosophy as an alternative account of love and its perfection to those represented by the other speakers, especially Agathon the poet who views love as the desire for the beautiful. The central dispute in the *Symposium*, and Plato draws our attention to this fact in the opening conversation, is the so-called quarrel between philosophy and poetry, declared in the *Republic*.[24]

Agathon is not the only poet at the party, however, and not even the poet who speaks best or in strongest opposition to Socrates.[25] Aristophanes, rather than Agathon, gives the strongest speech against Socrates' philosophical eros. While Plato presents the *Symposium* as primarily a contest between Agathon and Socrates (by putting these two names in the mouth of Apollodorus' friend), the more contentious quarrel takes place between Socrates and Aristophanes.

Alcibiades the patient

At issue in the quarrel between Socrates and the poets is the treatment of the passions. Rosen casts the quarrel in terms of the effects of philosophy and poetry on desire:

> The quarrel amounts to this: poetry encourages desire, and hence the will. It encourages production for the sake of satisfying the desires, or in other words defines completeness as satisfaction. Philosophy, on the other hand, advocates the restriction of the desires or the transformation of desire in accord with the definition of completeness as wisdom.[26]

Both poetry and philosophy, according to Rosen, are responses to the feeling of incompleteness brought about by desire. Each soothes this painful feeling by promoting a distinct notion of completeness. For poetry, completeness is the satisfaction of desire or the attainment of the desired object. Because the satisfaction of desire depends on the attainment of objects outside of one's control, the poetic account of completeness consigns individuals to a life where their happiness is hostage to the chancy outside

---

[24] Rep. 607b.

[25] The young Nietzsche makes this point, that Aristophanes is "the greater mind by far", and that Agathon "owes Plato his higher ranker over Aristophanes as a tragic poet: a judgement with which we would no longer agree" (Nietzsche, "On the Relationship of Alcibiades' Speech to the Other Speeches in Plato's Symposium," 4).

[26] Stanley Rosen, *The Quarrel between Philosophy and Poetry* (New York and London: Routledge, 1988), 13.

world. Poetry, by encouraging desire, disrupts the rational control of one's life. Philosophy, in contrast, takes the complete life to be one which is rationally directed. Since desire disrupts the exercise of rational control over one's life, according to Plato, desire is an impediment to completeness. The object of philosophy is the transform desire so that one can gain rational control over one's life.

In the *Symposium*, Alcibiades manifests the desirous lover. The intoxication of his love for Socrates underscores the fact that he is not in rational control of his life. Socrates offers Alcibiades a philosophical treatment of desire through which he might regain rational control of his life. Plato's selection of the dramatic dates of the dialogue —the timing of Apollodorus' conversations and of the party itself—serve to draw further attention to the figure of Alcibiades.

Nussbaum sets the date of Apollodorus' two conversations, first with Glaucon and then with his unnamed friend, in 404 BCE.[27] In the closing years of the fifth century BCE, Athens was on the verge of military defeat with seemingly the only hope for victory over Sparta and the restoration of democracy being the return of Alcibiades. The year 404 BCE is also the date of production for Aristophanes' *Frogs*, wherein he "testifies to the fear that not only political freedom, but poetic speech as well, are on the verge of extinction".[28] In this tense political situation, Critias—Plato's uncle and an associate of Socrates—leads the pro-Spartan, anti-democratic thirty tyrants to power, with the assassination of Alcibiades abroad soon to follow.

Agathon's party itself occurs in early 416 BCE, on the occasion of his first victory at the dramatic festival.[29] This date too evokes memories of Alcibiades. The following year, Alcibiades was implicated in two religious scandals: the mutilation of statues of

---

[27] Martha C. Nussbaum, "The Speech of Alcibiades: A Reading of Plato's Symposium," *Philosophy and Literature* 3, no. 2 (1979): 134–39.

[28] Nussbaum, "The Speech of Alcibiades," 136.

[29] Plato, *The Symposium*, ed. Frisbee C. C. Sheffield, trans. M. C. Howatson (Cambridge: Cambridge University Press, 2008), 2n6.

Hermes and profaning the Eleusinian mysteries at a drunken meeting.[30] Alcibiades was tried and found guilty in absentia, while on an ill-fated military expedition, and these scandals served for the Athenians as "the most egregious case of Alcibiades' lack of control over his actions, the recklessness and emotional disorder that were seen constantly to undercut his genius".[31] The events of 415 BCE led to Alcibiades long exile and ultimately to his assassination in 404 BCE.

Plato ties these two events together—the scandal of 415 BCE and the disastrous conclusion to Alcibiades' long exile in 404 BCE. Alcibiades was offered a therapy of his pernicious desires in 416 BCE. He failed to heed Socrates' therapy, and so a decade of estrangement from Athens culminated in the calamity of his death in 404 BCE. Contemporary readers of the *Symposium* could not have overlooked Alcibiades' need for the therapy which Socrates supplies.

Three uninspired speeches

Six speeches on love are recorded before Alcibiades' raucous entrance to Agathon's party. The first three, from Phaedrus, Pausanias, and Eryximachus, are what Strauss calls the dialogue's "uninspired" speeches.[32] The three praise love in terms of the human goods it might grant. Phaedrus, the first speaker, claims that love is the oldest god and "the source of our greatest blessings".[33] Pausanias praises love as the source of virtue and lawfulness in the city. Eryximachus expands the scope of love to all

---

[30] Plutarch (Alc. 18–19) and Thucydides (6.27–29) describe the accusations in detail. The Hermae were statues of the god Hermes, common in both private houses and in religious buildings. One night during preparation for the Athenian expedition to Sicily, the faces of many of the Hermae were mutilated. While no one witnessed the crime, attention turned to a group of licentious youths "in a drunken frolic", including Alcibiades, who were said to have mocked the religious rites of Eleusis (Thuc 6.28). The group was accused of parodying the initiation ceremony of the Eleusinian mysteries, with Alcibiades playing the role of the high priest. Alcibiades was saddled with responsibility for both crimes by his political enemies.

[31] Nussbaum, "The Speech of Alcibiades," 138.

[32] Strauss, *Leo Strauss On Plato's Symposium*, 121.

[33] Symp. 178c.

endeavours—love is that which brings about the reconciliation of opposites in any skilful profession [techne].

For all three speakers, love is praised as instrumentally useful for attaining some other good. Love is the best means to personal gain, civic virtue, and technical prowess. But, as Agathon later complains,[34] when the first three speakers praise love for its instrumental value, they overlook the nature of love itself.

Aristophanes makes a similar point when he jokes at Eryximachus' expense at line 189a. Aristophanes was to speak before Eryximachus, but was unable to because of an attack of hiccups. Eryximachus, the doctor, offers both to speak in his place and prescribes a number of treatments for his hiccups: first to hold his breath, to gargle water, and, if the first two treatments fail, to tickle his own nose.[35] Eryximachus praises the power of love to reconcile opposites—it produces "harmony and a blending in right proportions [sophron]".[36] At the conclusion of Eryximachus' speech, Aristophanes exclaims that his hiccups have been cured, but only when "the sneeze was applied to it".[37] Aristophanes wonders whether "the orderliness [kosmion] of the body desires these [disorderly] kinds of noises and ticklings".[38] He suggests that love, even if it aims at orderliness in the body, achieves its ends through disorderly, ugly, and base means. That love is instrumentally valuable does not guarantee its nobility in itself. This is the first indication that love might involve a mixture of higher and lower properties.

Aristophanes' joke marks the transition from the first three "uninspired" speeches to his own, Agathon's, and Socrates' "inspired" speeches. When he jokes at Eryximachus, Aristophanes (as a writer of comic poetry) refers to his art as a muse [moûsa] in

---

[34] Symp. 194e-195a.

[35] Symp. 189b.

[36] Symp. 188a.

[37] Symp. 189a.

[38] Symp. 189a.

contrast to Eryximachus' skill [*techne*]. The meaning of this distinction is that the musician is divinely inspired, while the technician is not.[39]

Love of the same

Aristophanes' account is intimately concerned with the bodily contingencies of love. His account takes seriously the experience that one has of love for a single particular individual and the danger passionate attachment to such an individual poses to our happiness. According to Aristophanes, lovers desire "to join with and melt into" a particular beloved.[40] The path to happiness depends on finding this individual, "which rarely happens at the present time".[41] Like many of the other speakers, he poses his account of love in the form of a mythic story. According to the tale he spins, humans were originally large spherical creatures with four arms, four legs, and a pair of faces on a single circular head. Each individual had a pair of reproductive organs, and each of these was either male or female, so that the individual had either two male organs, two female, or one of each. Thus these creatures were divided into three sexes. The two faces of each individual were oriented outwards, towards the being's two dorsal surfaces, as were the creature's genitals. These primordial humans were twice the size and strength of humans today, and were so powerful as to threaten the gods. Rather than annihilate the primordial humans in defence and lose the worship and sacrifices they provided, Zeus decided to slice each creature in half such that the newly formed individuals have half the limbs, a single face, and supposedly pose no threat to the gods. Zeus then asked Apollo to heal the wounds produced on the newly fashioned humans' abdomens, gathering their skin together into the navel "like a purse with a drawstring".[42] Apollo additionally rearranged the newly created humans' faces so that

---

[39] Symp. 189b.

[40] Symp. 192e.

[41] Symp. 193b.

[42] Symp. 190e.

they are oriented towards the abdominal scar, so that the sight of it reminds them to behave in moderation and obedience to the gods.

Love, according to Aristophanes, is the nostalgic yearning each person has for this lost primordial unity. Affection [*philia*], intimacy [*oikeiotes*], and love [*eros*] overcome those who happen upon their other half: a pair, once reunited, will happily spend the rest of their lives in an embrace, imitating the nature of their originary whole by holding each other at the abdomen. Pairs who had reunited in this manner—so goes Aristophanes' story—would not separate even to eat. Out of pity, and to prevent the humans trapped in a loving embrace from starving, Zeus moves the reproductive organs (hitherto in their original orientation on the new humans' backs) so that an embrace would subsequently beget new individuals through sexual activity. Aristophanes explains that thereby each of the pair "might achieve satisfaction from the union and after this respite turn to their tasks and get on with the business of life".[43]

Three principal characteristics emerge from Aristophanes' account. Firstly, he allows the bodily and the base into love's characteristic activity. Love arises out of the "painfully needy" body and the hope that these needs might be met through the "peculiar, or even grotesque" interpenetration of another.[44] While sexual activity grants temporary reprieve from the needs of the body, they soon return to distract the lover from the "business of life".[45] Mere interpenetration cannot re-establish the two lovers' originary unity; only the god Hephaestus could do that. Secondly, Aristophanes' love leaves the lover radically exposed to contingency. One loves a single other, and happening upon the right individual is an extreme piece of luck. Even if one does find the right individual this momentary success is fragile, subject to the threats of loss or jealousy. Lastly, there is a question over what might become of desire if one's originary

---

[43] Symp. 191c.

[44] Nussbaum, "The Speech of Alcibiades," 140.

[45] Symp. 191c.

whole were to be restored. Nussbaum suggests that were Hephaestus to join two lovers completely, the result would be "a wholeness that would put an end to all movement and all passion".[46] Indeed, this is what, according to Aristophanes, the lovers would profess—no one, having heard Hephaestus' offer, "would deny them or would admit to wanting anything else".[47] Yet Aristophanes also describes the behaviour of the original spherical creatures, and they do not resemble Nussbaum's static and emotionless artefact. The progenitors of humans were ambitious and impious. Indeed, Zeus's order to separate them was motivated by the fear that they would rebel against the gods. If the reunion of two lovers is the achievement of their original unity, then the reunited lovers would presumably regain their Promethean ambition against the gods. Thus for Aristophanes, the motive power of love is not quelled or exhausted by communion with the beloved, but continues excessively beyond such narrow bounds.[48]

In Aristophanes' tale this never occurs, because a union of two individuals necessarily eludes us as post-separation humans. Aristophanes' warning that the unruly passions will eventually lead to profanity would be read by Plato's contemporary readers, as mentioned, in light of the accusation that shortly after the party Alcibiades would deface the statues of Hermes.[49] This is not the only parallel between Aristophanes' account and the figure of Alcibiades. Alcibiades speaks about love by praising Socrates, because his experience of love is of a single individual, who affects him like no other. Alcibiades' "entire speech is an attempt to grasp and communicate that uniqueness, to make credible and imaginable for us an experience and a feeling that is by its nature difficult to describe".[50] Alcibiades love of Socrates, that individual

---

[46] Nussbaum, "The Speech of Alcibiades," 144.

[47] Symp. 192e.

[48] Anne Carson, *Eros the Bittersweet* (Princeton: Princeton University Press, 1986), 68.

[49] Nussbaum, "The Speech of Alcibiades," 138.

[50] Nussbaum, "The Speech of Alcibiades," 155–56.

who he praises as "completely unlike any other human being who has ever lived",[51] is of a kind with Aristophanes' account.

Aristophanes concludes by counselling piety, that one should arrest the excesses of love out of fear or respect for the gods. But as the *Symposium*'s reader would be aware, Alcibiades failed to heed this prescription, and suffered greatly for his irreverence.

Love of the beautiful

Agathon's "pretty but unmistakably superficial"[52] speech is the first to set out to praise the character of love itself, before making an appraisal of its human effects. As noted, he complains that the forerunning speeches have focused exclusively on love's utility for humans. But if Agathon's speech is novel in form, its content recycles the accolades the previous speakers have already announced: love is graceful,[53] just,[54] possessing self-control [*sophrosune*],[55] brave,[56] and wise in the arts [*moûsa*];[57] love is "not only supreme in beauty and goodness himself but is also the source of beauty and goodness in all other things".[58] Agathon's praise of love culminates in verse that encapsulates the first three speeches' unbridled veneration of love, that love creates

> Peace among humankind, windless calm on the open sea,
> Rest for the winds and sleep in sorrow.[59]

The first five speeches set the scene for the centrepiece of the *Symposium*, the speech of Socrates. The young Nietzsche of 1864 summarises the first five speeches as offering

---

[51] Symp. 221c.

[52] Glenn W. Most, "Six Remarks on Platonic Eros," in *Erotikon: Essays on Eros, Ancient and Modern*, eds. Shadi Bartsch and Thomas Bartscherer (Chicago: University of Chicago Press, 2005), 35.

[53] Symp. 196a.

[54] Symp. 196c.

[55] Symp. 196c.

[56] Symp. 196d.

[57] Symp. 196d-197b.

[58] Symp. 196c.

[59] Symp. 197c.

an account of love as "love of the Beautiful, a natural law aimed at producing the Good", an account "not substantially different" from the one which Socrates will go on to give.[60] Before moving to Socrates' speech, it is worthwhile to summarise the problems for an analysis of love thrown up by the first five speeches, to which Socrates will respond. Three of these are of particular importance in this chapter: i) the nature of love, ii) the object of love, and iii) the relationship with the world that love instils in the lover. First, as Agathon rightly points out, the nature of love is a neglected topic in the first four speeches. Agathon's posits that love's nature is supremely beautiful and good. As noted, however, when Aristophanes makes a joke at Eryximachus' expense, he suggests that love involves a mixture of higher and lower properties. We can read Aristophanes as contesting the other speakers' veneration of love as supremely noble in itself. Socrates spends a great deal of time arguing, against Agathon, that love is not beautiful, and involves a movement between higher and lower properties. The object of love is covered explicitly by each of the first five speeches, either a well-ordered arrangement, recuperation into a whole, or in Agathon's view, beauty and goodness themselves. This is the second point on which to analyse Socrates' speech. The third problem posed is the relationship between the lover and the sensuous life of the body. In Aristophanes' speech, base sexual desire functions to arrest the excess of love, while in Agathon's, love overcomes the brutish existence ruled—prior to its advent—by bare necessity. In all five speeches, love is an alternative to and an escape from the vulgarities of the sensuous. Since the everyday meaning of eros in Ancient Greece was, as its modern English cognates remain, intimately tied to sexual desire,[61] this aversion to the sensuous goes towards distinguishing a specifically *philosophical* love. With these three problems in mind we will now turn to Socrates's speech.

---

[60] Nietzsche, "On the Relationship of Alcibiades' Speech to the Other Speeches in Plato's Symposium," 3.
[61] Most, "Six Remarks on Platonic Eros," 33.

Socrates' love of wisdom

Socrates begins his speech by warning that he will not be able to offer the same unequivocal praise for love as the previous speakers, but only the truth.[62] And if Aristophanes gave voice to the baseness and fragility of the common experience of love, Socrates' account will be markedly revisionary. Socrates promises a love which escapes the Aristophanic predicament—the vulnerability of human erotic aspiration to the transient nature of its object. Socrates claims that this vulnerability stems from a failure to account for the true nature and object of love and that, properly understood, the highest lover can achieve stable and lasting happiness through the love of eternal and unchanging forms. By climbing Plato's ladder of love, the lover of the individual and particular might be cured of these attachments, and learn a love which grants self-sufficient and unshakeable happiness.

The nature of philosophy

Socrates first rejects that love itself is good or beautiful. Putting the object of love to the side, he identifies love as a kind of desire and, by means of an interrogation of Agathon, draws a number of conclusions. First, desire depends on the absence of its object: "there is no desire if there is no lack",[63] since a desire ceases if it is satisfied by possession of its object. There is an apparent counterexample in the situation when, for instance, a healthy person desires to be healthy, or someone with particular attributes "also *desire*[s] to have the attributes they have".[64] Socrates answers that in such a case, what is desired is not simply to possess a certain attribute, but to possess that attribute into the future. The healthy person desires to continue being healthy and desire, in general, is for the continued possession of an object.

---

[62] Symp. 199b.

[63] Symp. 200b.

[64] Symp. 200c, emphasis in original.

There is a riddle as to why, if love is devoid of beauty, as Socrates argues, it nevertheless takes beauty as its object. In his opening remarks he takes this thought from Agathon; in the body of his speech, he provides an explanation given to him by the priestess Diotima. According to Diotima, love is neither beautiful nor ugly, but an intermediary between the two, in the same way as correct belief exists at a midpoint between ignorance and wisdom (which requires both correct belief and a reasoned justification thereof). Diotima explains love's intermediary nature through a story concerning its parentage. While Phaedrus called love the eldest of the gods and Agathon named it the youngest, Diotima disputes that love is a god at all. Instead, love is the child of Poros [resource] and Penia [poverty]. Because it is the child of poverty, love *lacks* the beautiful, but because it is the child of resource, it is always "scheming to get what is beautiful and good".[65] Because of this fact of its birth, love is neither mortal nor godly, but daemonic—in an intermediary position between the mortal and the divine.

While this is a novel conception for Socrates within the setting of the *Symposium*, the notion that love involves an intermediary principle is not new in Greek thought. Carson discovers this idea in a poem from Sappho, two centuries before Plato.[66] The consequence of the intermediary nature of love for Carson, and for Socrates in the *Symposium*, is to give love a dynamic character. Platonic eros is not the "windless calm" praised by Agathon, but a movement between lover and beloved. Additionally for Socrates, love is an inspired movement—the lover is *daimonios* according to Diotima; that is, inspired by the divine.[67] The same notion of love appears in the *Phaedrus*, where Socrates praises it as an "inspired madness" which is "given by the gods".[68]

---

[65] Symp. 203d.

[66] Carson, *Eros the Bittersweet*, 12–17.

[67] Symp. 203a.

[68] Phaedrus 245b–c.

At a practical level, love as a *daimon* affects the lover as a "frenzy […] of heavenly origin".[69] In speaking of the 'demonic' character of love, Plato describes the way in which passionate engagements exceed and escape the control of sober, non-inspired deliberation. To speak of the philosopher as a lover, then, implies that the pursuit of wisdom is one such passionate engagement.

In order to distinguish philosophical wisdom from the disruptive and harmful passions which afflict, for examples, Alcibiades, Plato must explain how a philosophical love might conduce to rational self control. The passions disrupt practical reason by holding the course of one's life hostage to fragile and transient objects. If Plato can find a stable and omnipresent object of desire, he dissolves the difficulties of loving such fallible things. He finds precisely this in the divine form of the good—an eternal, unchanging object the desire of which allows him to rationally order his life. Socrates frees himself and others of passions for mortal objects by cultivating a singular devotion to the good.

The object of philosophy

There is an ambiguity in Socrates' speech: whether the object of love is the beautiful, as Agathon held, or the good. At first, Socrates borrows the notion that the object of love is the beautiful from Agathon during their initial dialogue,

> "I think you said something like this, that the interests of the gods were established by reason of their love of beautiful things; for there is no love of ugly things, you said. Didn't you say something like this?"[70]

This notion continues into Socrates' speech proper, the retelling of his dialogue with Diotima. At 204c, Diotima calls the object of love "supremely beautiful". Yet soon after, she draws a distinction between love of the beautiful and love of the good. When Socrates expresses confusion at what securing possession of the beautiful might grant the lover, Diotima shifts the discussion—"imagine that the object is changed, and the

---

[69] Denis de Rougemont, *Love in the Western World* (New York: Pantheon, 1956), 61.
[70] Symp. 201a.

inquiry is made about the good instead of the beautiful".[71] This is an easier question for Socrates to answer: secure possession of the good grants happiness to its possessor. This line of reasoning leads Diotima to claim that "the only thing people love is the good" and ultimately to conclude that "love is the desire to possess the good always".[72]

Socrates does not thereby abandon the beautiful in favour of the good. Immediately after concluding that "love is the desire to possess the good always", Diotima returns to a consideration of love as desiring what is beautiful. Even at the culmination of Socrates' speech, he calls the object of the philosopher's contemplation "beauty itself".[73] Socrates' speech "begins with a refutation of the assertion that love is of the beautiful and it ends with an unbelievable reassertion that love is love of the beautiful".[74]

Between these two assertions, Socrates fine-tunes the role the beautiful plays in love. Love is the desire, not just of the good, but of its perpetual possession. In order to possess the good perpetually, one must also desire some kind of immortality, since death dispossess us.[75] Diotima describes a number of ways in which mortal humans might achieve a kind of immortality: through rearing offspring, through fame, or through giving birth to the 'offspring' of the soul—wisdom and virtue.[76] The path to all three forms of immortality is through "continual generation".[77] According to Diotima, generation is only possible in the presence of the beautiful, and so the presence of the beautiful is necessary for the reproduction of the good. The ultimate goal of philosophical love is to give birth to and nurture true virtue:

---

[71] Symp. 204e.

[72] Symp. 206a; The phrase which, according to Singer, encapsulates all Platonic wisdom.

[73] Symp. 211d.

[74] Strauss, *Leo Strauss On Plato's Symposium*, 213.

[75] Symp. 207a.

[76] Symp. 209a.

[77] Symp. 207d.

> When he has given birth to and nurtured true virtue it is possible for him to be loved by the gods and to become, if any human can, immortal himself.[78]

Love, then—procreation in the presence of the beautiful—is the means by which mortals might live well. Philosophy posits the eternal form of the good as an object of desire in order that its followers can avoid the dangers of passionate attachment to (however beautiful) objects in the world. To "have an object of love and understanding that is perfectly unchanging and always available to be loved and contemplated" enables the philosopher to direct her life in a manner which the passions, supposedly, make impossible.[79] This is the distinction between philosophy and poetry which Rosen drew, above, that philosophy "advocates the […] transformation of desire in accord with the definition of completeness as wisdom" or practical reason.[80]

Diotima achieves a reconciliation of sorts between poetry (which loves the beautiful) and philosophy (which loves the good) "by interpreting the beautiful as an instrument or means to the good".[81] Again, recalling that the quarrel between philosophy and poetry in fifth-century Athens is a central theme of the *Symposium*, we can interpret this reconciliation politically. Plato depicts a settlement whereby poetry, and especially tragic poetry, could be used for philosophical ends. Socrates' expulsion of the poetry from the city in the *Republic* is made on the grounded of poetry's intemperance with desire. He excludes the "pleasure-seasoned Muse" for replacing the rule of *nomos* with the rule of pleasure and pain.[82] Yet, "if the mimetic and dulcet poetry can show any reason for her existence in a well-governed state, we would gladly admit her".[83] If poetry can be reformed of its harmful relationship with desire, it may be admitted back to the city. As Rosen observers, "Socrates does not actually, despite

---

[78] Symp. 212a.

[79] Nussbaum, "The Speech of Alcibiades," 150.

[80] Rosen, *The Quarrel between Philosophy and Poetry*, 13.

[81] Cooper, *Eros in Plato, Rousseau, and Nietzsche*, 80.

[82] Rep. 607a.

[83] Rep. 607d.

his explicit statement to that effect, expel poetry from his city but rather subordinates it to philosophy. [...] the philosopher must *imitate* the poet 'for the benefit of the city'".[84]

Such a possibility is realised in the *Symposium* itself. Plato exhibits great literary skill in its production—the dialogue is poetic—but the dialogue serves not only to beautify the life of Socrates, but also to draw the readers' eyes towards the good, so that by "[fixing their] gaze upon the things of the eternal and unchanging order" the reader "will [themselves] become orderly and divine in the measure permitted to man".[85]

The life of the Socratic lover

This account of love as the desire for the perpetual possession of the good gives rise to a particular way of life. This way of life is exemplified by Socrates as the dialogue's fourth manifest lover and its only lover of wisdom.

Plato foreshadows his account of the highest form of love as contemplation in his depiction of Socrates and Aristodemus on their way to Agathon's house. At some point, Socrates falls behind, becoming "absorbed in his own thoughts".[86] Later, having made his way nearly to Agathon's door, he again stops in thought, deaf to Agathon's attendants who beckon him to enter. Socrates is additionally praised for his capacity to drink without getting drunk,[87] walk over frost without footwear,[88] and resist Alcibiades' sexual advances.[89] Socrates seems able to escape the intoxication, painful compulsion, and temptation others would suffer in the same situations. In each of these cases, the ill can be traced to the body, and Socrates' success against it to the

---

[84] Rosen, *The Quarrel between Philosophy and Poetry*, 14.

[85] Rep. 500c-d.

[86] Symp. 174d.

[87] Symp. 220a.

[88] Symp. 220b.

[89] Symp. 217e–219c.

"psychological distance" between himself and his body as an object in the world.[90] In these moments Socrates shows his capacity for detachment and becomes, as Nussbaum notes, "actually forgetful" of the world.[91] Similarly he avoids the pains and distractions of passionate engagement to objects in the world, thus freeing himself from the danger of unhappiness threatened by their transience and frailty. This is the image of Socrates —self-sufficient and impervious to the outside world—which so seduces Apollodorus, Aristodemus, and Alcibiades. Socrates escapes the danger of passionate attachment to transient physical objects by directing his eros towards the stable and ever-present form of the good.

Socrates' speech is a lesson in how to attain such a state. He presents an ascent from the lowest desire of a beautiful body, to beauty in many bodies, in souls, in science and the arts, until eventually one desires "the vast sea of the beautiful" itself.[92] Importantly, the first rung on this ladder of love is merely the narrowest expression of the highest. The lowest lover loves another individual because, according to Plato, the beautiful individual participates in absolute beauty: for Plato "the lower that must be interpreted in light of the higher".[93] Thus, shaking off attachment to any particular individual, even one as striking as Socrates, is a way of ascending to a higher form of love.

Each step in the ascent is a sublimation of the lower desire into the higher.[94] In the *Republic*, Plato likens the upwards redirection of desire to a channeling of erotic energies.[95] The ascendant lover gradually transforms the love of objects in the world to more and more abstract objects, until striking upon an object which transcends the

---

[90] Nussbaum, "The Speech of Alcibiades," 151.

[91] Nussbaum, "The Speech of Alcibiades," 151.

[92] Symp. 210d.

[93] Cooper, *Eros in Plato, Rousseau, and Nietzsche*, 95.

[94] Following Kaufmann some Nietzschean interpreters argue that he defends a concept of sublimation (*Nietzsche: Philosopher, Psychologist, Antichrist* [Princeton and Oxford: Princeton University Press, 2013], 211–256) or that he helps to refine Freud's concept of sublimation (Ken Gemes, "Freud and Nietzsche on Sublimation," *Journal of Nietzsche Studies* 38 [2009]: 38–59). For the purposes of this chapter what matters is that Plato's sublimation of eros entails transcendence from temporality.

[95] Rep. 485d.

physical world altogether. At the first step, a lover becomes enamoured with another individual body:

> Then he will realise for himself that the beauty of any one body is closely akin to that of any other body, and that if what is beautiful in form is to be pursued it is folly not to regard the beauty in all bodies as one and the same.[96]

As Nussbaum observes, the first step on the ladder is a decision made on the basis of prudential reasoning.[97] It would be folly to remain attached to a single particular object, and so one should recognise other beauties, which resemble the object of one's desire, to be "one and the same". This redirection of desire, from the singular to the plural, diminishes the grip the first object has over our happiness:

> When he has understood this he should slacken his intense passion for one body, despising it and considering it a small thing, and become a lover of all beautiful bodies.[98]

The motive for starting the ascent (which means the motive of philosophy) is the inadequacy of untrained desire, which surrenders our happiness to transient objects beyond our control. In such a condition we have "the feeling that we are not what we ought to be".[99] Alcibiades admits that listening to Socrates convinces him that "[his] kind of life [is] not worth living".[100] On Plato's account, worldly existence is marked by the lack of the only thing that would grant us secure happiness, the divine form of the good.

Nevertheless, the form of the good provides a stable object of desire which allows us to regain rational control of ourselves and our lives. The rational life secures its practitioner from the "misery and the irrational tumult of personal erotic need".[101] The philosopher achieves this security through gradually removing himself from the

---

[96] Symp. 210a–b.

[97] Nussbaum, "The speech of Alcibiades," 147.

[98] Symp. 210b.

[99] Pierre Hadot, *What is Ancient Philosophy?*, trans. Michael Chase (Cambridge, MA: Belknap Press, 2004), 29.

[100] Symp. 216a.

[101] Nussbaum, "The Speech of Alcibiades," 150.

"mortal dross" of the natural world.[102] Not only does he abandon passionate attachments to worldly objects, in doing so he professes to transcend the mortal world itself and to partake in the immortality of the gods.[103] He eschews all that attaches to organic life—its embodiment, transience, and perspectival character—in favour of attachment to the eternal and universal forms. This attachment frees the philosopher from the anxiety of depending on anything in the natural world. The desire for perpetual communion with the eternal forms is only realised once the philosopher has purified himself of all natural attachments. In its most extreme case, this means purifying himself of life itself. Hence Socrates' last words in the *Phaedo* that he owes Asclepius, the god of medicine, a rooster.[104] A rooster was sacrificed to Asclepius when one was cured of a disease, so Socrates' words suggest death, according to Nietzsche, was a return to health.[105] As Nietzsche observes in the culminating sections of *The Gay Science*, Socrates saw death as a cure and life itself as a disease.[106]

The *Symposium* is Plato's treatment for the emotional disorder brought about by the passions. Within the dialogue Socrates is his exemplar of psychological health. Plato's philosophically trained eros, of which he claims all desire is merely a defective species, has three essential characteristics. Firstly, it grows from a poverty of the human soul. Love is a kind of neediness the exposes human inadequacy and motivates individuals to seek redemption from their narrow mortal lives. Secondly, the object of Platonic desire is the eternal form of the good, which offers a secure alternative to the

---

[102] Symp. 211e.

[103] Symp. 212a.

[104] Phaedo. 118a.

[105] Here Foucault disputes Nietzsche's reading of the *Phaedo*. On Foucault's account, following Dumézil, the disease which Socrates is cured of is not life, but "that corruption of the soul that results from following the general, ordinary opinion of mankind". (Arnold I. Davidson, "Ethics as Ascetics," in *The Cambridge Companion to Foucault*, ed. Gary Gutting [Cambridge: Cambridge University Press, 2005], 142.) See also Michel Foucault, *The Courage of Truth*, trans. Graham Burchall (Palgrave Macmillan, 2011), 95–116.

[106] GS 340; cf. Paul Loeb, *The Death of Nietzsche's Zarathustra* (Cambridge: Cambridge University Press, 2010), 32–44 on the relationship between Socrates' deathbed revelation, Zarathustra, and the affirmation of the eternal recurrence of life in GS 340–42.

transient and frail objects of the natural world. Thirdly, Platonic desire promises an escape from temporal existence. In contemplation one is able, like Socrates, to forget one's place in the world and participate in the divinity of the unchanging and eternal forms. Because the forms escape temporality, they can be experienced at any and every moment. When death comes, as it did to Socrates, one goes willingly, since the transience of life itself is an affliction to overcome.

The failure of Platonic eros

In *Twilight of the Idols*, Nietzsche turns his attention explicitly towards Platonic eros. This move is motivated by Socrates' deathbed judgement against (at least his own) life, and Nietzsche's therapeutic inclination, to read philosophical positions as indicative of conditions of health or sickness. More precisely, he asks of philosophers the same question he asks of artists in book five of *The Gay Science*, "is it hunger or superabundance that has here become creative?"[107] Reacting to Socrates' assessment of life itself as an illness, Nietzsche proposes to "take a closer look"—to carry out a thorough diagnosis—because "here at any rate there must be something *sick*".[108]

Nietzsche draws attention to an encounter between Socrates and the physiognomist Zopyrus, attested to in the *Tusculan Disputations*. Cicero tells us that Zopyrus publicly lists the inborn faults of Socrates: he declares that Socrates to hold a poor constitution, to be irascible, pitying, and envious by nature.[109] In Nietzsche's words, Socrates contains "every kind of foul vice and lust".[110] To this Socrates assents, "saying that [all manner of vices] were indeed inborn in him, but that he had cast them out by reason".[111] Socrates, according to Nietzsche, suffered from the disaggregation of his

---

[107] GS 370.

[108] TI "Socrates" 1, emphasis in original.

[109] Cicero Tusc. 4.80.

[110] TI "Socrates" 3.

[111] Cicero Tusc. 4.80.

drives. He thus epitomises what is, on both his and Nietzsche's accounts, the broader cultural malady of fifth century Athens: the drives which constitute the order (or disorder) of the soul were unruly, "in anarchy" and "becoming mutually antagonistic".[112] Socrates avoids the anarchy of the drives through the use of reason—he subdues and masters the drives and thereby masters himself.

Reason is the expression of the need for self-preservation against the "universal danger" of the *monstrum in animo*.[113] It was necessary to pose reason as a ruler over and against the drives because in their mutually antagonistic state; the alternative would have been the dissolution and destruction of the soul: "one had only *one* choice: either to perish or – be *absurdly rational*".[114] What results is a radical opposition between consciousness and reason on the one hand and the unconscious drives, desires, and passions on the other. Socratic reason is the single legitimate ruler of the soul—all legitimate motives and values derive their legitimacy from it.[115]

To cure the mutual antagonism of the drives, Socrates posits a *new* antagonism, between the drives and reason. This is why Nietzsche's diagnoses the Platonic treatment of eros—subjugation to reason and the eternal form of the good—as *reinforcing* the malady it purports to cure. As long as the Socratic opposition between reason and the drives persists, as long as one *has* "to combat one's instincts", one remains, according to Nietzsche, in a state of distress.

Nietzsche recognises nineteenth century romantic pessimism as the logical extension of Platonism. In Schopenhauer he identifies a Platonic conception of desire without the prospect of transcendence.

---

[112] TI "Socrates" 9.

[113] TI "Socrates" 9.

[114] TI "Socrates" 10.

[115] Compare above, that everything beautiful derives its beauty from participation in the form of the good.

Schopenhauer echoes Plato in claiming that all human desire arises "from a lack, from discontent with one's state".[116] For Schopenhauer, this lack is experienced as a painful absence of the desired object. Importantly, gaining possession of the object of one's desire grants only temporary cessation of this pain. Schopenhauer claims that "[a]ll satisfaction [...] is really and essentially only *negative* and never at all positive".[117] Satisfaction of a desire is merely its cancellation—gaining possession of an object of desire puts its possessor in precisely the state she was in before she formed her desire. The only consequence of desire is an intervening period of pain. Desire is unruly, disordered, and painful.

Schopenhauer's metaphysics of the will additionally prevents the will from experiencing—in addition to any *positive* notion of happiness—even the blissful state of *ataraxia* brought about by the elimination of desire.[118] All manifestations of will, including human desire, are characterised by a blind and constant striving, "to which no end is put by the achievement of any goal, which is therefore capable of no final satisfaction but can only be held up by impediments".[119] According to Schopenhauer, the satisfaction of one desire leads immediately to one of two conditions. Either one desires and thus experiences the painful lack of another object or, because of Schopenhauer's metaphysical premise that the will involves unending striving, lacks an object to strive for. In both cases one experiences a painful lack, and thus *ataraxia* is an impossible goal.

Schopenhauer agrees with Plato that desire cannot be tamed by satisfaction. For Plato, however, desire *can* be brought under rational control through the ascent to metaphysics. The metaphysical forms furnish Plato with a stable object of desire, the

---

[116] WWR 1.56.

[117] WWR 1.58, emphasis in original.

[118] cf. Epicureanism's negative hedonism, which identifies happiness with *ataraxia* or freedom from disturbance in chapter 2 of this thesis.

[119] WWR 1.56.

love of which allows for the rational conduct of life. Schopenhauer denies that the ascent to metaphysics achieves this goal.

For Schopenhauer, like Plato, metaphysics is an exercise in psychological detachment. Plato's Socrates succeeds in his ascent because it grants him freedom from the hardships of the world and the risks of loving mortal objects. The sight of the forms purifies Socrates of the infirmities associated with existing as a body in the world. For Schopenhauer too, in metaphysical contemplation an individual comprehends the world "purely objectively", shucking off the immediate concerns of will (and the body).[120] The aesthetic experience of pure contemplation gives an individual such a respite from the otherwise incessant press of desire. In such a state, which Schopenhauer explicitly links to contemplation of the Platonic forms, one becomes "entirely absorbed in [perception] and lets the entirety of consciousness be filled with restful contemplation of a natural object"—one loses oneself in the object of contemplation, becoming "pure, will-less, painless, timeless," and, according to Schopenhauer "no longer an individual".[121]

Schopenhauer's account of metaphysical contemplation diverges from Plato's in two important respects. Firstly, in contemplation the intellect "tears itself free" of the will and "is removed from any relation to the will".[122] In metaphysical contemplation, desire is entirely silenced. Whereas Plato claims that the ascent to metaphysics is like a channeling of desire, for Schopenhauer metaphysics is explicitly a project of subduing and eliminating desire. The object of aesthetic contemplation is not an object of desire, but stands "in no relation to our will".[123] Contemplation is only possible by escaping the will's demands. Schopenhauer recommends the radical cure of complete extirpation

---

[120] WWR 2.16.

[121] WWR 1.34.

[122] WWR 1.34.

[123] WWR 2.30.

because of his anti-teleological conception of the will—there is no object which would satisfy the will, as possession of the good would satisfy eros for Plato.

Secondly, for Plato the good is a stable and readily available object of desire. Accordingly, contemplation of the good grounds a stable and secure happiness—Socrates's perfect state of mind endures both the passage of time and threats from the outside world. For Schopenhauer, on the other hand, contemplation is only possible in "exceptional cases";[124] it is "difficult and therefore rare" and persists "only for a short time".[125] This is because of the organic nature of the intellect as an outgrowth of the will. On Schopenhauer's account, the capacity for metaphysical reflection is the latest fruit borne of the long process of the will's development. The intellect, which in other animals is merely "the medium of motives", in humanity develops into reason by divorcing itself from the immediate needs of the will.[126] This is why Schopenhauer refers to humans as the *animal metaphysicum*. The intellect nevertheless remains rooted in the will as the metaphysical grounds of all life. When the individual inevitably returns to the concerns of life, she must abandon the happiness granted by aesthetic contemplation:

> [A]s soon as the consciousness of one's own self, and thus subjectivity, i.e., the will, again obtains the ascendancy, a degree of discomfort or disquiet appears in keeping therewith; of discomfort, in so far as corporeality (the organism that in itself is will) again makes itself felt; of disquiet, in so far as the will, on the intellectual path, again fills our consciousness by desires, emotions, passions, and cares.[127]

All human life then, is marked by ineliminable suffering. In fact, since human life is the latest development of will, humans are "the neediest of all beings" and suffer the greatest.[128] Aesthetic contemplation grants the individual a momentary respite from this suffering, but it is only an intimation of a definitive cure: the complete silence of

---

[124] WWR 1.34.
[125] WWR 2.30.
[126] WWR 2.17.
[127] WWR 2.30.
[128] WWR 1.57.

the will. Human desire vacillates between painful absence and painful boredom: there is no object which could serve, as the form of the good did for Plato, to secure a stable happiness, either in life or outside it:

> So long as we are given over to the press of desires with its constant hoping and fearing, so long as we are subjects of willing, lasting happiness or rest will never come to be for us.[129]

The only palliative Schopenhauer offers for the almost ubiquitous pain of existence is the deadening of the will and the denial of the individual.

Schopenhauer picks out a unified force underlying all human striving, which he identifies with a painful deficiency in the human condition. This force finds its only temporary cessation in its own denial through metaphysical contemplation. Without the possibility of lasting satisfaction, Schopenhauer arrives at advocating the "denial and abandonment of all willing, and precisely thereby redemption from a world whose entire existence has shown itself to be suffering [...] a passage into empty *nothingness*".[130] For Nietzsche, this is the horizon of possibility for a Platonic conception of the passions. The Platonic–Schopenhauerian conception of the passions fails because it cannot sustain an attachment to life. He names this failure of desire nihilism.[131] To overcome nihilism, then, he requires a renovated conception of the passions *not* tied to the possibility of transcendence. We turn to the role of a rejuvenated account of the passions in *The Gay Science* in the next chapter.

---

[129] WWR 1.38.

[130] WWR 1.71.

[131] Robert B. Pippin, *Nietzsche, Psychology and First Philosophy* (Chicago: University of Chicago Press, 2006), 19–21.

4. *La Gaya Scienza*: Nietzsche and the Passions

Nietzsche's campaign to expose and overcome Platonism is one of the few constants in his oeuvre. He attacks the Platonic therapy of the passions as both misdirected and symptomatic of a distressed physiological condition. Plato's prescription of the ascent to metaphysics betrays the pain and poverty of his this-worldly life. In *Human, All Too Human* and *Dawn*, Nietzsche expresses an appreciation for Stoic self-mastery as an alternative to what he sees as the Platonic tyranny of reason. Nietzsche at this point has deep sympathies with the Stoic attempt to return to nature through the use of reason; he praises, for instance, the ideal of Epictetus as one who "believes strictly in reason": "the silent, self-sufficient man [...] who defends himself against the outside world and lives in a constant state of supreme bravery".[1] Contrary to the Platonic education of the passions, Nietzsche expresses an affinity to the Stoic who *renounces* the passions in order to gain control of himself.[2] Yet, looking back on this period eight years after the publication of *Human, All Too Human*, he characterises this affinity as both a great liberation and "at the same time a sickness that can destroy the man who has it".[3] Nietzsche judges that his experiments with Stoicism, Epicureanism, and the other Hellenistic therapies had instrumental value: they furnished him with techniques of self-control and self-cultivation, but they fail as comprehensive therapies in as much as they manifest a fundamental timidity towards the world.[4] They are symptoms of a deficit or impoverishment of life.[5]

Nietzsche's self-described convalescence of 1882 marks a distinct break with what he calls the Hellenistic ethics of timidity. In book four of *The Gay Science* Nietzsche

---

[1] D 546.

[2] See HH P 6: Nietzsche autobiographically describes his middle period as a time of renunciation.

[3] HH P 3.

[4] See GS 305 on the Stoics, BGE 198 on all the Hellenistic schools.

[5] GS 370.

formulates a new, fundamentally affirmative, ethical project. To open book four, he declares *amor fati* as his love thenceforth. The penultimate section of book four (and of *The Gay Science* in its first volume) confirms the amorous character of this project in Nietzsche's depiction of the fervent craving for the eternal recurrence of life as the sign of the best disposition towards oneself and one's life. Book four is bookended by these two formulations of an attitude which seeks to reinscribe value on this-worldly life.

Between his declaration of *amor fati* and the demon's revelation of the eternal recurrence, Nietzsche tells us how we might learn how to love fate and its eternal recurrence. In this chapter I elucidate the techniques and practices of love at work in book four of *The Gay Science* to argue that therein Nietzsche develops a rival theory of ascent to the Platonic-metaphysical ladder of love.

In the previous chapter I characterised Platonic love as having three parts. I set out Plato's particular account of the nature of love, the object in which it finds its fullest expression, and the relationship with the world such a perfection of love induces in the lover. In this chapter I analyse Nietzsche on the nature of love through his account of the passions [*Leidenschaften*]. I accomplish this in two parts. First, I trace the development of the term "passion" from its Greek origins, through Christian and secular developments to make clear what conceptions of the passions were available to Nietzsche at the end of the nineteenth century. Only by following the history of the passions can we make sense of Nietzsche's self-conscious allusions to the *gaya scienza* of the Provençal troubadours, who he claims invented passionate love.[6] Second, I chart Nietzsche's shifting valuation of the passions through the middle period, from *Human, All Too Human*, where passion is included in a list of "the worst of all methods of acquiring knowledge"[7] to *The Gay Science*, where Nietzsche characterises the philosophical drive to knowledge as both passional *and* constitutive of human

---

[6] BGE 230.
[7] HH 9.

flourishing.⁸ While Nietzsche makes room for the passions in the flourishing life—contra the Stoics—he nevertheless maintains that the passions are in need of treatment. His recuperation of the passions is not the indiscriminate production of passionate engagements, which he elsewhere characterises as romanticism.⁹ I pay particular attention to Nietzsche's declaration in book five of *Dawn* of a "new passion" for knowledge and the role of this passion in arranging the drives that constitute Nietzsche's well-ordered soul.¹⁰

In the following chapters, I use this account of Nietzsche's *Leidenschaften* to distinguish Nietzsche's affirmation of eros from the ostensibly similar Stoic attitude towards nature. I distinguish Nietzsche's affirmation from Stoicism's love of fate on the grounds that it involves an appreciation of the passions foreign to Stoicism, premised on a decidedly anti-Stoic account of nature (and naturalism). To underscore Nietzsche's contrast with Platonism, I finally set out Nietzsche's contention that *The Gay Science* supports a passionate affirmation of this-worldly life, contrary to the Platonic denial of and flight from the world.

Nietzsche's ascent

In the 1886 preface to *Human, All Too Human*, Nietzsche describes his own therapeutic experiments as an ascent on "a long ladder upon whose rungs we ourselves have sat and climbed—which we ourselves have at some time *been*!"¹¹ The first edition of *Human, All Too Human*, published eight years earlier, is one such rung. Nietzsche would come to describe it as a "melancholy-valiant" book, written while he was "surrounded by ills" and in a state of illness himself.¹² But in recognising *Human, All*

---

⁸ GS 290; GS 326.

⁹ GS P 1.

¹⁰ D 429.

¹¹ HH P 7.

¹² HH P 2.

Too Human as the work of a sickly author, Nietzsche does not repudiate its place in his philosophical development. Instead, Nietzsche considers the sickness of *Human, All Too Human, and* the overcoming of this sickness necessary precursors to his later philosophical health. The Stoic coldness of the text, its "hatred of love," and "such bad and painful things" all contribute to "the history of a great liberation".[13] The sickness of *Human, All Too Human* is instrumentally valuable in granting the free spirit control over her passions:

> You shall become master over yourself, master also over your virtues. Formerly *they* were your masters; but they must be only your instruments beside other instruments. You shall get control over your For and Against and learn how to display first one and then the other in accordance with your higher goal.[14]

It is essential to Nietzsche's therapeutic program that the free spirit does not remain cold and hostile to the passions. Rather, she undergoes a transformation, at the end of which she can deploy them in pursuit of her "higher goal".[15] This transformation constitutes the work of Nietzsche's middle period.

The promise of *Human, All Too Human*'s preface is that the long ladder of the middle period culminates in the purposive control of the passions. Nietzsche's project is then, according to Nussbaum, an attempt "to bring about a revival of Stoic values of self-command and self-formation within a post-Christian and post-Romantic context".[16] Yet as we have seen in his confrontation with Stoicism, it is precisely the overriding Stoic concern for self-control which Nietzsche singles out as harmful. The Stoic, unable to lose herself to the passions, cuts herself off from the fortuities of her own instincts and social goods including the teachings of others. For the Stoics, the passions were harmful because they cede control of our happiness to fortune; for Nietzsche, "one must be able to lose oneself" to reap the full harvest of life.[17]

---

[13] HH P 3.

[14] HH P 6.

[15] See Thomas Ryan and Michael Ure, "Nietzsche's Post-Classical Therapy," *Pli* 25 (2014): 104.

[16] Martha C. Nussbaum, "Pity and Mercy: Nietzsche's Stoicism," in *Nietzsche, Genealogy, Morality*, ed. Richard Schacht (Berkeley: University of California Press, 1994), 140.

[17] GS 305.

The gulf between Nietzsche and the Stoics as to the place of the passions in the highest human life depends importantly on their distinct conceptions of the passions. For the Greeks of antiquity, *pathos* denoted "a state of being afflicted, a state of being affected, a reception or a suffering"; its definitive characteristic was passivity.[18] The modern passions, on the other hand, are essentially active, storms and whirlwinds of the mind which are associated with passivity only inasmuch as they act upon a sufferer. To describe the modern passions, including Nietzsche's *Leidenschaften*, the Greeks would more readily use terms such as *epithymia* [desire] or *mania* [madness]. Indeed Plato eschews talk of the *pathê* altogether in the *Symposium*, and in the *Phaedrus* that which afflicts lovers [*erotikon pathos*] is a kind of *theia mania* [divine madness].[19] What remains from the earliest philosophical treatments through to Nietzsche is the close association between passion and suffering. One suffers from a passion, whether as pain, illness, or vulnerability. What is at stake in separating Nietzsche from the Stoics, then, is what sense can be made of his therapeutic project if it does not alleviate suffering?

Pathos, passio, Leidenschaft, passion

Erich Auerbach traces the gap between ancient *pathos* and modern *Leidenschaft* in his history of the latter term, "*Passio als Leidenschaft*", wherein he purports to explain the entrance of the modern sense of the passions into the semantic field of the *pathê*. According to Auerbach, Aristotle captures the classical understanding of *pathos* as passivity. On Aristotle's account, *pathos* means "everything that is passively taken in, received, suffered".[20] Thus Aristotle's *pathê* encompass a broad range of mental phenomena including sensation, strong and weak feeling, and experience. The important distinction is between an active doing and a passive receiving. As a

---

[18] Erich Auerbach, "*Passio* as Passion," trans. Martin Elsky, *Criticism* 43, no. 3 (2001): 289.

[19] Phaedrus 265b; Auerbach, "Passio as Passion," 290.

[20] Auerbach, "Passio as Passion," 290.

consequence, *pathos* is an ethically neutral term: one is neither praised nor blamed for one's *pathê*, since a *pathos* is an intervention of an outside cause. The very idea of controlling *pathos* is difficult on this account because the *pathê* are precisely what befall an individual. At best, one might influence the external causes one is receptive towards. In this sense, Aristotle's passions are susceptible to one's influence, but not direct manipulation.

The first significant development after Aristotle's account of *pathos* as passivity, according to Auerbach, occurs with the Stoics. Rather than simply passive, the *pathê* for the Stoics become restive and stormy perturbations that "destroy the tranquility of the wise".[21] Because these perturbations are themselves active psychological forces, they fall on the wrong side of Aristotle's active–passive distinction. The Stoics instead oppose *pathos* to reason, not action. The consequence of this shift is that, as we have seen in chapter one, the passions take on a strongly pejorative sense. Since, according to the Stoics, humans have a distinctly rational nature, it is the duty of humans to perfect this nature and bring the passions under the control of reason.

Whether a Stoic suffers a passion is, as we have seen in chapter one, under his control. This is because to suffer from a passion is to assent to certain judgements in the *hegemonikon*. This control, however, extends only so far as a Stoic can eliminate a passion, which means to reject the false impression it presents (in the case of desire, that a certain object is a good) and refrain from acting according to it (reaching for a desired object): control of the passions entails their elimination.

Auerbach states that it is only the Stoic conception of *pathos*, and not the Aristotelian, which is recognisable as modern passion.[22] As Nietzsche's commendation of the passions shows, however, the resemblance is imperfect. For the Stoics, the passions are universally destructive. Their effect is exhausted in disrupting their sufferer's mind. Yet Nietzsche's revaluation of the passions is clearly not a celebration

---

[21] Auerbach, "Passio as Passion," 291.

[22] Auerbach, "Passio as Passion," 291.

simply of irrational mental disturbance. Nietzsche's passions contain within them the possibility of nobility,[23] rapture, and the sublime.[24] For Auerbach, too, these are distinctive features of modern passion. Ancient terms, including *pathos* as well as terms such as *epithymia* and *mania*,

> lack the possibility of the sublime. Modern passion [*Leidenschaft*] is more than desire, craving, or frenzy. The word always contains as a possibility, often as its dominant meaning, the noble creative fire which extinguishes itself in either struggle or surrender, and next to which temperate reason at times appears contemptible.[25]

On Auerbach's account, this capacity for the sublime enters the passions through a tradition of Christian passion mysticism. Nietzsche, without mentioning Christianity, traces his conception of the passions back to the heirs of this tradition, the twelfth-century Provençal troubadours, who he claims "invented" the "European speciality" of passionate love.[26] The notions of passion operative in the troubadours' profane love poetry and in the Christian mystical tradition both derive from the transformation of the term at the hands of early Church fathers—a contribution exemplified by Augustine.

Augustine

Augustine broadens the Stoics account of the passions, both in regards to what counts as a passion, and their evaluative possibilities. On the extent of the *passiones*, Augustine notes that the Stoic claim that the wise person is not subject to passion depends on the notion of indifference: that the wise person may hold a preference for an object without considering that object a good. Such an object is an preferred indifferent. Augustine claims that this is a false distinction.

---

[23] GS 55.

[24] GS 105.

[25] Auerbach, "Passio as Passion," 290.

[26] BGE 260; Nietzsche's relationship with the troubadours will be revisited below. These "Provençal knight-poets" also gave Nietzsche the title of *The Gay Science*, and the subtitle to its second edition "*la gaya scienza*".

> The Stoic insistence that such things [as life and material existence] are not to be called 'good', but 'advantageous', should be regarded as a quibble about words, not a question of the realities they signify.[27]

He prefigures the argument by Schopenhauer, which we have already seen, that the notion of preferred indifferents is a means for the Stoics to "[sophisticate] themselves into all the amenities of life".[28] While he attacks the Stoic notion of indifference, he also rejects their distinction between passions—which follow from false judgements—and first-movements [*propatheia*]—involuntary jitters of the body or mind that precede but are not yet such judgements. This second notion is at play in an example Augustine recounts from the author Aulus Gellius, of a Stoic in danger of suffering shipwreck.[29] On a journey across the Ionian sea, a ship carrying Gellius and an eminent (but unnamed) Stoic encounters bad weather. Gellius reports on the behaviour of the Stoic as their ship is tossed to and fro:

> I beheld the man frightened and ghastly pale, not indeed uttering any lamentations, as all the rest were doing, nor any outcries of that kind, but in his loss of colour and distracted expression not differing much from the others.[30]

The Stoic, when challenged by Gellius, states that his loss of colour is merely a first-movement. This movement produces fantastic and terrifying images to which the Stoic claims he does not assent. Since assent to a false judgement is the key characteristic of Stoic *pathos*, the Stoic aboard Aulus' ship can claim that he does not suffer from fear.

Augustine rejects this account. As in the case of indifferents, he claims that the Stoic distinction is merely verbal, "so long as Stoic, no less than Peripatetic, trembles and grows pale [*pavescat et palleat*] at the thought of being deprived of [supposed indifferents]".[31] Augustine equates the Stoic first movements, bodily reactions such as growing pale or trembling, with briefly suffering a passion:

---

[27] De Civ 9.4.

[28] WWR 2.156.

[29] De Civ 9.4; the story is especially pertinent, as the Stoic founder Zeno was said to have turned to philosophy following such a wreck. His shipwreck was felicitous, since it led him to virtue: "I made a prosperous voyage when I suffered shipwreck" (DL 7.4).

[30] Gel. 19.1.1.

[31] De Civ 9.4.

> When these sensations arise from terrifying and awe-inspiring circumstances, the mind of even the wise man must unavoidably be disturbed, so that for a little while he either becomes pale with fear [*metu*] or is depressed by gloom [*tristitia*][32]

He justifies this equation with reference to Gellius and concludes that passions "do befall the Stoic wise person".[33] However, as Sorabji shows forensically, Augustine simply misunderstands Stoic terminology. This follows from Augustine's use of Gellius for an account of first movements and Gellius' use of the ambiguous term *pavor* [trembling]. Had Augustine turned to Seneca's *De Ira* for his account of first movements, he would have seen that in first movements, "fear [*metus*], anxiety, sadness [*tristitia*], and anger are not found, but only certain things like them".[34]

The consequence of Augustine's reading of the Stoics is that a much broader range of mental phenomena come to be called passions. Augustine shifts the conceptual core of the passions away from false judgements made by the faculty of assent, to the very presence of stormy undulations in the psyche. Augustine follows the Stoics in classifying four major passions depending on whether an object is considered a good or an evil and whether it is present or anticipated. But rather than locate, for instance, *laetitia* [joy or delight] in assent to a false judgement of a present good, he characterises it as the presence of a love which possesses and enjoys its object. The three other major passions are similarly characterised as modifications of love.[35]

Since even the wise person is susceptible to the passions (in the form of what the Stoics call *propatheia* and the preferred indifferents) the Stoic project of self-sufficiency is doomed to failure. While Augustine grants that freedom from passionate disruption is "clearly a good and desirable state", such a state does not belong to embodied this-

---

[32] De Civ 9.4.

[33] Richard Sorabji, *Emotion and Peace of Mind: From Stoic Agitation to Christian Temptation* (Oxford: Oxford University Press, 2000), 378.

[34] Sen. De Ira, 1.3.8.

[35] De Civ 14.7.

worldly life.³⁶ A life of bliss, free from fear and distress, "will not come until there is no sin in man"—until the life of eternity after death.³⁷

The Stoic attempt at self-sufficiency through the elimination of suffering is, for Augustine and the Christian tradition, a futile task: "all men, as long as they are mortals, must needs be also wretched".³⁸ Thus the good Christian abandons self-sufficient impassivity as a goal. What is important in the Christian transformation and recuperation of the passions and suffering is that the Christian suffers righteously. Love is the wellspring of the passions, and the good passions spring from the love of God. The Christian in this life is still vulnerable in precisely the way the Stoics sought to avoid—through passionate engagement with God, which can only be manifested in the frail and unreliable external world. But in cultivating a passionate vulnerability, through an ardent love of God, the Christian opens herself up to receive grace.

> Against the evil *passiones* of this world, they set neither Stoic apathy, nor the "good feelings" in order to arrive at the Aristotelian mean through rational balance, but instead they contrast it with something entirely new, until then unheard of: the *gloriosa passio* that derives from the burning love of God. The person who is *impassibilis* [incapable of suffering] is not perfect, but he is *perfectus in omnibus* [perfect in every way] [...] *quem caro iam revocare non posset a gloria passionis* [whom the flesh could no long retrieve from the glory of suffering]³⁹

Augustine rehabilitates passionate suffering through a transformation of the passions. Against the Stoic conception of the passions as entirely harmful perturbations, he makes the passions worthy of praise and cultivation. The passions become part of the best human life because they grant one access to the divine. To suffer the passions is to give oneself over to the grace of God—the only hope for the human to attain happiness. This is why the burning love of God gives rise to a compelling new passion: suffering the *gloriosa passio* redeems the painful and wretched experience of natural life. To reject this new passion, on the other hand, is to cut oneself off from the grace of

---

³⁶ De Civ 14.9.

³⁷ De Civ 14.9.

³⁸ De Civ 9.15.

³⁹ Auerbach, "*Passio* as Passion," 292.

God and from redemption from pain and all earthly suffering. The Stoic in *GS 305* cuts himself off from the full harvest of life by denying the passions. Augustine's Stoic similarly loses life's highest reward—eternal happiness in the next life—by refusing to loosen the reigns of his self-control.

For the Christian mystics of subsequent centuries, passion as stormy disturbance and passion as the ecstatic experience of the love of God merge.[40] To suffer a passion becomes simultaneously a moment of torment and one of divine rapture. Suffering becomes a means to experience the love of God and a source of redemption from the world. As a result, passionate disturbances themselves become noble, laudable experiences.

> In stark contrast to all ancient, especially Stoic concepts, [Christian] *passio* is praised and longed for; the life and stigmatization of St. Francis of Assisi concretely realize the union of passion and suffering, the mystical leap of one to the other. The passion of love leads through suffering to an *excessus mentis* and to union with Christ; whoever is without *passio* is without grace; whoever does not give himself over to the *passio* of the Savior lives in hardness of heart, *obduratio cordis,* and one finds in the mystical tracts much instruction about how to overcome this condition.[41]

Christian mystics, thus, seek to cultivate their capacity for suffering. They reject the Stoic project of self-sufficiency and promote their vulnerability to the external world.

Whether this capacity is realised, that is, whether one received grace, depends on the arrival of God's love. In this sense, the Christian *passio* strikes an Aristotelian tone: it denotes a receptive state rather than an wholly active force. The activity of the redemptive power of the passions originates in God alone, only entering those who have prepared themselves to receive the grace of God. The redeeming love of God, furthermore, "always originates from the heights or depths of superhuman forces and is received and suffered as a magnificent or terrifying gift".[42] The Christian mystic gives herself up to the terrifying power of God and it is in this manner that the Christian account of the passions heralds the possibility of the sublime.

---

[40] Auerbach, "*Passio* as Passion," 295.

[41] Auerbach, "*Passio* as Passion," 297.

[42] Auerbach, "*Passio* as Passion," 298.

God's love terrifies because of his overwhelming power. The love of God torments the one who suffers from it because, without a response from God we are stuck in our wretched state of neediness and if God answers our love, he would overwhelm us, "for God is too strong for the soul. If He took it to heart [...] the soul would die a *Liebestod* in real torment and real rapture at the same time."[43]

The early Christian account of the passions echoes Plato's amorous ascent in sanctioning a flight from the pains and sorrows of the natural world, whether into the arms of God or the ocean of beauty. In both cases, this is because our happiness depends on forming an attachment to a transcendent object. But, there is a crucial difference between the Platonic and Christian attitudes. For the Platonist, as we saw, each step on the ladder of love slackens the intensity of her passions until, at its apex, she achieves a perfectly secure tranquillity. The Platonic lover suffers less from the torment of the passions the closer she comes to the Platonic ideal. The closer the Christian mystic comes to God, however, the more severely she suffers—love *always* remains an affliction with the potential to prove fatal. The love of God reaches its apex in simultaneous torment and rapture; this terrifying prospect, of the overwhelming force of God's love, marks it out as an experience of the sublime. The "deepening" of suffering to include the possibility of the sublime is, according to Auerbach, the "incontestable" influence of Christian mysticism.[44]

Courtly love

The mystical account of the passions was taken up in profane love poetry, first by the Provençal troubadours and by later figures such as Dante. These poets repeat Christian mystics' insistence that the passions are the only route to a noble life, that the passions foster all virtue and insight, and importantly that the passions involve simultaneous rapture and torment that gives rise to the feeling of the sublime. Why

---

[43] Auerbach, "*Passio* as Passion," 298.

[44] Auerbach, "*Passio* as Passion," 300.

then, does Nietzsche claim that the troubadours *invented* passionate love, and why does he christen his most personal book with the Provençal term for the troubadours' love poetry, *gaia scienza*?[45] What distinguishes the troubadours' account love from its life-denying mystical precursor? While Auerbach devotes significant attention to the continuity between Christian mystical and secular poetic accounts of the passions and indeed finds them sometimes indistinguishable, there are important divergences between the two.[46] Making a clear distinction between what is novel in courtly love and what isn't will allow us to see what precisely Nietzsche is praising the troubadours for and the possibilities he sees in the passions.

Auerbach is correct to note a strong resonance between troubadour (or courtly) love and Passion mysticism. Both held that the highest form of human existence was to be found in sublime love—passionate devotion to an object with the potential for simultaneous torment and rapture. Courtly love differs most importantly from religious love in its selection of sublime object. Instead of God, the courtly lover of the twelfth century devotes himself to a woman he takes to embody and objectify "*in herself* beauty, goodness, and all the other goals of human aspiration recognised by the eros tradition".[47] Heterosexual love did not, of course, originate in the twelfth-century. Sexual relations are ubiquitous in the history of myth and literature because they are ubiquitous in human life. Even Plato accounts for heterosexual love as an attempt to secure immortality through children.[48] Such love and indeed all forms of interpersonal love, however, are for Plato subordinate to the higher love of beauty itself. For Plato interpersonal love is a step towards the perfection of *eros*, but as such it is only either instrumentally useful or a defective kind of love. In the Christian tradition too, Paul

---

[45] BGE 230; Although this claim has more recently been criticised as overly simplistic, it is widely held that the troubadours and the notion of "courtly love" have been one of the most influential sources of Western thinking about love. Nietzsche's position is not particularly distinctive. See Irving Singer, *The Nature of Love*, vol. 2, *Courtly and Romantic* (Cambridge and London: MIT Press, 2009), 19–36.

[46] Auerbach, "*Passio* as Passion," 299.

[47] Singer, *The Nature of Love*, 2.48, emphasis in original.

[48] Symp. 208e.

instructs married Christians to love one another, but only "out of reverence for Christ".[49] Paul sanctions interpersonal love as an imitation or subordinate form of the love of God. In courtly love on the other hand, the highest of human aspirations reside in the beloved, without reference to any transcendent object:

> About this more ultimate love the troubadours are remarkably unconcerned. Their beloved is indeed more than just another beautiful form in the external world: she is for them the supreme instance of beauty and that is why they love her. And yet, they do not love her for the sake of beauty, at least not beauty as an absolute or abstract entity. It scarcely occurs to the troubadours that love might be extended beyond the lady.[50]

Just as Christian-mystical passions spring from a burning love of God, devotion to the beloved inspires the emotional life of the courtly lover. The passions of the courtly lover are put in the service of his higher devotion. The beloved takes on the role of God as an absolute. This displacement has the consequence that courtly love encourages "a kind of autonomy or self-sufficiency of human love [...] a closed trajectory within itself".[51] If human love is self-sufficient, the human lover need not resort to the Christian-Platonic flight from the world as a radical cure for the passions. The Aristophanic predicament encountered in the previous chapter—the threat of the imperfect object—is surmountable within the human realm. The innovation of the troubadours regarding the passions is to ground them in the human world.

Gaya scienza denotes troubadour love poetry, which was of central importance to operation of courtly love. The troubadours practice *gaya scienza* when they use poetry to elevate the beloved as the unique exemplar of beauty, goodness and excellence in character. This aesthetic activity becomes the basis for the lover's desire; his longing for the beloved is underwritten by poetry showing the beloved to be worthy.[52] In the *Tractatus amoris & de amoris remedio* by Andreas Capellanus, the most systematic contemporary formulation of courtly love, we find an ambiguity over whether poetry

---

[49] Ephesians 5.21-33.

[50] Singer, *The Nature of Love*, 2.47.

[51] Singer, *The Nature of Love*, 2.47.

[52] Singer, *The Nature of Love*, 2.49.

produces the excellence of the beloved or *reveals* it. Love was certainly taken to have a transformative power. In a dialogue between a suitor and a woman who denies that she is outstanding in the way courtly love requires (the embodiment of beauty itself) the suitor claims that love changes the ugly into the beautiful by means of aesthetic falsification: "your beauty seems to me to put the charms of all other women in the shade, and to a lover love makes even an ugly woman appear most beautiful".[53] The beloved becomes beautiful (to the lover) through the power of his love. On the other hand, Capellanus also suggests that the beloved is objectively beautiful, and that "love is required [merely] as a means of detection".[54] So love makes the beloved beautiful or reveals her antecedent objective beauty. As Singer notes, this problem remains unresolved in the history of love until Romanticism abandons the belief in the antecedent objective beauty of the beloved.[55] But in either case, the significant point for our purposes is that courtly desire is stoked by the aesthetic means of *gaya scienza* (whether these means are productive or revelatory). We will be able to understand Nietzsche's use of aesthetic techniques to "make things beautiful, attractive, and desirable [...] when they are not" in these terms.[56]

In addition to idealising the beloved, the troubadours idealise themselves as lovers. They take their amorous state as itself a model of nobility. To take desire and longing as themselves worthy aspirations means that the courtly lover prolongs desire by deliberately frustrating it. Often the courtly lover takes a married woman as his beloved, so that their sexual continence testifies to both the moral virtue of the woman and the ennobling power of the lover's devotion. Jealousy is not a vice, but the condition of possibility for such a necessarily unrequited love.[57] The courtly lover

---

[53] Andreas Capellanus, *De Amore*, ed. and trans. P. G. Walsh (London: Duckworth, 1982), 49 (1.31).

[54] Singer, *The Nature of Love*, 2.72.

[55] Singer, *The Nature of Love*, 2.72.

[56] GS 299.

[57] Singer, *The Nature of Love*, 2.27.

thereby charts a course between the despair of being without love, and the terrifying prospect of rapture and *Liebestod* which, we have seen, attends to the notion of sublime passions the troubadours inherit. It is clear why Nietzsche would admire such lovers—they are strong enough to bear the sublime terror of their passion without shying away from their beloved, or falling into a rapture which destroys them both.

We can characterise courtly love, then, as the jealous love of an idealised woman, the experience of which makes life noble and worth living. It is, at the same time, an affliction which torments the lover and radically alters the orientation of the lover's life. In forging a passionate attachment to a particular other, the courtly lover becomes vulnerable to all of their familiar pains and sorrows. The courtly lover lives dangerously, but in pursuit of a higher plane of human existence.

Auerbach tells us that the courtly account of the passions was, at first, neglected. It takes until the seventeenth century for it to win out over its Aristotelian and Stoic rivals, when we are left with a descendant of the troubadours' anti-Christian turn of Passion mysticism best exemplified in the tragedy of Racine:

> The *passions* in seventeenth-century France are the great human desires, and what is particular about them is the clear inclination to regard them as tragic, heroic, sublime and worthy of admiration. At the beginning of the century, the pejorative Stoic judgment is still sounded quite frequently, yet it soon changes into a dialectic combination in which the terrible and the noble unite in the sublime. That is already to be sensed in Corneille and Pascal, perhaps already in Descartes, and it reaches its high point in the tragedy of Racine, whose goal it is to excite and glorify the passions. He speaks of *les belles passions* and *les passions généreuses,* and critics judged a tragedy according to the authenticity, depth, and beauty of the passions it represents; for the sensitive spectator, the torment and rapture of passion become the highest form of life.[58]

The passions of the seventeenth-century promise to elevate human life through an experience of the sublime. These are the coordinates within which modern discussion of the passions, including Nietzsche's, takes place. There remain two questions at issue in the remainder of this chapter. First, what does Nietzsche make of the very notion of such great human desires; is stoking the passions a viable hope for the elevation of human life? As I will show, Nietzsche only arrives at an affirmative answer to this

---

[58] Auerbach, "*Passio* as Passion," 302, emphasis in original.

question after much philosophical labour. Second, given this belated affirmative answer, which passion is capable of granting such elevation? I will show that Nietzsche proposes a *new* passion, the passion for knowledge, in book five of *Dawn*, and that in *The Gay Science* he elaborates the possibilities of this passion for the ennoblement of life.

Nietzsche's passionate development

Nietzsche provides his clearest characterisation of a passion in section 429 of *Dawn*, titled "*The new passion*". In this section he inaugurates the passion for knowledge. He describes a passion as a certain drive distinguished by its strength and intensity. Recall that for the Greeks, happiness [*eudaimonia*] served as the ultimate goal of life. When Diotima quizzes Socrates on the use of love, the value of happiness is beyond question: "the happy are happy by acquisition of good things, and we have no more need to ask for what end a man wishes to be happy, when such is his wish: the answer seems to be ultimate".[59] Nietzsche's passion for knowledge is a drive which usurps the motivational primacy of happiness. It is not the case, Nietzsche thinks, that satisfaction of this drive necessarily brings happiness. Nevertheless, the attainment of knowledge becomes a higher, more worthy goal than the Greek goal of happiness. The strength of a passion is so great that happiness without its object is undesirable: "even to imagine such a state of things is painful to us!"[60] One suffering a passion prefers the restless state of longing and torment to the tranquillity of Greek happiness—the tormented state is attractive in itself. Nietzsche specifically aligns this account of passion with the situation of unrequited lovers who, as we have seen in the courtly case, idealise their own state of unrequited desire. A passion "shrinks at no sacrifice and at bottom fears nothing but its own extinction".[61] Nietzsche suggests that even the prospect of death will not shake a

---

[59] Symp. 205a.
[60] D 429.
[61] D 429.

passion's hold. The question of the value of a passion comes down to a choice between two deaths: the glorious rapture of *Liebestod* or a contemptible, passionless end "in the sand".[62]

All the features of Auerbach's sublime passions are present in Nietzsche's depiction. And yet while in *Dawn* he celebrates the noble possibilities of the passions, this position undergoes multiple shifts and transformations throughout his philosophical development. We can elaborate Nietzsche's account of the sublime passions by examining the self-treatment he sets out in his prefaces. At the beginning of this chapter we noted the therapeutic program Nietzsche puts down in the preface to *Human, All Too Human*. This is one of five prefaces which Nietzsche writes for his earlier works in 1886. In each of these Nietzsche turns his attention to the states of philosophical health and sickness that work expresses. Thus, the prefaces to the two volumes of *Human, All Too Human*, in addition to the "Attempt at Self-Criticism" he attached to the second edition of *The Birth of Tragedy*, as well as the prefaces to the second editions of *Dawn* and *The Gay Science* provide a crucial insight into his proposed therapy and perfection of the passions.

Returning to *The Birth of Tragedy* a decade after its first publication, Nietzsche distances himself from the artistic metaphysics described therein. In *The Birth of Tragedy*, Nietzsche reflects, he sullied the Greek relation to suffering manifested by tragedy through his allegiance to Wagner and to German music.[63] In particular, he finds in the book's still-metaphysical outlook a "profound hatred of 'the contemporary age', 'reality' and 'modern ideas' [...] which would rather believe in Nothing, in the devil, than in 'the now'".[64] Nietzsche counterposes nothingness and "the devil" to the temporal world to show that his preference for nothingness over this world is a form of metaphysical consolation. This preference expresses the fearful attitude towards

---

[62] D 429.

[63] ASC 6.

[64] ASC 7.

suffering in the world which he so strongly rejects in his later thought. The preface is scathing about his early work, in the end warning that its romantic trajectory leads dangerously towards Christianity. However, Nietzsche's self-criticism is not merely a dismissal. He draws a distinction—as he does during the same period in *GS 370*—between Dionysian and Romantic pessimism. The substance of the distinction is in the two attitudes' response to suffering. The Romantic, Nietzsche says, devises metaphysical consolations, and offers to redeem the suffering of this world in another. Romantic pessimism exhibits an urge to escape from this-worldly suffering: for Nietzsche, from life itself. The Romantic detachment from life is such that it sanctions the "practical nihilism" of preferring oblivion to jealous suffering in "the now": "I would rather nothing were true than that *you* were right, that *your* truth should triumph!"[65] Nietzsche chides his earlier self for spoiling his treatment of pessimism with Romantic ideas and asks other young pessimists to learn from his mistake:

> You ought first learn the art of *this-worldly* consolation—you should learn to *laugh*, my young friends, if you are determined to remain pessimists; perhaps as laughers you will consign all metaphysical consolations to the devil —and metaphysics in front of all the rest![66]

Dionysian pessimism, then, is a pessimism which laughs. In book five of *The Gay Science* Nietzsche associates Dionysian pessimism with an overflowing vitality and strength.[67] Nietzsche's lament, in both the *Attempt at Self-Criticism* and section 370 of *The Gay Science*, is that his early estimate viewed the problem of Greek tragedy—the necessity of suffering—through a Romantic lens.

When Nietzsche claims that *Human, All Too Human* constitutes an "*anti-romantic self-treatment*", he refers to the broader project of that work to cool down the hot-headedness of the passions exemplified by *The Birth of Tragedy*.[68] From the vantage point of 1886, Nietzsche looks back on *Human, All Too Human* as an artefact of this

---

[65] ASC 7.

[66] ASC 7.

[67] GS 370.

[68] AOM P 3.

project. In the preface to *Human, All Too Human* he lays out his own philosophical evolution and states that finding the place of the work in this evolution will be a simple task for any "psychologist or reader of signs".[69] For once, Nietzsche's allusion is fairly straight forward. *Human, All Too Human* corresponds to his discussion of a midway condition between "morbid isolation" and a "*great* health".[70] This condition is characterised by a "bird-like freedom, bird-like altitude, bird-like exuberance" and "bird-like flights in cold heights".[71] It is the free-spirit, to whom *Human, All Too Human* is dedicated, who experiences this cooling down of the passions and the freezing of the ideals upon which they depend.[72]

We can garner a more nuanced understanding of Nietzsche's anti-romantic self-treatment by examining the sections of the work itself concerned with the passions. *HH 244* is central to this cooling project. In it, he offers Christianity, but also "philosophers, poets, [and] musicians" as responsible for the inflammation of the passions:

> If these are not to stifle us we must conjure up the spirit of science, which on the whole makes one somewhat colder and more sceptical and in especial cools down the fiery stream of belief in ultimate definitive truths; it is principally through Christianity that this stream has grown so turbulent.[73]

Nietzsche's position in this section is that the excesses of passion need to be tamed by the spirit of science. He opposes the fiery and turbulent passions to the scientific pursuit of knowledge. The passions are, indeed, impediments to this enterprise. They colour and distort the world and must be overcome if we are to climb the hundred-rung ladder of knowledge.[74] In *The Wanderer and his Shadow*, Nietzsche softens his tone somewhat, setting as his task to "take from the passions their terrible character

---

[69] HH P 8.

[70] HH P 4, emphasis in original. Note that the same year, Nietzsche closes volume two of *The Gay Science* with a penultimate section titled "The Great Health".

[71] HH P 4, P 5.

[72] EH "Books" HH 1.

[73] HH 244.

[74] HH 292.

and thus prevent their becoming devastating torrents".[75] He suggests that we might transform the passions [*Leidenschaften*] "one and all" into joys [*Freudenschaften*].[76]

Both volumes of *Human, All Too Human* exhibit an attempt to transform, moderate, and calm the passions. If this resembles a common Hellenistic treatment of the passions, we should not be surprised that Nietzsche explicitly considers the role of Hellenistic therapies. The Hellenistic schools are "experimental laboratories"[77] for the development of practical wisdom and the results of these experiments rightly "belong to us", in that we are entitled to practice Stoic, as well as Epicurean, techniques of living according to our own needs. Such practices of self-cultivation, which Nietzsche develops during the middle period are instrumentally useful in his own philosophical therapy.

> So far as praxis is concerned I view the various moral schools as experimental laboratories in which a considerable number of recipes for the art of living have been thoroughly practised and lived to the hilt. The results of all their experiments belong to us, as our legitimate property.[78]

A higher goal, however, is not to be found in *Human, All Too Human*'s "pale, subtle happiness [...] without yes [and] without no".[79] The first indication of such a higher goal emerges in book five of *Dawn*. There, as we have seen, Nietzsche declares a "new passion"—the passion for knowledge. He not only announces this passion but endorses it in the sublime ambivalence characteristic of his conception of the passions: it is both elevating a terrifying at once. If it were possible, a consummation of the passion for knowledge would prove fatal. *Dawn*'s passion for knowledge fearlessly strives towards this rapturous end. Nietzsche foresees that humanity will perish in a glorious *Liebestod* and indeed sees this as desirable: "we would all prefer the destruction of mankind to a

---

[75] WS 37.

[76] WS 37.

[77] KSA 9:15[59].

[78] KSA 9:15[59].

[79] HH P 4.

regression of knowledge".[80] In *Dawn* Nietzsche applauds unbounded sacrifice, including self-sacrifice, in service of the passion for knowledge.

The role of sacrifice in the search for knowledge is illuminated by an earlier section, titled "A tragic ending for knowledge".[81] In this section, Nietzsche advocates knowledge as a worthy goal for the self-sacrifice of humanity and supposed that the drive for knowledge will prove so strong that it "could drive mankind to the point of dying with the light of an anticipatory wisdom in its eyes".[82] The promise of consummation in death serves as a consolation for the pains of unrequited love in life.

The attitude to death manifested in Nietzsche's allusion to the romantic motif of the *Liebestod*, however, seems to shift as Nietzsche moves from *Dawn* to *The Gay Science*. In the latter work, the thought of death no longer offers any "anticipatory wisdom"; it no longer promises the consummation of a passion in the attainment of knowledge. Or, put in the terms of *An Attempt at Self-Criticism*, the thought of a glorious death no longer offers a metaphysical consolation for the pains of life. In section 278 of *The Gay Science*, expresses his reservations about such a thought, aligning it with a Christian "brotherhood of death" which finds consolation in the false hopes, fears and delusional beliefs produced by metaphysical speculation. Death is merely the conclusion, and not the secret goal, of life.

One of the most influential figurations of the *Liebestod* motif occurs in Wagner's *Tristan und Isolde*. *Liebestod* is the title of the opera's final aria, at the conclusion of which Isolde falls dead. The cause of her death is simply the power of her love for Tristan. While Tristan succumbs to the wound he willingly sustained when his love or Isolde is discovered, the death of Isolde is given no further explanation—her love for Tristan is sufficient. When the two die in each other's arms, they realise what has been the goal of their love all along.

---

[80] D 429.

[81] D 45.

[82] D 45.

> In Act I, Isolde and Tristan determinedly go through with what they believe to be an unspoken suicide pact [...]. In Act II they again want to die together. They are now openly in love with each other, and are longing for the only true oneness that is permanently available to them, the oneness of the noumenal state to which death will return them.[83]

The opera is suffused with Schopenhauerian metaphysics, to the extent that Nietzsche, in his essay *Richard Wagner in Bayreuth* calls it the "true *opus metaphysicum* of all art".[84] Wagner uses the *Liebestod* motif to illustrate the use of sexual love for the Schopenhauerian purpose of world-denial.[85] While Nietzsche's favourable treatment of Wagner is perhaps confined to his early works, BT and UM, his proposal to drive the mankind to the point of dying for knowledge in *Dawn 45* is hauntingly reminiscent of Wagner's *Liebestod*.

The redemptive *Liebestod* of *Tristan und Isolde* is undoubtedly one of the life-denying delusions about death which Nietzsche sets himself against in GS 278. So there is a puzzle whether there is a break in Nietzsche's thought between *Dawn* and *The Gay Science*, or whether Nietzsche alludes to some other notion of death in D 45 and D 429. Since he claims in Ecce Homo that both works are affirmative books, "deep but bright and gracious," we have reason to think the latter may be the case.[86] Nicholas Saul's "Love, death and *Liebestod* in German Romanticism" is instructive on this point.[87] On his account, the common romantic association of love and death is much more moderate than Wagner's use of the *Liebestod* would suggest. On Wagner's extreme conception, which we might call a teleological *Liebestod*, death is not only the chronological end but the aim of the passionate life. In death, lovers achieve the unity which they had been unable to achievable in the actual world, whether on metaphysical ground (the deceitful individuation of the phenomenal world, as Schopenhauer would

---

[83] Bryan Magee, *Wagner and Philosophy* (London: Penguin, 2001), 221.

[84] RWB 8.

[85] As Magee observes, this is not a connection that Schopenhauer himself makes. Nevertheless, the ends to which Wagner puts erotic love—mortification of the self and denial of the world—are undeniably Schopenhauerian.

[86] EH "Books" GS.

[87] Nicholas Saul, *The Cambridge Companion to German Romanticism* (Cambridge: Cambridge University Press, 2009).

have it) or because the adulterous relationships characteristic of romantic, following courtly, love offend against prevailing mores. This notion of the *Liebestod* illustrates the traditional association of romantic love with morbidity, the perverse, and sickness in general.[88] The Wagnerian *Liebstod* celebrates an "escape into the dream-world of beautiful, yet dead, art".[89]

However, according to Saul, this strong teleological account of *Liebestod* is not representative of the broader romantic tradition. He singles out Schlegel's semi-autobiographical novel *Lucinde* as featuring a more sophisticated approach to love and death. In a letter to his beloved Lucinde, the protagonist and stand-in for Schlegel, Julius dreams of her death and considers following her.

> The years slowly passed by and one event tiresomely succeeded another; one work and then another achieved its end, an end as little my own as my taking those events and works merely for what they seemed to be. They were only holy symbols for me, all of them referring to the only beloved one, who was the mediator between my dismembered self and indivisible eternal humanity. My whole existence was an uninterrupted divine service of solitary love.
>
> At last I realised that the end had come. My brow was no longer smooth and my hair had grown white. My life was finished but had not been completed. My most productive years were past and yet art and virtue still stood eternally unattainable before me. I would have despaired if I hadn't seen and worshipped both in you, most gracious Madonna! And seen you and your gentle godliness in myself.
>
> Then you appeared beckoning me with the summons of death. A heartfelt longing for you and for freedom seized me; I yearned to be back in my dear old homeland and was just about to shake the dust of the journey from me when I was recalled again to life by the promise and reassurance of your recovery.[90]

This passage doesn't seem vulnerable to the same easy objections as Wagner's so-called erotic death cult. Julius doesn't immediately rush to suicide. Rather the imagined death of Lucinde inspires him to a long life of what he calls divine service. He dreams that, at the chronological end of life, he completes life through a "simultaneously *ethical* and *aesthetic* act: the wilful foreshortening of the narrative thread of [his] biography".[91]

---

[88] Thus Goethe's dictum "I call the Classical the healthy and the Romantic the sick."

[89] Saul, *The Cambridge Companion to German Romanticism*, 163.

[90] Friedrich Schlegel, *Lucinde and the Fragments*, trans. Peter Firchow (Minneapolis: University of Minneapolis Press, 1971), 117–18.

[91] Saul, *The Cambridge Companion to German Romanticism*, 168.

What Schlegel is doing in this passage is mediating between the individual and the infinite (or indivisible eternal humanity). While we might retain some concerns about his "longing for dissolution and freedom" in death, as Saul notes, "the emphasis lies rather on the finite side of the equation". That is, as Novalis says, death becomes the romantic principle of life.

To return to Nietzsche, we can say that his characterisation of romanticism is at best unsubtle. On the other hand, if we keep in mind that the targets of his most emphatic polemics against romanticism are Schopenhauer and Wagner—his anti-romantic self-treatment is directed against that romanticism he himself had previously endorsed—these more moderate romantic positions show us how we might reconcile his statements about the passion for knowledge and death in *Dawn* with his rejection of metaphysical delusions in *The Gay Science*, namely by finding, for the thought of death, a this-worldly consolation.

Nietzsche thinks that knowledge can serve as such a consolation. In *Dawn*'s figuration of the passion for knowledge he makes just this claim: "mankind must believe itself to be more sublime and more consoled under the compulsion and suffering of [the passion for knowledge] than it did formerly".[92] There are two parts to the effect of the passion for knowledge on humanity. First, it gives a greater access to the feeling of the sublime than has previously been available. It achieves this by aestheticising the potential fatal consequences of the search for knowledge in the manner of a glorious *Liebestod*. In section 427, this is the task he sets for philosophy, to "discover the mightiest beauty in precisely the wild, ugly sides of science".[93] The consolation of knowledge is better expressed in *The Gay Science*, that with the principle that life can be lived as a means to knowledge—"one can live not only boldly but even gaily, and laugh gaily too".[94] What Nietzsche means is that the pains, sorrows,

---

[92] D 429.

[93] D 427.

[94] GS 324.

and disappointments of life can be redeemed under the understanding that they serve the search for knowledge.

There is an obvious tension internal to the passion for knowledge. Knowledge, on Nietzsche's account, inevitably dissolves our aesthetic productions.[95] This must include the sublime character of knowledge. Rather than reconciling this tension, Nietzsche enshrines it as a law of "ebb and flow". As he writes in a note from 1881:

> We must love and nurture error; it is the womb of knowledge. Art as the nurturing of illusions—*our* cult. To love and promote life for the sake of knowledge, to love and promote illusion for the sake of life. The fundamental condition of all passion for knowledge is to *give existence an aesthetic meaning, to augment our taste for it*. Thus, we discover here, too, a night and a day as the conditions for *our* lives: desiring knowledge and desiring error are ebb and flow. Ruled by *one* absolute, mankind would perish and *with it its capacities*.[96]

Conclusion

The distinction Nietzsche sketched in the *Attempt at Self-Criticism* between romantic and Dionysian pessimism is at the crux of his anti-Romanticism. In the *Birth of Tragedy*, and even, it might appear, in *Dawn*, Nietzsche countenances that death be preferable to the disappointment of a passion, and in particular any regression of knowledge. Even the slightest of disappointments for the jealous lover is intolerable in this world, and requires the radical cure of exit. This is precisely the practical nihilism Nietzsche describes in *ASC*, to prefer the oblivion of death to worldly suffering. In *The Gay Science* on the other hand, Nietzsche devises a means by which to both bear the disappointments of life and negotiate the dangers of the passion for knowledge.

Nietzsche proposes to frustrate the passion for knowledge in the service of life. In doing so he achieves the same as the troubadours, who refashioned the mystical love of god into a sublime this-worldly passion. Nietzsche takes and treats his own early romanticism, by perfecting his control of the passions, to achieve a new kind of philosophical health.

---

[95] GS 299.

[96] KSA 9:11[162], translated in Mazzino Montinari, *Reading Nietzsche*, trans. Greg Whitlock (Urbana: University of Illinois Press, 2003), 66, emphasis in original.

In the preface to *The Gay Science* we find Nietzsche's clearest enunciation of the relationship between philosophy and health. By engaging in philosophy, one inscribes one's own state of health or sickness onto "the heaven of concepts",[97] which can then be interpreted as signs or symptoms of the conditions of the philosopher's life. In this preface, Nietzsche turns his diagnostic eye back on his own work, and claims that *The Gay Science* is a work of a convalescent spirit, emerging from a period of severe sickness.

The Gay Science concludes Nietzsche's middle period and the so-called free spirit trilogy—during which Nietzsche practiced "long and dangerous exercises of self-mastery".[98] It marks the emergence of a "new happiness"[99] which stands in stark contrast to *Human, All Too Human*'s "pale, subtle happiness [...] without yes [and] without no".[100] The happiness of *The Gay Science* is a fundamentally *affirmative* happiness; the free spirit trilogy reaches its apotheosis in book four with the double yes-saying of *amor fati* and the eternal recurrence. These affirmations flow from a revival of the passions. That Nietzsche recovers from the romanticism of *The Birth of Tragedy* and the Stoicism of *Human, All Too Human* depends the recuperation and incorporation of the passions and his courtly contortion of the passion for knowledge in *The Gay Science*.

---

[97] GS P 2.
[98] GS P 3.
[99] GS P 3.
[100] HH P 4.

5. Diagnosing Eternity

Nietzsche's recuperation of the passions, and specifically the passion for knowledge, furnishes him with the means to develop a novel ethics of affirmation. Hitherto, he claims, philosophy has only been rendered life valuable in relation to 'higher' metaphysical or theological principles. That is, life has only been conditionally affirmed. Under his diagnostic eye, these higher principles have been exposed as symptoms of weakness or impoverishment. Nietzsche's task is to revalue conditions of human existence which previous philosophies simply efface.

In the previous chapter I set the passion for knowledge as Nietzsche's post-Christian and post-Romantic renovation of the traditional philosophical drive to truth, which he re-conceives as passional in the mould of the troubadours' passionate courtly love. As both Plato and Nietzsche agree, the passions put eternity at stake and the passion for knowledge is no different.[1] Nietzsche challenges Plato's account of the passions, however, by developing a novel conception of eternity. This conception, he claims, arrests the philosophical flight from transience. In this chapter I examine in turn the objections Nietzsche levies against Plato, Stoicism, and Epicureanism, through the lens of their respective figurations of transience and eternity. In doing so I set the stage for the next chapter, in which I show how the doctrine of the eternal recurrence undergirds the ethics of passionate affirmation we find in *The Gay Science*.

Nietzsche contests the characterisations of eternity present in the main ethical traditions of antiquity, because he argues these characterisations express pathological judgments on the value of existence. In Platonism, the eternal is conceived as unchanging, perfect, and immune to the passage of time. In Stoicism, the eternal appears as the dynamic, but lawful and rational procession of nature. In Epicureanism, eternity figures in the infinite descent of dead atoms through void, as the painlessness

---

[1] Compare Symp. 206a "love loves the good to be one's own for ever" and GS 295 where a "faith of passion" is "faith in eternity".

before birth and after death to which the philosopher aspires. Nietzsche holds that these figures' veneration of the unchanging, the rational, and the painless entails a concomitant contempt for transient particulars and the natural lives these transient particulars comprise. Nietzsche develops the thought of the eternal recurrence as an expression of an ethics which affirms our this-worldly entanglement with transient particulars. Bernd Magnus poses the thought of the eternal recurrence as an "eternalistic counter-myth" to classical figurations of eternity.[2] Such figurations are expressions of an inherent aversion to time and transience, which he terms *kronophobia*. Classical figurations palliate *kronophobia* by positing an eternity which escapes the failings of temporal existence—vulnerability to change, to contingency, and painful yearnings of desire—and setting this escape from temporality as the highest human aspiration. In Nietzsche's words, they express a spirit of revenge against the temporal world itself. As a philosophical therapist he seeks to treat this traditional philosophical aversion to transience and return our attention to the temporal world.

Plato

As I have shown in chapter three, Nietzsche reads Platonic ethics as an attempt to escape the sorrows of transient existence. Socrates escapes the danger of passionate attachment to transient physical objects by directing his eros towards the stable and ever-present form of the good. The task of philosophy is to follow Socrates up the *scala amoris* thereby transcending the mortal world, and partaking in the immortality of the gods.[3] In chapter three our focus was on the proper structure of a philosophical life according to Plato; in the current section I attend to Plato's conception of eternity in justifying this life and to Nietzsche's eternal recurrence in disrupting it.

---

[2] Bernd Magnus, "Nietzsche's Eternalistic Counter-Myth," *The Review of Metaphysics* 26, no. 4 (1973), 615.

[3] Symp. 212a.

Recall that Plato's aim is to resolve the predicament in which non-philosophical human love finds itself with regards to the transient nature of its object, namely the discrepancy between human erotic aspirations—for eternal possession—and natural possibilities—of failure, loss, and death. On the one hand, the human lover wants her object in perpetuity; on the other, the finitude of natural objects prevents the satisfaction of this desire. Plato claims to have solved this predicament by finding a realm in which the aspirations of human desire can be met. He promises to do away with the pains of worldly attachments if only the unhappy human lover directs her attention towards the realm of the perfect eternal forms. Contemplation of the forms grants the philosopher a stable happiness, and secures her from the dangers of loving, even valuing, transient particulars. As Hannah Arendt notes, Plato's inauguration of eternity as the highest human aspiration displaces the drive to immortality of earlier Greek religion. Plato and Socrates develop a way of life that aims at deliverance from time, rather than infinite duration. Since this Platonic (or, as Arendt suggests, Socratic) impetus, philosophy has fabricated a series of contemplative objects named eternity which compensate in the ideal for the failings of temporal existence.[4]

The forms provide Plato with stable objects of love. The forms are not only stable but perfect. That is, they are complete in themselves and could never be otherwise to what they are. We might say that the forms do not admit of counterfactual hypotheses. This gives rise to an opposition between the forms as manifestations of perfection and transient particulars in the natural world as imperfect, deficient copies. The perfection of the forms both draws one's attention away from the natural world and instills contempt for transient particulars *as* deficient. Plato posits the realm of the forms as a better existence that the natural world fails to live up to.

Plato develops this account of the philosophical life, as we have seen in chapter three, in response to cultural conditions in fifth century Athens. He offers up Socrates

---

[4] Hannah Arendt, *The Human Condition* (Chicago: University of Chicago Press, 1958), 17.

as an alternative to Homeric ethical models, most especially the hero Achilles. But not only is Socrates an alternative, Plato presents him as a rival to Achilles' heroism: Socrates trumps Achilles with a new heroic ideal. Achilles subordinates life to immortal honour, when he stays to fight in Troy.[5] Socrates subordinates life to reason, being "the kind of man who listens to nothing within [him] but the argument that on reflection seems best".[6] They share the "absolute subordination of everything each values to one superlatively precious thing".[7] Besides this continuity, however, Socrates is unlike Achilles in almost every respect. Most importantly, the site of his heroism is his struggle to overcome, masters, and extirpate the savage and unruly passions that characterise Achilles. Achilles' grief over the death of Patroclus, and his vengeance against Hector's corpse, allow Homer to claim the passions as the only source of a life worthy of immortality. Socrates trumps Achilles by finding a form of immortality impervious to fortune and immune to grief. "Desiring the kind of happiness [Socrates] does, he can't lose".[8] In chapter six we will see Nietzsche return to grief like that of Achilles, in his own anti-Platonic ethical model.[9]

Plato, then, teaches the purification of eros of attachments to transient particulars for the elimination of grief. The highest form of love is directed at an object with no temporal existence, arrived at through pure intellection. Turning to *The Gay Science*, we see that Nietzsche *also* considers coming to love as a process of purification, most clearly in *GS 334*. In this section, entitled "One must learn to love", Nietzsche describes how we fall in love with a tune and, by extension, all things that we now

---

[5] Hom. Il. 9.410–16.

[6] Pl. Crito 46b.

[7] Gregory Vlastos, *Socrates, Ironist and Moral Philosopher* (Ithaca, NY: Cornell University Press, 1991), 234.

[8] Vlastos, *Socrates, Ironist and Moral Philosopher*, 235.

[9] For an extended discussion of the contest between Plato and Homer and their respective avatars Socrates and Achilles, see Angela Hobbs, *Plato and the Hero: Courage, Manliness, and the Impersonal Good* (Cambridge: Cambridge University Press, 2000), especially chapter 7 "The threat of Achilles".

love, "even he who loves himself".[10] It is, he claims, only by patient attention that we first come to distinguish and isolate an object from its surrounds. With hospitality, goodwill, and gentleness towards it, the object "sheds its veil and turns out to be a new and indescribable beauty".[11]

We can note a number of consequences of the account contained in this section. First, the object of love throughout the purification of love remains a worldly particular. Where Plato's ascent proceeds *from* a transient particular *to* its idealised perfections by means of pure intellect, the purification that Nietzsche offers works by *striping away* counterfactual hypotheses. Through goodwill and patient attention, the transient particulars we encounter appear beautiful, indispensable, and necessary. An object of love charms us as "enraptured lovers who desire nothing better from the world than it and only it".[12]

Second, while *GS 334* speaks the language of revelation (and, recall the troubadour's ambiguous position between revelation and production of beauty), earlier in book four Nietzsche comes down firmly, with the Romantics, on the side of beauty as an artefact of human production.[13] Some part of the troubadour's ambiguity survives, however, in Nietzsche's analysis of how the contemplative type bestows value on the world in *GS 301*. The contemplative, he thinks, always overlooks her own active contribution to the world of value; she considers herself *only* a spectator and listener, without recognising her creative power in fabricating the variegated world. In fact, she is both fashioner of and spectator on the world. This forgetfulness is not so much a failure on the part of the contemplative, but a mark of her success—her aesthetic contribution to the world is so enchanting as to fool its very author.

---

[10] GS 334.

[11] GS 334.

[12] GS 334.

[13] See GS 299 and 301.

A Platonist might defend a metaphysical account of love by claiming it does account for a love of transient particulars *inasmuch as* it participates in the eternal form of the beautiful. As shown in chapter three, it is questionable whether the purest Platonic lover remains attached to any of the particulars on which she started her ascent. Nevertheless, the human production of beauty provides an additional point of difference for Nietzsche's account. Beauty, along with "the whole eternally growing world of valuations, colours, accents, perspectives, scales, affirmations, and negations," is given to nature through artistic means.[14] Artists may lie when they layer beautiful appearances over things (that are never beautiful in themselves)[15] but, as Nietzsche describes in an important passage from book two of *The Gay Science*, an appearance draped over an object, over time, "gradually grows to be part of the thing and turns into its very body".[16] In artistic production, according to Nietzsche, appearances become essences, and over time the poet's words become flesh.

Not only are the objects of love subject to transience; so too are the value predicates which attach to them. Nietzsche's lover is thus doubly exposed to the vicissitudes of temporality. Not only can harm or death come to a beautiful particular, as a Platonist may well concede. Value-predicates, as human fabrications in a transient world, are themselves just as vulnerable to the passage of time as the particulars to which they lend their lustre.[17]

The *gaia scienza* of the troubadours translated religious forms of veneration into the human realm. In a similar manner, Nietzsche's gay science contends to translate love—conceptually grounded in the Platonic tradition on an affirmation of another metaphysical world and a concomitant negation of nature—into a this-worldly affirmation.

---

[14] GS 301.

[15] GS 299.

[16] GS 58.

[17] In connection with this possibility see GS 328.

Stoicism

Nietzsche connects his this-worldly account of love to eternity in a complex manner. In order to do so, in the context of his rejection of Platonic transcendence, he requires a figure of eternity that does not stand against the temporal world. He finds this in the thought of the eternal recurrence. Nietzsche himself acknowledges that this thought is not entirely foreign to the history of philosophy, claiming to have detected "traces of it" in the Stoics.[18] Although the eternal recurrence finds its popular presentation as a practical doctrine in *GS 341*, the thought first occurs earlier in that volume, at *GS 109*. Nietzsche introduces his doctrine in a discussion of the scientific de-deification of nature which opens book three of *The Gay Science*. This book begins with section 108's announcement of the death of god. Despite god's demise, Nietzsche warns, his "shadows" will remain projected on the world thousands of years hence.[19] Nietzsche's point, here and in the related section 125, is that because God has stood as a transcendent guarantor of meaning and purpose, disbelief in God also threatens "supposedly secular truths that have nonetheless lost their pedigree and intellectual warrant".[20]

The task Nietzsche sets in the following sections, most importantly *GS 109*, is to dispel belief in unwarranted theological claims. Nietzsche catalogues such shadows of god, including the beliefs that the universe is an organism, that existence has a purpose, and the nature operates lawfully. More generally he attacks our "aesthetic anthropomorphisms" [*ästhetischen Menschlichkeiten*] as ultimately depending on divine or metaphysical warrant.

---

[18] EH "Books" BT 3.

[19] "There may still be caves for thousands of years in which [God's] shadow will be shown" (GS 108).

[20] Lawrence Hatab, "Nietzsche, Nature, and Life Affirmation," in *Nietzsche and the Becoming of Life*, ed. Vanessa Lemm (New York: Fordham University Press, 2015), 36.

> "The total character of the world, however, is in all eternity chaos—in the sense not of a lack of necessity but of a lack of order, arrangement, form, beauty, wisdom, and whatever other names there are for our aesthetic anthropomorphisms"[21]

Nietzsche attacks the application of anthropomorphic predicates to the world as a whole or judgements on the "total character" of existence. Under the eye of knowledge, such judgements are vacuous—"None of our aesthetic or moral judgements apply to [the universe]".[22] Science, he says, reveals only the world as a chaotic tumult of bare necessities to which the application of anthropomorphic predicates is an error. The progress of science will "de-deify" nature, correcting these errors, on the way to delivering nature "pure, newly discovered, [and] newly redeemed".[23] The de-deification of nature, Nietzsche suggests, will grants us the means to "naturalise" humanity or to reconcile humanity with nature.

In this difficult section, Nietzsche appears to sanction the wholesale dissolution of aesthetic predicates that have hitherto attached value to the world. Paul Loeb suggests as much in his analysis of the thought of the eternal recurrence. In *GS 109*, Loeb claims, Nietzsche first reveals the truth about the universe—that underneath all appearances lies the chaotic reality of eternally recurring flux—and recommends the extraction of aesthetic predicates which have preserved life hitherto.[24] Loeb devotes significant attention to Nietzsche's contention that, "judged from the vantage point of our reason" the universe is a "*Spielwerk*" (a plaything or musical mechanism) whose eternally recurrent tune "must never be called a melody".[25] This passage is the first published reference to the thought of the eternal recurrence (preceding *GS 285* and the celebrated *GS 341*) and has the advantage, on Loeb's account, of lending itself to a cosmological reading of the doctrine. The truth of the eternal recurrence is opposed to

---

[21] GS 109.

[22] GS 109.

[23] GS 109.

[24] Paul Loeb, "Eternal Recurrence," in *The Oxford Handbook of Nietzsche* (Oxford: Oxford University Press, 2013), 656.

[25] GS 109.

a collection of false predicates given to the world by our theological and aesthetic projections. Science dissolves these predicates by showing that they have no objective basis. The discipline of science therefore liberates us of our attachment to erroneously-valued objects in the world.

It would seem, then, as if *GS 109* establishes a prohibition of the projection of aesthetic predicates in favour of a world stripped of colour and melody. If so, we should read it as an endorsement of the disciplined Stoic withdrawal of value from externals. Nietzsche makes the connection between the solvent power of science and Stoic withdrawal explicit in *GS 12*, where he claims both Stoicism and modern science serve the same goal: purifying us of both the pleasures and pains caused by our investments in transient particulars. Reflecting on science in the second volume to *The Gay Science*, he considers the natural-scientific interpretation of the world as a bare mechanism to yield an "essentially *meaningless* world".[26] Natural scientists who evacuate the world of value fail to grasp the rich ambiguity of existence and "nothing of what is 'music' in it".[27]

If Nietzsche in 1886 turns away from the intellectual Stoicism of his natural scientist contemporaries, we have pause to consider whether this marks a change in position from the earlier *GS 109*, or whether *GS 109* can avoid a charge of Stoicism. We have a second reason for care in interpreting *GS 109*'s relation to Stoicism, namely the difficulty the extraction of aesthetic predicates would pose for Nietzsche's ethical program in book four. We have already seen that Nietzsche conceptualises love in musical terms. In *GS 334* he claims there is "no other way" to come to love another or oneself but by a process modelled on coming to love a musical figure. If *GS 109* establishes a prohibition on the application of aesthetic (and especially musical) predicates in general, this threatens the aesthetic grounds for an affirmation of life. The following section asks whether knowledge can be incorporated into life. If the chaotic

---

[26] GS 373, emphasis in original.
[27] GS 373.

and eternally recurrent flux Nietzsche describes in *GS 109* rules out the aesthetic techniques and practices involved in every means of learning to love, then the answer to the question is no, before any experimentation has taken place. Nietzsche does not draw this immediate conclusion, and indeed considers its unsettledness one of life's greatest temptations.[28]

Nietzsche employs musical metaphors to describe two contrasting aspects of his account of the progress of science. He celebrates the absence of melody in the scientific world view, but decries that along with melody, modern science has lost an ear for all musical qualities. Returning to *GS 109*, we can come to terms with this passage and the intellectual Stoicism it appears to condone, by giving attention to the significant yet puzzling distinction Nietzsche draws between *Weise* (tune) and *Melodie*. If the eternal recurrence has a tune, but not a melody, this contrast will point the way towards reconciling scientific disenchantment (with *Melodie*) with the amorous enchantment he describes in terms of *eine Weise* in *GS 334* and how this reconciliation might recuperate the notion of eternity into this-worldly, temporal life.

Nietzsche's prohibition on *Melodie* in this context recalls the caution towards music he expresses in *Human, All Too Human*. This work, in which Nietzsche sets his erstwhile romanticism on ice, contains reflections deeply skeptical of the promises of music, and of art more generally. In contrast to *The Birth of Tragedy*'s treatment of art as the "true metaphysical activity of this life," in *Human, All Too Human*, Nietzsche subjects both the production and experience of art to naturalistic, psychological investigation. Nietzsche now considers the artist's claim to privileged epistemic access to the very essence of the world as a mere pretence, reinforced by the praise of her successfully deceived audience.[29] The pretence and deception of art strain the

---

[28] "I find [life] truer, more desirable and mysterious every year—ever since the day when the great liberator came to me: the idea that life could be an experiment of the seeker for knowledge" (GS 324).

[29] HH 32.

intellectual conscience, as Nietzsche illustrates with reference to the music of Beethoven:

> *Art makes the thinker's heart heavy.* - How strong the metaphysical need is, and how hard nature makes it to bid it a final farewell, can be seen from the fact that even when the free spirit has divested himself of everything metaphysical the highest effects of art can easily set the metaphysical strings, which have long been silent or indeed snapped apart, vibrating in sympathy; so it can happen, for example, that a passage in Beethoven's Ninth Symphony will make him feel he is hovering above the earth in a dome of stars with the dream of immortality in his heart: all the stars seem to glitter around him and the earth seems to sink farther and farther away. - If he becomes aware of being in this condition he feels a profound stab in the heart and sighs for the man who will lead him back to his lost love, whether she be called religion or metaphysics. It is in such moments that his intellectual probity [*intellectualer Charakter*] is put to the test.[30]

The danger of art is in tempting us back to religion and metaphysics. Nietzsche evocatively describes the way in which Beethoven's Symphony no. 9 draws its audience up to a fictitious cosmic perspective, at a remove from earthly concerns and interests. In this state one feels as if one is taking part in a rational ordered cosmos, and the dream of immortality displaces the fear of death. Music is particularly seductive according to Nietzsche, even for those who have cultivated a stringent intellectual probity. Modern music tempts us with such a promise of joy, grandeur, and moral ecstasy that "even the noble and self-controlled always drink from it a drop too much".[31] Music's danger, and the danger of describing the world as a *Melodie*, is capitulation to metaphysics.

Nietzsche's focus on music and, more specifically, *Melodie* echoes the central position these concepts occupy in Schopenhauer's aesthetic system, expounded in book three of *The World as Will and Representation*. Sketching out this position will require a brief explanation of Schopenhauer's philosophy of art.

The general purpose of art, according to Schopenhauer, is to engender "a special kind of consciousness or perception which is uniquely aesthetic".[32] He counterposes this aesthetic experience to the ordinary experience of the world by the distinctive character of both its subject and object. In the course of ordinary experience, one

---

[30] HH 153. Note that this passage predates Nietzsche's use of the term *Redlichkeit*, honesty or probity, from *Dawn* on.

[31] AOM 159.

[32] Julian Young, *Nietzsche's Philosophy of Art* (Cambridge: Cambridge University Press, 1992), 1.6, p10.

considers oneself an empirical individual, occupying a particular body, surrounded by objects similarly located in space and time. Schopenhauer inherits from Kant the notion that a metaphysical substratum exists in-itself, antecedent to the empirical world. Experience comes about when the thing-in-itself is determined according to the various necessary conditions of appearance, including the categories of space, time, and causality. For Schopenhauer, unlike Kant, the body plays an important role as the locus of this determination: relations between an individual and her surrounds is mediated by a body "whose affections constitute its starting-point, and which is itself only willing made concrete".[33] The subject of ordinary experience, then, is this time-bound individual who experiences the world through the incessant and painful demands of the body, expressing the ceaseless striving of the underlying metaphysical will. The objects of ordinary experience also relate, in the end, back to the will. Cognition, perception, and sensibility are, "just like the other parts of organic beings, expressions of the will" at higher levels of objectivation.[34] Consequently, "the representation which arises through them also serves the will as a means for achieving its now complicated ends of maintaining a creature with diverse needs".[35] Schopenhauer's conclusion is that the individual of ordinary experience always considers objects from the perspective of her diverse needs. Ordinary experience is always "interested".[36]

Aesthetic experience involves a transformation of both the subject and object of ordinary experience. As Schopenhauer summarises,

> there are *two inseparable components* of the aesthetic way of looking at things: cognition of the object, not as a particular thing but rather as a Platonic *Idea*, i.e. as a permanent form of this whole

---

[33] WWR 1.32.

[34] WWR 1.33. I follow Norman, Welchman, and Janaway's coinage of "objectivation" for the process whereby the will, the thing-in-itself, "becomes object" in the world of appearance (WWR I, l).

[35] WWR 1.33.

[36] As Julian Young (1992, 6) notes, Nietzsche recognises and celebrates this feature of Schopenhauer's thought. The "instrumental" character of ordinary consciousness according to Schopenhauer resurfaces in Nietzsche's developmental explanation of the origins of knowledge in life-preserving errors (GS 110).

genus of things; and then the self-consciousness of the one who has this cognition, not as an individual, but as *pure, will-less subject of cognition*.[37]

When the subject undergoes aesthetic experience, she finds not a representation of a particular thing in space and time, to which she relates according to her own interests, but one of the Ideas, the "original, unchanging forms and qualities" of particular things.[38] Following Plato, Schopenhauer claims that particulars are merely deficient imitations of the forms. He also claims that the Ideas stand in some relation to the will, which he identifies with Kant's thing-in-itself. Schopenhauer reconciles the Platonic and Kantian characterisations of the Ideas in the claim that Kant overlooked "being-an-object-for-a-subject" as a necessary conditions of appearance.[39] The Ideas are, according to Schopenhauer, the thing-in-itself made object. Because "being-an-object-for-a-subject" is "the first and most universal form of all appearance", the Ideas stand behind each and every particular appearance, as Plato had it.[40] Nevertheless, they represent the will subject to the condition of being-an-object-for-a-subject, they stand at a remove from the Kantian thing-in-itself. As the "immediate and therefore adequate" objectivation of the will, the Ideas stand outside of time.[41] In aesthetic experience, then, one is confronted not by a particular landscape, tree, cliff, or building, but by the eternal species to which such particulars belong.

Cognition of the Ideas transforms the subject of aesthetic experience. The subject is gripped by contemplation of the forms. Schopenhauer describes how one loses oneself in the object of contemplation completely: "we forget our individuality, our will, and continue to exist only as pure subject, the clear mirror of the object [...] a *pure*, will-

---

[37] WWR 1.38.

[38] WWR 1.30.

[39] WWR 1.32.

[40] WWR 1.32.

[41] WWR 1.32. For Schopenhauer, as for Plato, transience is the chief deficiency of particulars. Time is "merely the scattered and dismembered perspective that an individual being has of the Ideas that are outside of time and therefore *eternal*".

less, painless, timeless *subject of cognition*".[42] This state involves the suspension of almost all conditions of appearance (most importantly time) except objectivation, which conditions even the Ideas. Through the intellect, one momentarily escapes the world populated by transient particulars and ruled by the will. Schopenhauer illustrates this freedom from the will with the sculpture of Apollo Belvedere, whose head sits "so freely on its shoulders that it seems entirely wrenched away from the body and no longer subject to its cares".[43]

This is the general structure and function of art, according to Schopenhauer. Different art forms are distinguished by the degree of clarity and perfection with which they represent the essence of the will, mediated by the Ideas. Schopenhauer enumerates the arts from the crudest, architecture, concerned with the interplay of Ideas such as gravity and rigidity, to poetry, which faithfully represents the essence of humanity.

Uniquely among the arts, music does not use the Ideas to indirectly represent the essence of the will. Instead, Schopenhauer claims that music is an *"unmediated objectivation and copy of the entire will"*.[44] Whereas the non-musical arts invite cognition of the Ideas in order to represent the will, music grants direct access to the metaphysical world. Because music bypasses both the Ideas (as fractured objectivations of the will) and the world of transient particulars (as the will conditioned by time, space and causality under the aegis of the principle of sufficient reason), Schopenhauer concludes that music provides direct insight into existence purified of these perspectival distortions.[45] Music allows one to cognise the "essence" of the will and not merely its "shadows".[46]

---

[42] WWR 1.34.

[43] WWR 1.33.

[44] WWR 1.52, emphasis in original.

[45] Music "could in a sense still exist even if there were no world at all" (WWR 1.52).

[46] WWR 1.52.

Melodie occupies a privileged position within music, according to Schopenhauer, due to the clarity with which it contributes to this cognitive task. Recall that the non-music arts indirectly represent the will, by means of Ideas, in ascending grades of clarity and perfection. The plurality of the Ideas comprise a total objectivation of the will, encompassing the basest (gravity, rigidity) through to the grandest (humanity) of Ideas. Since both the plurality of the Ideas and music are "copies" of the will, Schopenhauer concludes that there must exist an analogous grading of musical voices to the grades of Ideas. The lowest notes of harmony, like the aesthetic apprehension of architecture, express the lowest grades of the objectivation of the will. In like manner, *Melodie* directly expresses what poetry only achieves by means of the Ideas, the essence of the will at its highest grade of clarity in human affairs.

> In *melody*, the high-singing, principal voice that guides the whole, moving forward with unhindered freedom so as to join everything from beginning to end seamlessly together into a *single*, meaningful thought, a principal voice presenting a whole, – in this I recognize the highest level of the objectivation of the will, the thoughtful living and striving of human beings. Only human beings, being endowed with reason, keep looking forwards and backwards over the course of their actual life as well as their countless possibilities, thereby achieving a life course that, in being thoughtful, is a coherent whole: – correspondingly, only *melody* is joined up from beginning to end in a way that is full both of purpose and significance.[47]

This passage on the importance of melody clarifies the position that Nietzsche is arguing against when he prohibits the application of melody to existence. Melody represents the will at its highest grade of clarity in human affairs. Schopenhauer thinks this is evidenced by the manner in which a melodic line departs, deviates, and eventually returns to the tonic. The manifold different intervals and arrangements possible within a melody express "the many different forms of the striving of the will", while its return to the tonic expresses satisfaction.[48] In the creation of a melody the composer unveils "the deepest secrets of human willing and sensation".[49] The musical function of the melody is to tie a range of disparate voices into a coherent whole. It

---

[47] WWR 1.52.

[48] WWR 1.52.

[49] WWR 1.52.

grants a piece of music a single unifying narrative, full of purpose and significance: melody bestows order on the whole of a musical piece.

In addition to expressing deep truths about the human will, Schopenhauer claims on the basis of the analogy he draws between music and the non-musical arts, that music conveys deep *metaphysical* truths. We recognise in melody, according to Schopenhauer, the unity, purpose, and significance of the metaphysical will's ceaseless striving. *Melodie* tells us that the world comprises a single meaningful whole and invites us to cognise this whole by an analogy with the human will, namely in terms of a continual striving towards satisfaction. This is precisely the invitation, and temptation, that Nietzsche warns against when he prohibits *Melodie* from his aesthetic projects.

Loeb refers to Nietzsche's use of music in *GS 109* as an allusion to the "Pythagorean tradition of using music to explain the cosmos" and associates the putatively-cosmological discussion of the eternal recurrence in this section with his "earlier explicit discussion of the Pythagorean cosmological theory of eternal recurrence" in the second untimely meditation.[50] He associates the figure of the music box with Pythagoras to buttress his cosmological interpretation of *GS 109* whereby, as we have seen, the de-deification of nature implies the Stoic withdrawal of false value-predicates.

The passage Loeb cites occurs within Nietzsche's second *Untimely Meditation* on history. In this essay, Nietzsche examines the practical use of history in response to three sets of human needs. He outlines three corresponding modes of historical activity. The reference to Pythagoras occurs during the discussion of "monumental" history—history as it pertains to human action and striving. Monumental history depicts a chain of human greatness "like a range of human mountain peaks", the sight of which stirs ambition and courage in the present.[51] For those who need monumental history, "looking to the past impels them towards the future" in order that they repeat, or

---

[50] Loeb, "Eternal Recurrence," 657.
[51] HL 2.

attempt to repeat, that greatness once more.[52] It reminds those in the present of the breadth of the horizon of the possible, "that the greatness that once existed was in any event once possible and may thus be possible again".[53] This mode of history bears practical fruit inasmuch as the example of past greatness provokes action in the present. Those hoping to transform culture in Germany, for example, might take heart from a monumentalised Renaissance as evidence that their task is possible. Immediately, however, Nietzsche qualifies the prospect of historical repetition:

> And yet - to learn something new straightaway from this example - how inexact, fluid and provisional that comparison would be! How much of the past would have to be overlooked if it was to produce that mighty effect, how violently what is individual in it would have to be forced into a universal mould and all its sharp corners and hard outlines broken up in the interest of conformity! At bottom, indeed, that which was once possible could present itself as a possibility for a second time only if the Pythagoreans were right in believing that when the constellation of the heavenly bodies is repeated the same things, down to the smallest event, must also be repeated on earth[54]

Monumental history gives us hope for the repetition of an event resembling a past monumentalised event. It does not, importantly, promise the recurrences of identical particular events. It always deals in "approximations and generalities", makes "what is dissimilar look similar" and "diminish[es] the differences of motives and instigations" so as to present the past as "something exemplary and worthy of imitation".[55] Monumental history relies on the falsification of the past. It aims at the incorporation of history into practical life in order to transform that life. The success of monumental history hinges upon this practical transformation. In the foreword to this essay Nietzsche poses the impetus to history in these practical terms: "we need [history] for life and for action".[56]

Because it serves a practical need, monumental history stops short of an attempt to depict the past in absolute veracity. An unconditional will to historical truth, a

---

[52] HL 1.

[53] HL 2.

[54] HL 2.

[55] HL 2.

[56] HL F.

hypertrophy of the historical sense, is indeed the target of the essay. A scientific approach to history, which sought to fully understand relations of historical cause and effect, "would only demonstrate that the dice-game of chance and the future could never again produce anything exactly similar to what it produced in the past".[57]

Nietzsche uses the Pythagoreans not to endorse their musical cosmology, but to illustrate failure of history. We might take monumental history as indicative of the return of identical particular events only by closing our eyes to its approximations and distortions—at the cost of the regression of scientific knowledge—once "astronomers have again become astrologers".[58] Nietzsche also indicates the dependence of Pythagorean theory of recurrence on a parallelism between events on earth and a recurrent celestial order. This is precisely the position Nietzsche warns against in *GS 109*—"positing generally and everywhere anything as elegant as the cyclical movements of our neighbouring stars".[59] At best, the second *Untimely Meditation* remains neutral on the cosmological issues disputed in *GS 109*.

Nietzsche uses music, and in particular melody, in *GS 109* to single out the aesthetic experience of a deified nature. And, *pace* Loeb, this experience is not a revelation of the essence of existence, but a mystification which modern science purports to dispel. The experience of nature as melody is underwritten by the beliefs, with which Nietzsche begins his enumeration of the shadows of god, that the universe is an organism, that existence has a purpose, and that nature operates lawfully. "God is dead" rejects transcendent theism.[60] *GS 109* warns against the application of derivative theological predicates to nature, that is, pantheism.

---

[57] HL 2.

[58] HL 2. Compare D 429: "we would all prefer the destruction of mankind to a regression of knowledge!"

[59] GS 109.

[60] GS 108.

Nietzsche opposes pantheism with the claim that nature is chaotic, "in the sense not of a lack of necessity but of a lack of order".[61] During the preparation of *The Gay Science*, Nietzsche frequently puts his opposition to pantheism in these terms. A note sketching the structure of the forthcoming Zarathustra from 1881 has the first book describing "*Chaos sive natura*".[62] Nietzsche modifies, and parodies, Spinoza's slogan for pantheism *Deus sive natura* by substituting chaos for god.[63] While Nietzsche had only just seriously encountered Spinoza for the first time (an encounter that left him overjoyed), he would have been familiar with Schopenhauer's polemic against Spinoza's pantheism.[64]

Nietzsche's engagement with Stoicism during the early 1880s provides another occasion for him to mount an objection to pantheistic beliefs and commitments. This is especially apparent in the case of "cosmic" Stoicism, the strain of Stoic thought in which one finds alleviation from the fear of mortality and temporality through communion with a purposive and rational cosmic whole. This form of Stoicism formulates a concept of eternity that enables the Stoic to become indifferent to temporality.

Cosmic Stoicism, exemplified in chapter one by Marcus Aurelius, grounds Stoic indifference in attaining a cosmic point-of-view of the whole, whereby the emotional travails of earthly life shrink into comparative (and actual) insignificance. Marcus reminds himself of his power,

> to strip away many superfluous troubles located wholly in [his] judgement, and to possess a large room for [himself] embracing in thought the whole cosmos, to consider everlasting time, to think of

---

[61] GS 109.

[62] KSA 9:11[197].

[63] Stanley Rosen, *The Mask of Enlightenment: Nietzsche's Zarathustra* (New Haven and London: Yale University Press, 2004), 18.

[64] WWR 2.47. For the continuity of Spinoza's pantheism with Stoic pantheism in relation to the ethical systems of both, see WWR 1.16. On Nietzsche's primarily second-hand acquaintance with Spinoza, see Andreas Urs Sommer, "Nietzsche's Readings on Spinoza: A Contextualist Study, Particularly on the Reception of Kuno Fischer," *Journal of Nietzsche Studies* 43, no. 2 (2012): 156–84 and Thomas H. Brobjer, *Nietzsche's Philosophical Context: An Intellectual Biography* (Urbana and Chicago: University of Illinois Press, 2008), 77–82.

the rapid change in the parts of each thing, of how short it is from birth until dissolution, and how the void before birth and that after dissolution are equally infinite.[65]

This passage makes explicit the connection in Stoicism between the striping away of perspectival aesthetic predicates, and the belief in an underlying cosmic order which is thereby revealed. The importance of the rapidly changing part of nature, including those parts of ourselves subject to transience and eventual dissolution or death, pale in comparison to the cosmic grandeur of everlasting time. The figure of an eternal natural order palliates against the pains caused by investing transient particulars with value and compensates for our impending dissolution into the "great sea of being".[66]

Cosmic Stoicism clarifies the temptation present in the false cosmological beliefs Nietzsche details in *GS 109*—why we need not only *reject* the shadows of god but *beware* of them. To follow Marcus in holding nature as "a single living organism […] with a single purpose" is to treat this anthropomorphised nature as if it were the possible source of a deep and abiding satisfaction.[67] By ascending to a cosmic point of view, where one identifies with the organic, purposive whole, Marcus escapes from the disorder of the passions caused by the perspectival distortions of aesthetic value predication. Pantheism provides him with a means of reaping pleasure from the experience of nature, at the same time as eliminating pain. Cosmic Stoicism protects Marcus from the vagaries of temporality with an image of eternity as the rational order of the cosmos.

Recall that in chapter one, cosmic Stoicism was opposed to "human" Stoicism, in which one finds relief from the fear of death and temporality through the attainment of complete rational self-possession that makes one impervious to time. Time can take nothing from one who is already complete or in complete self-possession. This notion

---

[65] Marcus Aurelius 9.32.

[66] Marcus Aurelius 4.43.

[67] Marcus Aurelius 4.40.

of self-completion furnishes human Stoicism with a conception of eternity in terms of indifference to external temporal goods.

The two conceptions of eternity considered so far—Platonic transcendence and Stoic pantheism—give eternity a cosmological character. The conception of eternity at play in human Stoicism is different in that it posits an escape from temporality from an evaluative, rather than cosmological, perspective. The emphasis of Seneca's counsel in his *Epistles to Lucilius* is firmly on the need for fortitude in the face of an 'indifferent' external world. Seneca instructs Lucilius to put his own mind in order so as to endure external events.[68] Lucilius is to cultivate his capacity for a particular kind of joy, which hinges on distinguishing true goods from mere indifferents (or, as Seneca derisively refers to them, "useless things").[69]

The description of the Stoic *telos* as joy, as we have seen, comes under sharp criticism from Nietzsche as a "casuistic delicacy".[70] Seneca himself admits that it is a "a stern [or severe, *severa*] matter".[71] Nevertheless, Seneca recommends Lucilius to turn away from the enjoyment of externals and to "cast aside and trample under food all the things that glitter outwardly".[72] Rather than the imaginative expansion of perspectives, which comprised the therapy of Marcus, Seneca finds the grounds for a rejection of external objects in a "true good [...] which comes from [one's] own store".[73] By learning "how to feel joy" from his own store, Lucilius will attain a state of internal self-completion which leaves him impervious to time.[74]

---

[68] Elsewhere, for instance in the Natural Questions, Seneca adopts a more 'cosmic' perspective. The compatibility of these two poles of the Stoic system is discussed below.

[69] Sen. Ep. 23.1.

[70] GS 12.

[71] Sen. Ep. 23.4.

[72] Sen. Ep. 23.6.

[73] Sen. Ep. 23.6.

[74] Sen. Ep. 23.3.

Seneca's consolation to Lucilius, then, offers him a form of perfection as completion in the moment. We saw that Stoic pantheism ascends to a state of perfection by identifying with an eternal cosmic order. This identification grants the perfection of the whole to the Stoic sage in the moment. Lucilius is offered the same perfection or completion, without reference to the cosmic order. If Lucilius achieves this completion, he has nothing to fear from death. That a complete life is possible in the present moment shows that absent goods, whether future or past, are not necessary for happiness. Thus Seneca's instruction to "live every day as if it were a complete life".[75] The complete life is not defined by its duration, but by its self-sufficiency—it "depends neither on our years nor upon our days, but upon our minds".[76]

Eliminating the fear of death has the effect of freeing us from any kind of temporal attachment. Lucilius conceptualises the passage of time as itself a kind of death. Inasmuch as time passes, it is lost to us—"all past time is lost time".[77] Every day "a little of our life is taken from us" and thus "we die every day".[78] Seneca provides us a verse of Lucilius' own,

> Not single is the death which comes; the death
> Which takes us off is but the last of all.[79]

In the context of ubiquitous death, deliverance from the fear of death is both more urgent and a more powerful psychological remedy. If death is not to feared, then neither is the loss of any other object by the passage of time. Indeed, because such objects are not real goods, their passing is no real loss. One can meet death and the passage of time cheerfully, according to Seneca, if the present moment is the only time to which we ascribe value. Time "means nothing" to one who enjoys the present "to the

---

[75] Sen. Ep. 61.1.

[76] Sen. Ep. 61.4.

[77] Sen. Ep. 24.19.

[78] Sen. Ep. 24.19–20.

[79] Sen. Ep. 24.21. Seneca repeats a verse belonging to Lucilius back to its author.

full".[80] One who does so is free of care or greed for future, and has "no need of added years".[81]

Against the constant presence of death (which is itself simply a consequence of the passage of time) Seneca sets the possibility of living a complete life in the present moment. That is, he suggests Lucilius can transcend temporality by fashioning within himself a perfectly organised whole, impervious to the passage of time. Seneca develops a sense of self-completion entirely independent of temporality.

Nietzsche clearly rejects the Stoic project of fabricating a rationally organised whole, independent of transience. Lambasting the Stoics as poor physicians of the soul, he counterposes radical Stoic withdrawal to the "innumerable palliatives against pain" with which one might treat one's losses. While the Stoics deny the possibility of loss, for Nietzsche admits our vulnerability to loss, if equivocally: "a loss is a loss" if only for "barely an hour".[82] Nietzsche's equivocation—a loss in the moment can be easily recuperated in a short period of time—gives us pause in our consideration as to exactly how far he departs from Stoicism. He steadfastly rejects the Stoic's faith in reason and flight from temporality. Duration and other extra-rational means are necessary components of Nietzsche's philosophical therapy.[83] Yet at some points his goal does resemble a form of completion—the fabrication of perfect whole, where loss, sickness and injury are reinterpreted "immediately or very soon" as an essential component of a whole.[84]

We might also note that Seneca himself sometimes goes beyond the strict Stoicism of the letters to Lucilius. In his *Consolation to Marcia*, Seneca denies that he plans to "filch from [Marcia] any of [her] sufferings".[85] In the same letter he distances his

---

[80] Sen. Ep. 32.

[81] Sen. Ep. 32.

[82] GS 326.

[83] See the list of anaesthetics in GS 326.

[84] GS 277.

[85] Sen. Marcia 1.5.

consolation from "precepts of the sterner sort" which "bid [Marcia to] bear a human fortune in inhuman fashion".[86] In the *Consolation to Polybius*, Seneca describes the wisdom of those who "deny that the wise man will ever grieve" (that is, especially, the Stoics) as "harsh rather than brave".[87] Whatever the means, self-completion is still certainly Seneca's goal in these more eclectic consolations. The good of self-completion is that it delivers us from the disorderly conduct caused by emotional commitments to objects outside our own control.

We will return to a consideration of Nietzsche's eternal recurrence, and whether it gives him an ethical goal in the form of self-completion, in chapter six. For now, we should keep in mind that inasmuch as Nietzsche's appreciation of duration and extra-rational means of consolation echo Seneca, they both depart from Stoic orthodoxy.

Human and cosmic Stoicism present different approaches of the Stoic ethics of indifference. Marcus describes time as "a kind of river" and "an irresistible flood".[88] By adopting a cosmic perspective, Marcus escapes the disruption of local turbulences. Seneca maintains an individual point of view, but relies on the strength of an internal "guiding purpose" for the heroic endurance of violent currents and whirlpools.[89] Despite this contrast, both arrive at an ethics of indifference towards transient particulars on the basis of a principle of order impervious to time. This agreement should not be surprising, given the connection the Stoics draw between the rationality of human nature and the rationality of the universe. It is the same regulative principle that rules in the individual and the cosmos, and so the difference between human and cosmic Stoicism is one of emphasis, rather than essence.[90]

---

[86] Sen. Marcia 4.1.

[87] Sen. Polybium 18.5.

[88] Marcus Aurelius 4.43 (see also ibid. 2.17).

[89] Sen. Ep. 23.8.

[90] Sellars helpfully frames this difference in emphasis as between the two non-ethical parts of Stoic philosophy. A focus on Stoic physics raises the question of how to situation oneself within the cosmos, while Stoic logic is concerned with the use of representations. John Sellars, *Stocism* (Chesham: Acumen, 2006), 160.

Nietzsche diagnoses both aspects of Stoicism in turn as expressing, and masking, a fear of the disorder of the passions.[91] By fashioning eternity as an perfectly ordered whole and projecting this upon the self and the cosmos, the Stoics seek to protect themselves from the dangers of transience. To return to the inauguration of the eternal recurrence in *GS 109*, if this is to be Nietzsche's figure of eternity—an undergirding principle of a Dionysian life of the passions—his doctrine must leave one open to the vagaries of temporality and human finitude.

Epicureanism

Nietzsche returns to the theme of *GS 108–9* at the outset of book four of *The Gay Science*. He again warns against both the belief in a personal god "who is full of care and personally knows every little hair on our head" and belief in any "providential reason and goodness" in nature.[92] There is neither a transcendent, nor an immanent, world order; only the "beautiful chaos of existence".[93] While *GS 108–9* enumerates the theological and pantheistic beliefs we must guard ourselves against, *GS 277* describes the circumstances which tempt us to such beliefs. *GS 277* gives us the occasions that require us to exercise the caution advised in the earlier sections. The moment of greatest temptation, Nietzsche writes, occurs at "a certain high point in life" where "everything that befalls us continually turns out for the best".[94] Our luck and happiness seems to demand that nature and its parts are organised for our own benefit. At this moment, Nietzsche exhorts us to remember the gods of Epicurus who are wholly indifferent to our fate and entirely removed from the human world. In place of providence, Nietzsche identifies two factors necessary for our happiness: first, one's own contribution to the active fabrication of the human world by artistic means; and

---

[91] In the case of cosmic Stoicism, *GS 109* and more explicitly *BGE 9*. For human Stoicism, *GS 12* and *GS 305–6*.

[92] *GS 277*.

[93] *GS 277*.

[94] *GS 277*.

second, "good old chance", which bears responsibility for the most surprising and beautiful parts of the "wonderful harmony" of our lives.[95] That our artistic powers alone are insufficient for happiness draws into question whether Nietzsche's ethics can be described as a form of *self*-completion or "artistic" Stoicism, even before considering the elevation of the Epicureans above the Stoics in book four.

Nietzsche's call to remember the Epicurean gods echoes his positive appraisal of Epicurean physics in *Human, All Too Human*. Modern science, Nietzsche says, has sided with Epicurus over Christianity "point by point".[96] Most importantly for the current discussion, modern science and Epicurus both reject, at least on Nietzsche's account, the existence of a rational ordering of nature. The Epicureans denied that nature required any supernatural agency to regulate the turbulent descent of atoms through the void.[97] Rather, the atoms and composite bodies fall in a straight line, except when they are knocked off course by collisions with each other, or diverted by the unpredictable influence of the *clinamen* or swerve. The total image of Epicurean nature is of an unstable, chaotic tumult of atoms falling purposelessly through the void. Epicureanism does without both the providential divinity of Stoicism and the interventionist gods of Greek myth (and later Christianity). Because they live wholly removed of our affairs, we have no reason to fear the gods.

In *Dawn*, Nietzsche shifts his focus from the physical to the moral parallels between Epicureanism and modern science. This involves a shift of emphasis from the Epicurean remedy against the fear of the gods to that against the fear of death. In particular, Nietzsche paints science's rejection of a life after death as a new triumph for Epicurus.[98] Because we meet our definitive end at death, we have nothing to fear from religious prophesies of the afterlife. In particular, we needn't fear punishment in hell as

---

[95] GS 277.

[96] HH 68.

[97] Catherine Wilson, *Epicureanism at the Origins of Modernity* (Cambridge: Cambridge University Press, 2008), 37.

[98] D 72.

retribution for conduct in this life. Punishment in hell is just one of the harms to which religious believers imagine death will expose them. Eradicating this belief is just one part of the broader Epicurean project to dispel the fear of death in general.

That death is not a harm follows from the Epicureans' negative hedonism and their materialist view of the soul. The experience of pain is the only harm, and death is the dissolution of the experiential subject. Since there is no subject to experience pain at or after death, death is not a harm (at least, to the one who 'suffers' it).

The Roman Epicurean Lucretius answers a series of objections centred on the contention that death harms by depriving the one who dies of the goods of life. Lucretius claims that death can only count as a harm by means of an imaginative projection of the still living individual to a time after death. Death can only count as a harm, he argues, if there is a subject of that harm. One who worries about deprivation in death illicitly considers the ante-mortem individual subject to post-mortem harms. Normal deprivations like hunger or thirst are harms because they produce a painful longing for particular goods. To count the deprivation of life as a harm, then, is to imagine that some part of us survives death and that the surviving part is subject to painful longing for the goods of life.

Lucretius answers this objection with a comparison of death and sleep. In particular he describes the restful, dreamless sleep in which we enjoy none of the goods of waking life and yet feel no painful longing to recover them.[99]

> Death is therefore to be regarded as something much less, if there can be anything less than what we can see to be nothing, because a greater disturbance and dispersal of matter ensues at death, nor does anyone wake and rise once the chill severance of life has overtaken him.[100]

No one suffers just by virtue of dreamless sleep, which puts us at a remove from both the goods of waking life and the painful desire for their possession and

---

[99] In the Apology, Socrates claims that if death were such a dreamless sleep, it "would be a wonderful gain" (Plat. Apol. 40d). In the Odyssey, Penelope wishes that "holy Artemis would grant me a death as gentle as" her "wonderful sleep", to save her from a life of anguish and longing for the missing Odysseus. (Hom. Od. 200).

[100] Lucr. 3.926–30.

enjoyment. Death removes us even further from desire's painful longings—in the case of the peaceful dream we will eventually be brought back to consciousness and waking neediness. In the case of death we are permanently free from desire.

The weight of this comparison is carried by the finality of death, and the eternity of painless non-existence which follows. While the analogy between death and sleep serves to extend the indifference in which we hold sleep to death, a more forceful Epicurean response draws an equivalence between death and the eternity of non-existence before birth. Just as no one has been harmed by the eternity of non-existence before birth, no one will be harmed by the eternity of non-existence after death. There is nothing to fear in the post-mortem void because the only harm is in pain and suffering, and non-existence precludes suffering.

Keith Ansell-Pearson has drawn attention to the presence of a cosmological recurrence in Lucretius' discussion of the fear of death.[101] Considering the "past expanse of measureless time," Lucretius suggests that "you could easily come to believe that these same seeds of which we are now composed have often been placed in the same arrangement as they are now".[102] Unlike Nietzsche's presentation in *GS 341*, the thought of the eternal recurrence is no great cause of anxiety for Lucretius. We retain no memories from before birth, and so the sufferings of past qualitatively identical individuals cannot cause us distress. It cannot simply be the case that we lack epistemic access to past lives, however, since Lucretius grants that we might easily come to believe in the regular recurrence of particular configurations of atoms, including those of which we are composed.

The dominant position in the classical scholarship is to ascribe Lucretius an account of personal identity in which psychological continuity is a necessary condition. In a critical edition of *De Rerum Natura III*, Brown claims that the break in conscious self-

---

[101] Keith Ansell-Pearson, "A Melancholy Science?: On Bergson's Appreciation of Lucretius," *Pli* 27 (2015): 98.

[102] Lucr. 3.855.

remembrance would "give our 'recycled' selves a different identity from our own".[103] Without psychological continuity, qualitatively identical individuals in the past and future are not "us" and hence not the object of our self-directed concern. This concurs with Epicurus' claim that "We have been born once and cannot be born a second time; for all eternity we shall no longer exist".[104]

Warren offers an alternative reading of this section which does not ascribe to Lucretius a position on the problem of personal identity. Instead Lucretius offers the stronger claim that *were* we brought back to life by the return of the atoms which presently make up my body to their present configuration *then* "this would not affect us in any way".[105] On this reading, *even if* an identity holds between recurrences, the Epicurean need not fear the eternal repetition of worldly pain. "Even if these future individuals are identical with me, the fact that no memory is retained from one instantiation to the next ensures that none of these identical individuals should be concerned about what has happened or will happen to others".[106] The break in memory between recurrences allows Lucretius to avoid the thought of my pains recurring on to eternity, but we may question whether it necessarily excludes my concern for future or past individuals like, or identified with, myself. As we will see in chapter six, when Nietzsche considers the possibility of recurrence this allows him the imaginative projection of the self into the future and past. Lucretius and Nietzsche's starkly different responses to the thought of the eternal recurrence signals the divergence between Nietzsche and Epicurean philosophical therapy. We can use Nietzsche's formulation of the eternal recurrence as a diagnostic tool to discover the failings—in his eyes—of Epicureanism. Nietzsche's recurrence leaves no place for the tranquil equanimity towards death and eternity which the Epicureans, like the other

---

[103] P. Michael Brown, *De Rerum Natura III* (Warminster: Aris & Phillips, 1997), 193. E. J. Kenney concurs in *De Rerum Natura Book III* (Cambridge: Cambridge University Press, 1971), 196.

[104] VS 14.

[105] James Warren, "Lucretian Palingenesis Recycled," *The Classical Quarterly* 51, no. 2 (2001): 502.

[106] Warren, "Lucretian Palingensis Recycled," 503.

Hellenistic schools, prize dearly. On Nietzsche's telling, the thought of eternal recurrence will induce either sublime rapture or despondency in those it seizes. If the Epicureans fails Nietzsche's test, we can ask what it is about life that prevents them from passionately longing for its return.[107]

In his letter to Menoeceus, Epicurus concerns himself primarily with philosophical purgatives. There, Epicurus counsels his reader to rid himself of unnatural desires (which are vain and empty) and temper natural desires so that they are easily satisfied. Once they have been reigned in, natural desires (whether those which strike of necessity or not) will not be experienced as a source of pain or mental disturbance. Epicurus is a hedonist in that he takes pleasure as the highest good, but he is a *negative* hedonist in that he identifies pleasure with the removal and absence of pain. The end result of elimination of pain is *ataraxia*, the "painless state that Epicurus prized as the highest good and the state of the gods".[108]

> The voice of the flesh cries, "Keep me from hunger, thirst, and cold!" The man who has these sureties and who expects he always will would rival even Zeus for happiness.[109]

For Epicurus the happiness of the gods is identical to the highest human aspiration, an identification the Epicureans signal by their preference for the term *makaria* or blessedness over *eudaemonia*.[110]

Benjamin Farrington tells us that there is "no more important concept in Epicurus than that of the blessed life".[111] Howard Caygill, writing on Nietzsche's interpretation of Epicurus, focuses on blessedness as the grounds on which to build an rapprochement between the two. To this end, he argues that Epicurean blessedness, *makaria*, is a state beyond *ataraxia*. Whereas the negative ideal of *ataraxia* stands for the Epicurus

---

[107] We might note that the impossibility of *my* recurrence, according to the argument at Lucr. 3.855, does not necessarily bear on its desirability.

[108] WWR 1.38.

[109] VS 33.

[110] Julia Annas, *The Morality of Happiness* (Oxford: Oxford University Press, 1995), 345n34.

[111] B. Farrington, "The Meanings of *voluptas* in Lucretius," *Hermathena*, no. 80 (1952): 26.

Nietzsche castigates as another kind of Christian tranquilliser, a focus on blessedness allows for what Caygill calls a "Dionysian reading of Epicurus".[112]

Farrington's inspection of Lucretius lends support to this account. While he doesn't find a Latin equivalent for *makaria* (he claims Cicero's later coinages *beatitas* and *beatitudo* were unavailable for "metrical reasons"), he identifies certain uses of *voluptas* with, on the one hand, run of the mill pleasure or *hedone* and others, especially in the phrase *divina voluptas* with "this most exalted state of feeling known to [Lucretius]," "that state of blessedness for which Epicurus would have used the word *makaria*".[113]

Caygill develops an account of a distinction between *ataraxia* and *makaria* on the basis of the Vatican Sayings.[114] In these fragments, he detects an "intimation" of blessedness "beyond the therapeutic consolations of ataraxia".[115] "Blessedness," Caygill claims, "is not identical to ataraxia".[116]

Returning to Epicurus' letter to Menoeceus, this distinction becomes difficult to make out.

> He who has a clear and certain understanding of [Epicurean precepts] will direct every preference and aversion toward securing health of body and tranquillity of mind, seeing that this is the sum and end of a blessed [*makarios*] life.
>
> When we are pained because of the absence of pleasure, then, and then only, do we feel the need of pleasure. Wherefore we call pleasure the alpha and omega of a blessed [*makarios*] life.[117]

The sum and end of a blessed life is pleasure, which "reaches its limit in the removal of all pain".[118]

---

[112] Howard Caygill, "Under the Epicurean Skies," *Angelaki* 11, no. 3 (2006): 111.

[113] Farrington, "The Meanings of *voluptas* in Lucretius," 28.

[114] Whether or not Caygill establishes a distinction between *ataraxia* and *makaria*, these sources, discovered in 1888, could not furnish Nietzsche with such a distinction.

[115] Caygill, "Under the Epicurean Skies," 113.

[116] Caygill, "Under the Epicurean Skies," 112.

[117] DL 10.128.

[118] PD 3.

Epicurus has a good reason for identifying blessedness with *ataraxia*. *Ataraxia*, as the absences of disturbance, resists quantification. That is, it doesn't make sense to speak of having more or less *ataraxia*, as we might speak of the magnitude of a kinetic pleasure. As Cicero reports, while static pleasures may vary in kind, they cannot in intensity or degree.[119] Later, Cicero attributes to Epicurus the stronger position that not even protraction in time increases the amount of static pleasures: Epicurus "maintains that long duration can not add anything to happiness, and that as much pleasure is enjoyed in a brief span of time as if pleasure were everlasting".[120]

As Julia Annas explicates, this has the consequence that pleasure "does not make a longer life any better, and thus more desirable, than a shorter life".[121] Even everlasting Jupiter is no happier than Epicurus (as long as we grant that Epicurus actually achieved *ataraxia*). Again, from Epicurus' principle doctrines: "Unlimited time and limited time afford an equal amount of pleasure, if we measure the limits of that pleasure by reason."[122]

This counter-intuitive identification of the happiness of the gods and the happiness of *ataraxia* plays a fundamental role in establishing the Epicurean slogan that "death is nothing to us". Namely, since duration is irrelevant to happiness, one can live a complete life in the moment: "If you are already happy, then further time cannot give you anything you don't now already have, so you have no reason to prefer having further time to dying now."[123] If blessedness were a positive notion beyond the zero-point of *ataraxia*—one that gave rise to a conception of happiness as protracted in time—the immortality of the gods *would* grant them a richer harvest of existence than any mortal, and a premature death *would* be harmful to the one who dies.

---

[119] Cicero De Fin 1.39.

[120] Cicero De Fin 2.87–8.

[121] Annas, *The Morality of Happiness*, 344.

[122] PD 19.

[123] Annas, *The Morality of Happiness*, 345.

Both both *ataraxia* and blessedness are protected from duration because neither include desires for goods that nature does not readily provide. The Epicureans avoid protracted desires precisely to escape the "implacable sense of risk and exposure" that Caygill correctly ascribes to Nietzsche.[124] This leads us to the striking conclusion that, since Nietzsche refuses the Hellenistic indifference to duration, he must count death, at least some of the time, as a harm. And this is right: if any of our temporally-extended projects can be harmed, then death at an inopportune time will harm them.

As I will argue in the next chapter, where Nietzsche does develop his own conception of blessedness [*glückseligkeit*], he both evokes and contests the sympathetic portrait of the blissful Epicurus drawn in GS 45.

Epicurus, like the Stoics, conceives of happiness in terms of completion on the moment or indifference to duration. While they purport to thereby do away with the longing for immortality, the Epicureans smuggle in an escape from mortal life through the godliness of *ataraxia*. We can understand this escape from temporality, as in the case of Stoic self-completion, as a figure of eternity, in this case an eternity of non-existence or the void. The culmination of Epicurus' ethical letter is the promise that "man loses all semblance of mortality by living in the midst of immortal blessings".[125] By exercising Epicurean precepts, we can hope to escape the pains of mortal life, chief among them the painful turbulence of desire.

Fear of Time

Plato, the Stoics, and the Epicureans each develop a distinctive conception of eternity. In each case, this figure of eternity functions as a consolation for or an escape from necessary features of temporal life. Plato shies away from change and unsettledness of the human world. The Stoics deny the chaos of nature. The Epicureans avoid the press of desire. These are three distinct refractions of the philosophical fear of time expressed

---

[124] Caygill, "Under the Epicurean Skies," 113.
[125] DL 10.135.

in the inauguration of eternity. Each exposes an acute awareness of and hostility to the pains of transient existence. Nietzsche diagnoses this hostility as a symptom of distress. His task, which I will examine in the next chapter, is to develop a novel conception of eternity that is properly therapeutic.

6. Nietzsche's Eternity: A Voluptuous Art of Living

In the newly added preface to the second edition of *The Gay Science*, Nietzsche describes that whole work as emerging under the influence of an intoxication of convalescence from an "interlude of old age at the wrong time".[1] *The Gay Science* describes a renewed vitality and vigour—a return to youthfulness—which finds expression in the work's hope and anticipation for the future. Set against the Hellenistic flight from temporality analysed in the previous chapter, in *The Gay Science* Nietzsche re-situates himself and his readers within a temporal horizon. The eternity of antiquity expressed the possibility of living a complete life in a single moment: Stoics and Epicureans considered the tranquility of old age both possible and desirable at any moment of life. Nietzsche's return to youth signals a revaluation of the future and the *incompleteness* of the present.

The thaw of *The Gay Science* grants Nietzsche a renewed appreciation of eros and the passions, after his disappointment with Wagner's romanticism led to a Hellenistic "icing up in the midst of youth".[2] In contrast to the secure tranquillity offered by the Hellenistics, Nietzsche sets necessarily fragile hopes and anticipations for the future. His erotic attachment to life requires an anti-Hellenistic affirmation of transience.

In the preceding chapters I have set out, first, the general contours of Nietzsche's middle-period stance towards Stoicism (chapter one) and Epicureanism (chapter two), and then his case against Romanticism traced back to its Platonic origins (chapter three). In chapter four I investigated his recuperation of eros, against both Stoic *apatheia* and Platonic transcendence, in the secularised love poetry of the troubadours. Chapter five tightened the focus of Nietzsche's break with the ancients to the role of eternity in consoling for the fear of death. In this chapter, I present Nietzsche's alternative, anti-Hellenistic ethics of eternity: a youthful and voluptuous art of living,

---

[1] GS P 1.

[2] GS P 1.

youthful in the sense that it implies vigorous action for the sake of the future and voluptuous in the sense that it implies a passionate sensitivity to transience. I argue that this art of living must be specified in terms of the eternal recurrence.

Youth

With *The Gay Science's* praise of youth, Nietzsche returns to a theme to which he had first attended in the second *Untimely Meditation*, *On the Utility and Liability of History for Life*. Compared with the broad target of *The Gay Science*, in the essay on history Nietzsche's critical focus is more narrowly directed towards the state of his contemporary historical culture. The study of history has taken on a quasi-religious character within this culture, according to Nietzsche, in two senses. Firstly, history tells the story of a grand cosmic process. Through history, we study the trajectory of this process and hope to uncover the meaning and secret goal of existence. The second sense in which history has become religious is by purifying itself of practical imperatives. History as a 'pure science' takes historical knowledge as an end in itself. Nietzsche criticises such an unconditional will to historical knowledge because it glorifies the past at the expense of the present and future. History raised to the level of a 'pure science' "would be for humanity a kind of conclusion to life and a settling of accounts".[3] This historical religiosity has promoted an expansion of popular historical consciousness at the same time as it has exposed a crisis in the use of historical knowledge.[4] Nietzsche epitomises this crisis in the persona of Eduard von Hartmann.

Nietzsche diagnoses von Hartmann's conception of history with a congenital greyhairedness: the intrusion of old age into all phases of life.[5] As in his criticism of

---

[3] HL 1.

[4] For an account of the political dimension of this crisis in the aftermath of the Franco-Prussian war of 1870-71, see Christian J. Emden, "Toward a Critical Historicism: History and Politics in Nietzsche's Second "Untimely Meditation," *Modern Intellectual History* 3, no. 1 (2006):1–31.

[5] Nietzsche refers to Hesiod's apocalyptic prophesy: "But Zeus will destroy this race of speech-endowed human beings too, when at their birth the hair on their temples will be quite gray" (Hes. WD 180).

Hellenistic senescence in *The Gay Science*, Nietzsche opposes this expansion of old age with a figuration of youth. In this section I pull apart his criticism of von Hartmann in order to better understand his deployment of youth against the Hellenistic schools. Youth, for Nietzsche, expresses a vitality dependent on anticipation of the future.

Von Hartmann provides the theoretical underpinnings of the historical sensibility Nietzsche attacks with a teleological, developmental conception of history. He likens world history to the stages of individual development, moving from the childhood of early societies to the contemplative maturity of nineteenth century Germany.[6] The motive force in history is, reminiscent of Schopenhauer, the operation of the metaphysical Will, which over the course of history gradually comes into consciousness. Von Hartmann expands Schopenhauer's momentary experience of the intellect silencing the will in aesthetic contemplation to a historical scale. The historical epoch of the nineteenth century corresponds to the closing stages of a cosmic struggle between Idea and Will, at the conclusion of which will come the "redeeming triumph" of the former over the latter.[7]

As Shapiro notes, while Nietzsche ridicules the ontological extravagance of von Hartmann's position, the weight of his opposition to von Hartmann is "from the standpoint of ethical and political action".[8] Nietzsche's attention, then, is focused on the practical consequences of historical cultivation. He diagnoses a crisis in historical culture in terms of the kind of life it promotes. The kernel of his criticism of von Hartmann's historiography is that it promotes a life in the service of history, rather than a history in the service of life.

A life devoted to the accumulation of historical knowledge is primarily contemplative. The historical occupation is "that of looking back, of reckoning up, of

---

[6] Gary Shapiro, *Nietzsche's Earth: Great Events, Great Politics* (Chicago: University of Chicago Press, 2016), 38.

[7] Michael J. Inwood, "Hartmann, Eduard von (1842–1906)," in *The Oxford Companion to Philosophy*, ed. Ted Honderich, 2nd ed. (Oxford: Oxford University Press, 2005), 361.

[8] Shapiro, *Nietzsche's Earth*, 39.

closing accounts, of seeking consolation through remembering what has been".[9] Under von Hartmann's conception of history, this is the form of life appropriate to the end of history, near the final triumph of consciousness over the will. The contemplative historian embodies the *telos* of the *Weltprozess*.

Nietzsche identifies three moods attendant on such historically cultivated individuals. At first, understanding oneself as the culmination of the history produces an ecstatic pride. They themselves, as the most historically cultivated and conscious individuals, are the culmination and perfection of world history. They constitute the completion of a cosmic process stretching back over the life of the universe: "even in the deepest depths of the ocean", according to Nietzsche, they "discover the traces of [themselves] in living slime".[10] As with the Stoic sage, who encompasses within himself the entirety of the cosmic whole, the highest representatives of historical culture can pronounce "we have reached our goal; we are the goal; we are nature perfected".[11]

Nietzsche's contemporaries are proud of their historical cultivation because it allows them to encompass the whole of the past (*as* a perfect historical whole) in thought. This historical knowledge inevitably reveals a discrepancy, however, between their own condition and that of the significant figures of history. Because they consider the goal of history to lie in contemplation, modern historians adopt a *spectatorial* relation to history. Yet, as Nietzsche argues, exceptional lives are marked by their historically significant *actions*. Significant historical figures *act* precisely inasmuch as they rise "against that blind power of the factual and tyranny of the actual and [submit] to law that are not the laws of the fluctuations of history".[12] The tension between the position of the spectator and actor in history produces what Nietzsche calls an "*ironic self-*

---

[9] HL 8.

[10] HL 9.

[11] HL 9.

[12] HL 8.

consciousness" in modern historians.[13] The important distinction between the two position concerns their causal power. The historical *actor* is a causal agent (their actions bear historical consequence) while the historical *spectator* is an epiphenomenon of history. That is, modern historians are a byproduct or effect *of* history, but not a cause *in* history:

> The expression of individual Will does not significantly affect history or culture in any period of world history but, rather, only contributes in a minuscule way to the unfolding of universal and already determined cultural, historical, philosophical, or even biological and environmental movements.[14]

The strivings of modern historians are, on their own account, necessarily ineffectual.

The historian's ironic self-consciousness is stultifying in suggesting that the great feats of human history lie in the past, and that nothing remains to do except contemplation of the world process's final stages.[15] In this mode, history takes the form of a nostalgia for the now lost capacity for action: while previous generations could hope to carry out great tasks, the current generation is condemned to document and reflect on the past. In addition, this ironic sensibility eats away at the pride of the historically cultivated. Being merely a byproduct of history, the historian's insignificance to the process of history undercuts his pride at being its ripest fruit.

The third mood produced by historical cultivation follows when, on Nietzsche's telling, the individual can no longer endure the psychological tension of the ironical state. Instead of the position of the spectator as a special case, the end and competition of history, these individuals generalise their impotence backwards, and consider all prior historical figures as epiphenomenal to the world-process: "as things are they had to be, as men now are they were bound to become, *none* may resist this inevitability".[16]

---

[13] HL 8, emphasis in original.

[14] Anthony K. Jensen, "The Rogue of All Rogues: Nietzsche's Presentation of Eduard von Hartmann's Philosophie des Unbewussten and Hartmann's Response to Nietzsche," *Journal of Nietzsche Studies* 32 (2006): 49.

[15] Jensen, "The Rogue of All Rogues," 49.

[16] HL 9, emphasis added.

Nietzsche attaches von Hartmann's exhortation for the "total surrender of the personality to the world-process" to this resignation in the face of history.[17]

The upshot of Nietzsche's analysis of historical cultivation is the connection he draws to Schopenhauerian resignation. The total effect of von Hartmann's historiography is to expose as illusion all claims to historical agency. This is the same effect of Schopenhauer's doctrine of the Will. Nietzsche's presentation of Von Hartmann is of an historically distended Schopenhauer. The constellation of pride, irony, and resignation together serve to rob Nietzsche's contemporaries of vitality. In historical knowledge "there is no longer any support for […] life".[18] Von Hartmann's history functions, from the standpoint of ethical and political action, as an enervating spiritual exercise.

Nietzsche's claim in the history essay is that history need not have this devitalising effect. Indeed, the "active and powerful human being" "shrinks from resignation and uses history as a means to combat it".[19] The first half of the essay sets out how three modes of history can be deployed against resignation. Monumental history can inspire action, antiquarian history can teach how to preserve life through tradition, and critical history reveals the existing state of things as historically contingent and amenable to change. Each mode of history contains its own dangers, and Nietzsche explains at length the possibility of their misuse. The malady of historical cultivation is a failure to press each kind of history into the service of life, brought about by von Hartmann's misguided quasi-religious historiography.

Nietzsche offers two remedies for the historical malady: the ahistorical and the supra-historical. The supra-historical remedy is to adopt a perspective outside of time, indifferent to the course of history. This perspective is exemplified by the melancholy Italian poet Giacomo Leopardi who, nauseated by the "infinite superabundance of

---

[17] HL 9.
[18] HL 9.
[19] HL 2.

events",[20] calls for a tranquillity insulated from history: "Nothing exists that is worthy / of your emotions, and the earth deserves no sighs".[21]

While this perspective may combat the hypertrophy of the historical sense by lifting one out of the fluctuations of history, it achieves this at the cost of turning one away from life. The supra-historical character reaches a standpoint outside of history by grasping the ultimate vanity of all endeavour. Jenkins explains this as a consequence of Nietzsche's contention that in addition to pursuing particular ends, life is always also directed towards the expression and expansion of its drives, whatever they may be.[22] On Jenkins' account, supra-historical wisdom is the recognition that the content of one's particular drives, and hence the particular values these drives produce, are arbitrary from the perspective of this second-order drive (which the late Nietzsche will conceptualise as the will-to-power). This second order drive is indifferent to which particular drives it seeks the expression and expansion of, and so "any *particular* drive, and any action based upon it, is superfluous in the sense that it could, in principle, be replaced by another".[23] Apprehending the superfluity of all of life's particular endeavours "leads to disgust or nausea [Nietzsche's *Ekel*] in the supra-historical person, accompanied by a reluctance to go on living".[24]

In a revealing intimation of the doctrine of the eternal recurrence, Nietzsche asks whether his contemporaries "would like to relive the past ten or twenty years".[25] The supra-historical character, Nietzsche claims, would refuse, because of her indifference towards the future: "What could ten more years teach that the past ten were unable to

---

[20] HL 1.

[21] Giacomo Leopardi, "A Se Stesso," quoted in HL 1.

[22] Scott Jenkins, "Life, Injustice, and Recurrence," in *Nietzsche and the Becoming of Life,* ed. Vanessa Lemm (New York: Fordham University Press, 2015), 125.

[23] Jenkins, "Life, Injustice, and Recurrence," 126.

[24] Jenkins, "Life, Injustice, and Recurrence," 124.

[25] HL 1.

teach!"²⁶ This reluctance to go on living is indicative of her poor disposition towards life. Since the supra-historical practice of history does not find the individual's salvation in surrender to the *Weltprozess*, and indeed destroys this false hope, it does treat the particular historical malady that Nietzsche targets. It nevertheless facilitates a "withdrawal from life and action".²⁷ In the context of the entire essay then, it must "arouse our intense hatred", following Goethe's dictum with which Nietzsche opens his text: "Moreover, I hate everything that only instructs me without increasing or immediately stimulating my own activity."²⁸

Schopenhauer praises Leopardi as having been "entirely imbued and penetrated" with the misery of existence and for treating this subject more "thoroughly and exhaustively" than any of his contemporaries.²⁹

Following his description of the supra-historical character, Nietzsche asks his reader to "leave the supra-historical human beings to their nausea [*Ekel*] and their wisdom".³⁰ Here, wisdom necessarily leads to resignation. Nietzsche instead pursues an ahistorical remedy under the title of "youth". Nietzsche's youthfulness tempers the historical malady in the recognition that "the ahistorical and the historical are equally necessary for the health of an individual, a people, and a culture".³¹ The ahistorical is necessary for the health of individuals and collectives because of the effect that historical knowledge has on one's endeavours. Namely, historical knowledge reveals these endeavours to be superfluous, to either the historical totality (for von Hartmann) or the drive to express and expand one's power (for the supra-historical individual). From both perspectives, particular actions lack any significance. This fact undermines our commitments to particular values or projects leading to, as we have seen, resignation or

---

[26] HL 1.

[27] HL F.

[28] HL F.

[29] WWR 2.46.

[30] HL 1.

[31] HL 1.

a turn away from life. Youth escapes resignation by enveloping itself in an protective "ahistorical atmosphere". Within this atmosphere, it retains a capacity for action that an overabundance of historical knowledge destroys. Youth retains it's "most beautiful privilege"—"the power to plant, overflowing with faith, a great thought within itself and letting it grow into an even greater thought"—because it does not recognise and so is not discouraged by the universal vanity of all endeavour.[32] This active forgetfulness is essential to the project which Nietzsche sets for youth in the close of the essay, of producing a "happier, more beautiful cultivation [*Bildung*] and humaneness [*Menschlichkeit*]".[33] In *On the Utility and Liability of History for Life*, only youth, in its folly, is well-disposed enough towards life to plant the seeds of the future.

Stoics and Epicureans

The preceding section set out how Nietzsche diagnoses a malady in his contemporaries' attitude towards history, namely an incapacity to use the past as a source of nourishment in the present. This malady expresses itself in resignation, which Nietzsche figured as a kind of congenital senility. We saw that 'youth' designates a healthier historical sensibility, capable of acting for the sake of the future. In *The Gay Science* Nietzsche modifies his account of youthful vitality, directing it against the Hellenistic aversion to transience. Against the Hellenistic position, Nietzsche expounds sensitivity to transience as a necessary condition of joy.

Nietzsche returns to a consideration of the historical sense in an important section towards the end of GS IV, titled *"The 'humaneness'* [Menschlichkeit] *of the future"*. Again, he considers the practice of history deeply ambiguous from the perspective of life: it is his present day's "distinctive virtue *and* disease".[34] Nietzsche restates the danger that writing the history of earlier humanity will become a means to distract

---

[32] HL 9.

[33] HL 10.

[34] GS 337, emphasis added.

from and deflate present drives and goals—an escape from the demands of life. He restates the possibility that the historical sense will become a "marvellous growth with an equally marvellous scent" that will make life more agreeable.[35] But now Nietzsche reveals that this danger and this possibility are two aspects of the one sensibility. GS 337 brings this prospective historical sensibility into a sharper focus. There are a number of conclusions Nietzsche reaches in this rich and expressive passage.

To start, history is the means by which one can incorporate experiences of the past into one's own life. As we have seen in the history essay, Nietzsche criticises his contemporaries for accumulating historical knowledge without any effect on the outward form of their lives. The practice of history that Nietzsche describes in "*The 'humaneness' of the future*" grasps not just the factual, but the experiential and emotional register of past events. History grants access to historical perspectives such that one might "experience the history of humanity as *[one's] own history*".[36] It extends recollection beyond the limits of an individual's experience. Here we should note a contrast with the Epicurean position on the past. The Epicurean's indifference to (pains after) death is mirrored by their indifference to events before birth.[37] Whereas the Epicureans restrict the scope of desirable recollections to pleasant experiences from one's life,[38] Nietzsche radically expands this scope to encompass the sum of past experiences, both pleasant and painful.

This expansive historical attitude helps bring out the implicit criticism of Epicureanism in GS 306. As we have seen, in this section Nietzsche expresses a *preference* for an Epicurean sensitivity to the world over Stoic indifference. It *also* brings Epicurean modesty to the foreground, in that it reveals the strong Epicurean need to reduce their exposure to outside events by restricting their horizon of

---

[35] GS 337.

[36] GS 337, emphasis in original.

[37] In one formulation, the argument against the fear of death is *premised* upon the indifference with which we hold the eternity before birth.

[38] DL 10.137.

experience. The Epicurean enjoys the "unextended present" and "momentary comfort" (and "does everything he can to maintain these") that Schopenhauer grants to the limited human individual in a discussion of the tumultuous sea of existence.[39] In Schopenhauer's description of the sensibility, the *principium individuationis* protects the individual from the tumult of existence, allowing for a calm repose in the midst of "a world full of sorrow [...] with its infinite past and infinite future".[40] Nietzsche cites this passage in *BT 1* in connection with the tranquillising effect of the Apollonian dream. At first glance, the Nietzschean historian of *GS 337* looks much closer to the Stoic rather than the Epicurean of *GS 306*, in insofar as both Nietzschean and Stoic aspire to expand the boundaries of the self and incorporate an ever greater sum of experiences, and, on the coordinates of The Birth of Tragedy, to a Dionysian intoxication with the world.

In one respect, this incorporative stance also aligns the Nietzschean historian with the supra-historical individuals of *HL*, whose digestion of the painful, terrible, and questionable segments of the past, as we have seen, has a profound effect on their lives. However, Nietzsche's sensibility differs from Leopardi's supra-historicism in its response to the unfathomable sum of historical grief. Instead of resignation, Nietzsche imagines the heroic endurance of suffering. In illustrating this endurance, he lists various unhappy occasions of historical reflection—nostalgia for lost health, yearning for an absent lover, the injury and the death of a friend—which his expansive historical sense exposes one to:

> But if one endured, if one *could* endure this immense sum of grief of all kinds while yet being the hero who, as the second day breaks, welcomes the dawn and his fortune, being a person whose horizon encompasses thousands of years past and future, being the heir of all the nobility of all past spirit—an heir with a sense of obligation, the most aristocratic of old nobles and at the same time the first of a new nobility—the like of which no age has yet seen or dreamed of; if one could burden one's soul with all this—the oldest, the newest, losses, hopes, conquests, and the victories of humanity; if one could finally contain all this in one soul and crowd it into a

---

[39] WWR 1.63.

[40] WWR 1.63.

single feeling—this would surely have to result in a happiness that humanity has not known so far[41]

Nietzsche goes as far as to describe this happiness as godlike, in the extent of its "power and love", full of both "tears and laughter".[42] These terms set high demands on Nietzsche's new human happiness—so high as to qualify as a kind of divinity. Nietzsche's model is a military hero who, after losing a friend in an indecisive battle, returns to the field the next day.[43] Nietzsche's analogy between the military hero and the historian incorporating the whole of the past underlines how this godlike happiness or nobility entails incorporating intense grief over a seemingly pointless, absurd, cruel loss. The hero's loss is not redeemed by subsequent victory,[44] but neither is it followed by at least the resolution of defeat.[45] The "power and love" of Nietzsche's hero—his attachment to even the painful, terrible, and questionable aspects of life—makes it possible for him to return to the fray. While we will return to this issue below, we might presently make a distinction concerning the role of suffering in this vignette. We could either conceive of heroic endurance as valuable for its own sake or as instrumental to obtain some other good. I will suggest below that we should understand Nietzsche to be endorsing the latter: the magnitude of suffering the hero endures or can endure indexes his love of life.

We can make more sense of this distinction by turning to Nietzsche's comments in GS 12, "*On the aim of science*".[46] In that earlier section, he alludes to the Romantic doctrine that pleasure and pain are so intertwined that "whoever *wanted* to have as much as possible of one *must* also have as much as possible of the other".[47] If we

---

[41] GS 337.

[42] GS 337.

[43] Here Nietzsche seems to allude to Achilles' loss of Patroclus.

[44] As is, for instance, the sacrifice of Decius Mus. (Liv. 8.9).

[45] Compare this with GS 285's renunciation of any "ultimate peace" in favour of the "eternal recurrence of war and peace".

[46] See Thomas Ryan and Michael Ure, "Nietzsche's Post-Classical Therapy," *Pli* 25 (2014): 91-110.

[47] GS 12.

accept this assertion then there are two possible responses. The first, which he attributes to modern science and to ancient Stoicism, would seek to diminish one's capacity for pleasure as a means of protection against pain, yielding a conception of happiness as cool tranquillity. Motivated by this tranquillising goal, science serves to protect or insulate one from the dangerous excess of the passions. The second, Romantic position would sanction the intensification of pain in the pursuit of a higher feeling of pleasure. The means to this intensification is the expansion of one's vulnerability to the passions.

Nietzsche's explicit claim in GS 12 is only that science [*Wissenschaft*] can serve either set of interests. While his sympathy for the Romantic intensification of both pleasure and pain is clearly apparent, the desirability of a "joyful science" motivated by such a goal is left as mere suggestion. In the early sections of *The Gay Science*, Nietzsche simply sets the coordinates of two general approaches science can take regarding our vulnerability to objects of desire, either tranquillising (in fear of suffering) or expansive (in pursuit of joy), to which he will return. When he does return to this question in GS IV, however, he makes explicit his aspirations that the sciences (more specifically in GS 337, history) will serve the expansive ideal.

We can discern a development in Nietzsche's position on the use of history from *Untimely Meditations* to *The Gay Science*. In the former work, three historical approaches are canvassed. Both von Hartmann's progressive historiography and Leopardi's supra-historicism, Nietzsche argues, lead to nausea and resignation. Only youth, encased within a protective ahistorical atmosphere, avoids such a turn away from life. This atmosphere insulates Nietzsche's vigorous youth from the sorrows of history. In *The Gay Science*, on the other hand, Nietzsche deploys the conception of the passions he has developed through the middle period to allow for the endurance of suffering caused by historical reflection. In the later work, Nietzsche turns away from the protection offered by the ahistorical, in favour of attachment, sensitivity, and exposure to history. His task remains, in both works, to affirm life. In the former this is achieved only by means of blind love or folly, in the latter by means of a more sophisticated pedagogy of eros. In *Untimely Meditations*, youthful vigour is made possible by a lack of cognitive capacities. In *The Gay Science*, Nietzsche shows how a passionate engagement with the world can be one more such capacity.

Nietzsche's erotic revaluation of suffering finds expression in the section following 'The humaneness of the future'. In the context of a polemic against "those who feel pity [*die Mitleidigen*]", Nietzsche complains that an attempt to alleviate outward signs of suffering (as he analyses pity both here, and in more depth at sections 131-139 of *Dawn*) fail to account for the "personal necessity of distress".[48] The objection to pity is two-fold. First, because it is targeted at outward signs of suffering, pity is satisfied with any treatment which does away with its symptoms. And Nietzsche claims that these are the treatments which *die Mitleidigen* pursue, accusing them of outrageous "intellectual frivolity" for not undertaking the slow and subtle psychological enquiry necessary for understanding and treating the causes of another's psychic distress: "one simply knows nothing of the whole inner sequence and intricacies that are distress for *me* or for *you*".[49] Pity, as a form of moral "quackery", is unlikely to successfully treat suffering even on its own measure (that is, alleviation).[50] The second part of Nietzsche's objection follows from what the pitier's hasty and superficial analysis misses, namely, that from the perspective of the "whole economy of [the] soul" many necessary and indeed valuable psychic occurrences can give rise to outward signs of suffering. As examples Nietzsche lists "the way new springs and needs break open, the way in which old wounds are healing, the way whole periods of the past are shed".[51] Because the pitier seeks, however clumsily, to arrest any psychic process which gives rise to outward

---

[48] GS 338.

[49] GS 338.

[50] AOM 68.

[51] GS 338.

signs of suffering, it aims to interrupt or anaesthetise the pitied to painful processes of life (growth, convalescence, and forgetting, respectively). They act without regard for the role of these processes in the economy of the soul or, more prosaically, that the benefits of these processes outweigh the harm of the pain they cause. The point, at this juncture, is not a valorisation of suffering, but the claim that internal events that give rise to external signs of distress play a role within "the whole economy of [the] soul".[52]

The Stoic might well accept the general point that hardships and painful experiences can be endured as either instrumentally preferred (such as the aches of growth or the return to health, a preferred indifferent) or necessary from the perspective of the whole. However, Nietzsche's examples make it clear he has a much broader idea of distress's role within the economy of the soul than Stoicism. "Terrors, deprivations, impoverishments, midnights, adventures, risks, and blunders" are all listed as candidates for *personal* necessities, a view unthinkable on the Stoic conception of the self identified with the *hêgemonikon*.[53] Indeed, the necessity of unpleasant or threatening experiences such as these is grounded in Nietzsche's much more sophisticated, post-Romantic conception of the self. While the Stoic is satisfied to embody universal reason, Nietzsche's project requires the capacity to view oneself from an "artistic distance" and "occassionally find pleasure in [one's] folly".[54] More generally, throughout book four Nietzsche likens his project of the self to musical composition—the self as an improvisational, creative construction bringing diverse parts into a harmonious whole.[55] We will return to this project of the self below. For now it is sufficient to recognise the instrumental role of suffering in a project of self-formation.

---

[52] GS 338.

[53] GS 338.

[54] GS 107.

[55] See GS 277, GS 303, and GS 334.

Nietzsche admits that in *GS 338* he puts his point "mystically".⁵⁶ The contrast with Stoicism is made explicit in *GS 305*. There, Nietzsche criticises ethics of self-mastery for their aversion to "natural stirrings and inclinations". The Stoic, on guard against his passions, cuts himself off from "the most beautiful fortuities of his soul" and "all further *instruction* [*Belehrung*]".⁵⁷ The demand for self-mastery freezes up the hydraulics of the soul, so to speak. The Stoic cannot enjoy the vicissitudes of the passions as dramatic material or tap the passions for knowledge of oneself or the world. In *GS 338* these beautiful fortuities, insights, and personal necessities come under the banner of the "voluptuousness of one's own hell".⁵⁸

He mentions the "voluptuousness of hell" [*Wollust der Hölle*] at only one other location in the published works, and only once in the *Nachlass*. The published use occurs in the later *Ecce Homo*, in a discussion of Wagner's *Tristan*. There, Nietzsche praises Wagner's *Tristan* for causing him profound suffering: "and, given the way I am, strong enough to turn even what is most questionable and dangerous to my advantage and thus to become stronger, I call Wagner the great benefactor of my life".⁵⁹ Nietzsche makes the bold statement that his disposition has enabled him to transform suffering to his advantage, restating the claim of *GS 338* in the first person. The unpublished use of the phrase, from 1888, occurs in a notebook of poetry. The line reads "By the voluptuousness of hell no sage [*Weisen*] has yet gone".⁶⁰ We can see here that in praising the "voluptuousness of hell" as the condition of the highest joy, Nietzsche is clearly aiming for an ethical ideal sharply distinct from classical figurations of the sage.

To reinforce the anti-Stoic resonance of the "voluptuousness of hell" we might note that Nietzsche uses the same term, *Wollust*, to describe Epicurus in *GS 45*. In that

---

⁵⁶ GS 338.

⁵⁷ GS 305, emphasis in original.

⁵⁸ GS 338.

⁵⁹ EH "Clever" 6.

⁶⁰ KSA 13:20[103].

section, voluptuousness refers to the pleasure Epicurus takes in the "tender, shuddering skin of the sea [of existence]".[61] Nietzsche suggests that the comparative calm Epicurus has achieved through his regimen of small pleasures grants him a new perspective on the modest suffering that remains (for instance, desires for food and conversation). While Nietzsche's tone is poetic, there is also a touch of melancholy. Epicurus represents the weary "afternoon of antiquity".[62] His modesty testifies to his will to "rest, stillness, calm seas, [and] redemption from" himself.[63] In book four of *The Gay Science*, Nietzsche opposes the Epicureans' "subtle irritability" [*feine Reizbarkeit*] to Stoic insensitivity.[64] The Epicurean disposition connotes a propensity for irritation, but also for excitement, for provocation and for stimulating anticipation. When Nietzsche cites the "voluptuousness of hell" in *GS 338*, he refers to an intensification of this erotic sensitivity to the world and the "accidents of existence".[65]

Throughout *The Gay Science*, Nietzsche uses Stoicism and Epicureanism to triangulate his own position. In sections 12 and 338 he makes his case against the Stoic rejection of *eros*. Section 306 privileges Epicureanism above Stoicism for its modest erotic sensibility, but a comparison of the portrait of Epicurus in section 45 and the Nietzschean historian in section 337 clearly explicates the limitations of Epicurean *ataraxia*. Epicurean modesty stands in stark contrast to the immodesty of Nietzsche's voluptuousness. Where Stoicism *withdraws* and Epicureanism *contracts* one's sensitivity to transience, Nietzsche's voluptuousness implies an anti-Hellenistic *expansion*, in both scope and intensity, of one's exposure to time through sensible interaction with transient objects. Nietzsche arrives at the anti-Hellenistic position that sensitivity to transience is a necessary condition of joy.

---

[61] GS 45.

[62] GS 45.

[63] GS 370.

[64] GS 306.

[65] GS 306.

Eternal recurrence

In *The Gay Science* Nietzsche deploys a more sophisticated account of the passions under the banner of youthfulness than the blind folly under consideration in *Untimely Meditations*. His recuperation of eros also furnishes him with a more sophisticated, and more demanding, test for the affirmation of life. While in *On the Utility and Liability of History for Life* Nietzsche dismissed the historical and supra-historical sense because he conceives them as inducing a nausea that made it impossible to wish to relive "the last ten or twenty years", in *The Gay Science* his question concerns the entirety of life, relived in repetition to eternity.[66]

We gain a richer understanding of Nietzsche's ethics of affirmation by connecting Nietzsche's conception of eros to the doctrine of the eternal recurrence. Throughout book four Nietzsche develops what we might call a musical project of the self. He describes a process of self-formation akin to musical composition. To affirm life, one must fashion the self into a beautiful, integrated, harmonious whole. In the previous section, we saw how Nietzsche's affirmation is indexed by an anti-Hellenistic form of pleasure. This form of affirmation implies a recuperation of eros and the passions. It also allows us to make sense of the eternal recurrence as the necessary culmination of Nietzsche's project of the self. When Nietzsche turns the question of affirmation back onto the self, what results in the successful case is a passion for life that necessarily entails a longing for its return. I want to suggest that the voluptuous disposition examined in the previous section allows us to make sense of the specific affirmation canvassed in *GS 341* within the context of *The Gay Science*, in a way that is consistent with the near unanimous rejection of a literal cosmological reading of the eternal recurrence. It is not that one loves life because it is eternal, but one wants life in repetition to eternity because one loves it.

---

[66] HL 1.

In the remaining section, I connect Nietzsche's anti-Hellenistic voluptuousness to the doctrine of the eternal recurrence, rejecting a 'cosmological' account of the latter. I show how this connection challenges the popular 'heroic' reading of Nietzsche. Against Nietzsche's purported heroism, I emphasise the 'erotic' dimension of the eternal recurrence as the test and measure of one's attachment to life.

Nietzsche first sets out the doctrine of the eternal recurrence in any detail in section 341 of *The Gay Science*. Famously, the reader is confronted with the warning that their life will recur *ad infinitum*, including all its sorrows and joys, and "everything unutterably small and great".[67] The demon who delivers this message mocks the reader: "The eternal hourglass of existence is turned upside down again and again, and you with it, speck of dust!".[68] Nietzsche asks how the reader would respond to such a confrontation. As Janaway astutely notes, he asks this apropos two distinct instances.[69] Firstly there is the question of one's immediate reaction to the demon's warning. Nietzsche, and the demon, suggest the default response will be one of crushing despair, that the reader would "throw themselves down and gnash [their] teeth and curse the demon who spoke thus".[70] The only alternative *immediate* response canvassed by Nietzsche is an ecstatic affirmation, the exclamation that "You [the demon] are a god and never have I heard anything more divine".[71] Nietzsche's phrasing refers back to a *previous* tremendous moment when one *would* have answered affirmatively, drawing the reader back to the Nietzsche frequent depictions of the life-affirmation throughout book four. This response comes, on Janaway's telling, before one subjects the demon's message to critical scrutiny, or any reflective thought. The second instance comes if and

---

[67] GS 341.

[68] GS 341.

[69] Christopher Janaway, "The Gay Science," in *The Oxford Handbook of Nietzsche*, eds. Ken Gemes and John Richardson (Oxford: Oxford University Press, 2013), 261.

[70] GS 341.

[71] GS 341.

when "this thought [of the eternal recurrence] gained possession over you".⁷² At issue then is "a huge transformation in one's life, a long-sustained attitude of joy or despair towards oneself".⁷³ In *this* moment, the question is one of disposition: "how well disposed would you have to become to yourself and to life *to crave nothing more fervently* than this ultimate eternal confirmation and seal?"⁷⁴

We might note, at this stage, that Nietzsche does not countenance the possibility of a equanimous response to the demon's shocking pronouncement. We might also note that, while the passage features Nietzsche's familiar bifurcation into life-affirmation and life-denial, it does not by itself tell us why affirmation and denial take on their particular characters. Why, we might ask, does Nietzsche conceive of affirmation as a fervent craving for repetition and not, for instance, as tranquil assent? We can answer this question by focusing on Nietzsche's use of eros through *The Gay Science*. In doing so I will show the inadequacy of existing accounts of the eternal recurrence and provide a distinctive reading of Nietzsche's ethics of affirmation.

The final sentence of section 341 is crucial to grasping the role of the doctrine of the eternal recurrence within Nietzsche's ethics of affirmation. It reads: "how well disposed would you have to become to yourself and to life *to crave nothing more fervently* than this ultimate eternal confirmation and seal?"⁷⁵ For Nietzsche, the necessary condition for affirming the eternal recurrence is that one is sufficiently well-disposed to life and to oneself. While this condition may seem vague if we restrict ourselves to section 341, or to the closing triptych of book four,⁷⁶ Nietzsche in fact provides ample detail on what it takes to come to this affirmative disposition. We can analyse the condition in two

---

⁷² GS 341.

⁷³ Janaway, "The Gay Science," 261.

⁷⁴ GS 341, emphasis in original.

⁷⁵ GS 341.

⁷⁶ Paul Loeb claims that sections 340–342 form a triptych allegedly narrating a contest between Socrates and Zarathustra over the affirmation of life at the point of death. The interpretation presented in this chapter shows that we need to grasp the whole of Book 4, especially its anti-Hellenistic erotic pedagogy, to properly understand section 341. See Paul S. Loeb, *The Death of Nietzsche's Zarathustra* (Cambridge: Cambridge University Press, 2010), 32–44.

parts. What does it take to be well-disposed to life, and what does it take to be well-disposed to oneself?

In section 291 Nietzsche singles out the builders of Genoa as "well-disposed towards life, however ill-disposed they often may have been towards themselves".[77] While the Genoese may not pass the test of the eternal recurrence, they nevertheless provide a model for the partial fulfilment of Nietzsche's ethical ideal. Nietzsche praises the Genoese for a desire to go on living. This desire, he thinks, is evidenced by the longevity of their architectural constructions, "built and adorned to last for centuries and not for the fleeting hour".[78] To be well-disposed towards life is to desire to go on living, but it is not only the durability of Genoese architecture that Nietzsche praises. In Genoa the landscape has been transformed according to the personal styles of its inhabitants. The Genoese imbue their "villas and pleasure gardens" with personality to the extent that Nietzsche recognises "*faces* that belong to past generations" and "images of bold and autocratic human beings" in the built environment of the city.[79] In their architecture, the Genoese give full expression to a desire to incorporate, transform and possess their world. The Genoese exemplify the creative virtuosity Nietzsche celebrates throughout *The Gay Science*. In *On the Utility and Liability of History for Life* he calls this "plastic power":

> the capacity to develop out of oneself in one's own way, to transform and incorporate into oneself what is past and foreign, to heal wounds, to replace what has been lost, to recreate broken moulds.[80]

Nietzsche draws a contrast between Genoa and the cities of northern Europe which —so he claims—have been laid out according (or obedient) to an orderly city-wide plan. The contrast turns on the uniquely personal style of Genoese architecture. The personality in the Genoese buildings expresses, according to Nietzsche, a strong "lust

---

[77] GS 291.

[78] GS 291.

[79] GS 291, emphasis in original.

[80] HL 1.

for possession and spoils".[81] The Genoese come to possess the landscape by fitting it into their own plan. Nietzsche emphasises the individuality of the Genoese style: "All this [the city, the sea, and the contours of the mountains] they want to fit into *their* plan and ultimately make their *possession* by making it part of their plan".[82] The spoils of this refashioning are the pleasures and satisfactions of "the moments of a sunny afternoon when [the Genoese builder's] insatiable and melancholy soul does feel sated, and only what is his and nothing alien may appear to his eyes". The Genoese builder takes an aesthetic pleasure at the sight of his own reflection—the entire landscape becomes "a feast for his eyes".[83]

The Genoese disposition towards life is proved by their willingness to undertake the fabrication of enduring artefacts of their own design. They do not shy away from acting for the sake of the future, as Nietzsche accuses both the classical tradition and his historically-fevered contemporaries of doing. The "personal infinity" they lay between their neighbours and themselves exists both spatially, encompassing the entire landscape, and temporally, enduring long after their own time.

Because the Genoese direct their creative activity outside of themselves they do not satisfy the second half of the necessary condition for the affirmation of life. The Genoese are like the artists Nietzsche describes in section 299, with whom "this subtle power usually comes to an end where art [or architecture] ends and life begins; but we want to be the poets of our life".[84] Where the Genoese arrange bricks, mortar, and soil into an all-encompassing personalised landscape, to pass the test of the eternal recurrence one must organise the elements of one's life into a unified, idiosyncratic, harmonious self. Indeed, section 291 immediately follows the well-known section 290, wherein Nietzsche, parodying Luke 10:42, declares "giving style" to oneself the "*one*

---

[81] GS 291.

[82] GS 291.

[83] GS 291.

[84] GS 299.

thing [...] needful".⁸⁵ The parody implies that fashioning the self into a pleasurable sight to behold is on par with the eternal redemption offered by Christianity.⁸⁶

Nietzsche begins book four of *The Gay Science* by describing a "high point in life" when we can take in the view of the "wonderful harmony created by the playing of our instrument" brought about by a combination of "our own practical and theoretical skill in interpreting and arranging events" and "good old chance".⁸⁷ In section 303 he depicts an *"improviser of life"* who, like "masters of musical improvisation" are "ready at any moment to incorporate into their thematic order the most accidental tone to which the flick of a finger or a mood has driven them, breathing a beautiful meaning and a soul into an accident".⁸⁸ He again likens the fashioning of the self to a musical composition in section 334. The claim in that section is that all loves, even self-love, develop just like the love of a musical composition, after a slow, patient process of acquaintance and digestion.

Conceiving Nietzsche's ethics as an art of self-fashioning has, of course, received significant attention in the scholarly literature, since Alexander Nehamas's *Life As Literature*.⁸⁹ However, by focusing on Nietzsche's figuration of the self as a kind of musical composition we gain a sharper insight into how it differs from classical projects of the self, particular that of the Stoics.⁹⁰

Nietzsche's musical self has three important characteristics. As we've already seen, Nietzsche's project of the self is the fashioning of an idiosyncratic, unified whole. A

---

⁸⁵ GS 290, emphasis in original.

⁸⁶ Daniel Came, "The Themes of Affirmation and Illusion in *The Birth of Tragedy* and Beyond," in *The Oxford Handbook of Nietzsche*, eds. Ken Gemes and John Richardson (Oxford: Oxford University Press, 2013), 218.

⁸⁷ GS 277.

⁸⁸ GS 303.

⁸⁹ See Alexander Nehamas, *Nietzsche: Life As Literature* (Cambridge, MA: Harvard University Press, 1985).

⁹⁰ On this point also see John Carvalho, "Improvisations, on Nietzsche, on Jazz," in *Nietzsche, Philosophy and the Arts*, eds. Salim Kemal, Ivan Gaskell, and Daniel W. Conway (Cambridge: Cambridge University Press, 1998), 187–211.

musical understanding implies a first characteristic, that this self is a diachronic entity. Nietzsche conceives the self as the result of a dynamic process that develops through time. The personal necessity of "terrors, deprivations, impoverishments, midnights, adventures, risks, and blunders" only makes sense within such a temporal order.[91] In this sense, a complete life requires duration and Nietzsche's ethical program cannot be identified with a Stoic or classical flight from temporality. The second characteristic suggested by a musical understanding of the self is that its composition involves the integration, or harmonisation, of plural voices. Nietzsche criticises the monistic rationalism of the Stoics as monotonous.[92] While the Stoic strives to identify the self solely with universal reason, Nietzsche rightly observes that in doing so he cuts himself off from the most beautiful fortuities of his soul. Nietzschean *eudaimonism* incorporates a wider range of drives and experiences than the singular focus of Stoic *apatheia*.[93] The third characteristic concerns the manner of composing the musical self. As we've already seen, Nietzsche likens life to musical *improvisation*. The explicit comparison in section 303 is with the ability to incorporate mistakes and missteps into a thematic order and in so doing "[breath] a beautiful meaning and a soul into an accident".[94] Adroit improvisers know how to quickly remedy pains and losses and so do not require the "radical cure" of Stoic rationalism.[95] Nietzsche's praise of improvisation makes sense of his claim in section 277 that chance plays an essential role in the beautiful harmony of the soul. Improvisation allows for the incorporation of the new and unexpected. It is only through improvisation that one can fabricate the "new, unique, incomparable" self that Nietzsche advocates in section 335.[96]

---

[91] GS 338.

[92] WS 313.

[93] See Michael Ure, "Sublime Losers: Stoicism in Nineteenth Century German Philosophy," in *The Routledge Handbook of the Stoic Tradition*, ed, John Sellars (London: Routledge, 2015), 297.

[94] GS 303.

[95] GS 326.

[96] GS 335.

From this view of the self, we can make sense of the necessary condition to desire the eternal recurrence noted above. One desires the eternal recurrence of life—"this life as you now live it and have lived it", in the words of the demon—only if one is successful at fashioning the self into a unique, diachronic, harmonic whole.

Why is this the case? In section 334 Nietzsche elaborates his pedagogy of eros, taking as his model the love of a musical figure. He explains that once we have learnt to love such a tune, we "desire nothing better from the world than it and only it".[97] Its harmony "continues to compel and enchant us" such that we become "enraptured lovers".[98] While we sense that "we should miss it if it were missing," our desire is stoked by the enjoyment of the tune: it does not depend on the object's absence.[99]

Nietzsche explicitly affirms the application of this erotic pedagogy to the love of the self. The image of rapturous desire painted in section 334 repeats that of section 278, of "thirsty life and drunkenness of life"[100] and 292, of the "insatiable lust for possession and spoils".[101]

Bernard Williams asks, introducing *The Gay Science*, "if there is anything in this test [of the eternal recurrence] at all, why would willing one recurrence not be enough?"[102] Williams' question helps bring out the importance of insatiable desire for Nietzsche. A thirst for life that could be quenched by just one, two, or any finite number does not measure up to Nietzsche's conception of passionate love. If one loves life then one must wish for its eternal recurrence.

This understanding of the doctrine of the eternal recurrence as expressing the passionate love of life coheres better with the other elements of Nietzsche's philosophy

---

[97] GS 334.

[98] GS 334.

[99] GS 334.

[100] GS 278.

[101] GS 292.

[102] Bernard Williams, ed., *The Gay Science: With a Prelude in German Rhymes and an Appendix of Songs*, (Cambridge: Cambridge University Press, 2001), xvi.

than two influential interpretations, the 'cosmological' and the 'heroic'. These two interpretations fail to connect the doctrine with Nietzsche's voluptuous art of living and the centrality of eros to that art.

Paul Loeb's cosmological reading of the doctrine is premised on the notion that Nietzsche has discovered the recurrence of life.[103] From this it follows that to affirm life, one must affirm it as it is, that is, as eternally recurrent. Putting to one side the details of Nietzsche's alleged proof of the eternal recurrence as a cosmological doctrine, this claim sits uncomfortably with the affective dimension of the demon's message in section 341. If one affirms life by wishing for its eternal recurrence on the basis of a demonstration of recurrence, why would recurrence become the object of fervent craving? If the eternal recurrence was a demonstrable cosmological doctrine, this might generate tranquil assent to life's recurrence as a fait accompli. It is difficult to see how a proof of recurrence could generate the anxious craving for life that Nietzsche depicts both in section 341 concerning recurrence, as well as throughout book four as a sign of health.[104]

In the 1886 preface, Nietzsche associates his "new happiness" with a jealous love for someone that "causes doubts in us".[105] Nietzsche's love is "dangerous" in that he asks us to love life even after "the trust in life is gone".[106] That is, the Nietzschean lover remains unsure of whether life will return her good will (despite the optimism of *GS 334*). In other words Nietzsche is skeptical that life possesses any properties which guarantee that it is loveable. Nevertheless, apparently this loss of faith in the world is not a reason for gloom. Nietzsche's passion doesn't hinge on the demonstration that life eternally recurs. To "live dangerously" as Nietzsche exhorts in *GS 283* requires a voluptuous attachment to life. The passionate suffering of the jealous lover itself entails

---

[103] Loeb, *The Death of Nietzsche's Zarathustra*, 11–31.

[104] As above, see GS 278; GS 292.

[105] GS P 3.

[106] GS P 3.

a kind of pleasure. This pleasure is located at the very process of desire, not in the overcoming of resistance to desire. We might say that Nietzsche conceives a kind of voluptuous suffering that is its own reward.

When he returns in 1886 to appraise *The Gay Science* in a preface, as we have seen, Nietzsche considers the whole work an expression of convalescence. The gambit of the work is whether the stakes of philosophy are something other than "truth".[107] Philosophical positions, and especially the "world affirmations or world negations *tout court*" in which Nietzsche criticises *and* participates, are to be read "first of all as the symptoms of certain bodies".[108] The preceding chapters of this work have focused on how these remarks shed light on his criticism of Hellenistic philosophies as expressions of sickness or deprivation. We should not overlook, as a result, that Nietzsche also countenances how health or richness philosophises. Nietzsche declares that such a voluptuousness would have to "inscribe itself in cosmic letters on the heaven of concepts".[109] Nietzsche's allusion to the Platonic heaven of concepts makes clear that he plans not just to jettison, but replace, the eternity of the forms with the eternal recurrence. The eternal recurrence is an expression of a voluptuous attachment to life which "desire[s] nothing better from the world than it and only it".[110] It is not that one loves life because it is eternal, but one wants life in repetition to eternity because one loves it.

In Bernard Reginster's terms, because the eternal recurrence indexes the scope and intensity of one's attachment to life, it is a 'practical' doctrine. Reginster takes the doctrine to express the highest possible regard for life by representing a moment of perfection where one overcomes resistance to a desire. One affirms life, on this account, if one desires the continual overcoming of resistances to one's will. Reginster likens his

---

[107] GS P 2.

[108] GS P 2.

[109] GS P 3.

[110] GS 334.

affirmative character to a Olympian competitor, who wants victory, but also for "their victory to be short lived and to be an opportunity for new games".[111] Counter-intuitively, Reginster's account implies a desire "that one not succeed in that satisfaction without resistance—preferably great and painful resistance—to overcome".[112] Since life is an arena for the heroic overcoming resistance, greater resistance generates a stronger attachment to life.

Reginster explains the eternal recurrence in reference to Zarathustra's roundelay, that "all joy [*Lust*] wants eternity".[113] He characterises joy as the experience of a perfect moment, and perfection as that which leaves nothing to be desired.[114] In such a moment, one experiences momentary and total satisfaction. Reginster takes the doctrine of the eternal recurrence to express a wish for the endless concatenation of such momentary satisfactions.

In identifying perfection as that which leaves nothing to be desired, however, Reginster inadvertently capitulates to a Schopenhauerian conception of desire, namely of satisfaction as the cancelation of desire. As we have already seen, Nietzsche's joy involves the enjoyment, intoxication and intensification of desire. Nietzsche rejects the Schopenhauerian premise that enjoyment cancels desire. On the contrary, Nietzsche is aligned with the Romantics' idealisation of desire, such that he could say with Rousseau that desire "is sufficient in itself, and the anxiety it inflicts is a sort of enjoyment that compensates for reality [...] *Woe to him who has nothing left to desire.*"[115] Nietzsche's idealisation of desire undermines Reginster's account of the eternal recurrence because it rules out the perfection of a state free from desire.

---

[111] Bernard Reginster, *The Affirmation of Life: Nietzsche on Overcoming Nihilism* (Cambridge, MA: Harvard University Press, 2006), 137.

[112] Robert Pippin, review of *The Affirmation of Life: Nietzsche on Overcoming Nihilism* by Bernard Reginster, *Philosophy and Phenomenological Research* 77, no. 1 (2008): 287.

[113] Z III "The Other Dance Song" 3; Z IV "The Sleepwalker Song" 12.

[114] Reginster, *The Affirmation of Life*, 224.

[115] Jean-Jacques Rousseau, *Julie, or, The New Heloise*, (Hanover, NH: University Press of New England, 1997), Part 6, Letter VII, emphasis added.

We can level three main criticism at Reginster's account. Firstly, his ethics is too formal, in that it could endorse any arbitrary pursuit from the banal to the abhorrent, so long as there is resistance to overcome. Secondly, it is ascetic, in that such pursuits are valued according to the suffering they induce. Thirdly, his account of the eternal recurrence is enervating, in that it idealises the absence of desire.

Reginster's account fails because it does not consider the central role of eros in the doctrine of the eternal recurrence. In the doctrine of the eternal recurrence Nietzsche venerates desire. One longs for the eternal recurrence of life if and only if one has learned to love oneself in Nietzsche's sense of the intoxication of unquenchable desire. The doctrine implies the enjoyment and intensification of the desire for nothing but one's life repeated into eternity.

Conclusion

In chapter five we saw how Nietzsche uses the concept of eternity as a diagnostic tool. The eternities venerated by Plato, the Stoics, and the Epicureans expose an underlying state of distress. Eternity plays an analogous role in Nietzsche's art of living, except for the crucial difference that in this case longing for the eternal recurrence is an indication or expression of health, not sickness. In the doctrine of the eternal recurrence, Nietzsche ventures to "paint [his] *happiness* on the wall".[116]

In this chapter we have traced the development of Nietzsche's thinking regarding the necessary conditions for the affirmation of life. In book four of *The Gay Science*, Nietzsche presents us with a youthful and voluptuous art of living, the success of which is indexed by a longing to relive life in repetition to eternity. The doctrine of the eternal recurrence is the central achievement of this project of the self because it is the necessary expression of an erotic attachment to life. The account of the eternal recurrence elaborated in this chapter advances on existing accounts in the literature by

---

[116] GS 56, emphasis in original.

more closely linking the doctrine to Nietzsche's broader ethics of affirmation and to his recuperation of eros and the passions. It avoids the ontological extravagance of literal or cosmological readings of the doctrine, as well as addressing the shortcomings of heroic readings. Rather than the formal criterion of activity for activity's sake, it emphasises the substantive value Nietzsche places on beauty. Rather than the ascetic valorisation of suffering, it admits the instrumental value of suffering to the formation of a beautiful dramatic harmony of the self. Rather than idealising the absence of desire, it celebrates the intoxication of desire as the only path to "new galaxies of joy".[117]

---

[117] GS 12.

Conclusion

The Gay Science marks Nietzsche's radical break with classical philosophical therapeutics. By naming this work after *la gaya scienza* of the troubadours he signals the central role that passionate love comes to play in his post-classical art of living. Passionate love becomes Nietzsche's measure of what it takes to affirm life. Nietzsche challenges classical philosophies for their exclusion of eros. Because they eliminate, diminish, or transcend eros respectively, Nietzsche diagnoses Stoicism, Epicureanism, and Platonism as themselves forms of sickness.

Nietzsche's long antagonism with Plato is a commonplace in the literature. According to Nietzsche, Plato inaugurates an idealist philosophical tradition that has its logical and historical culmination in Arthur Schopenhauer's romantic pessimism. Platonic love can be satisfied only by an unchanging and ever-present object. Secure possession of such an object promises to release Plato's lovers from their anxious longing. Platonic lovers want to secure perpetual possession of their beloved. Chapters three and four make it clear that Nietzsche follows Schopenhauer in believing Platonic love necessarily fails, but that he also develops a profoundly anti-Platonic pedagogy of eros: "one loves differently" and discovers "a new happiness".[1]

Nietzsche takes the jealous lover as his model. Without the security of the ideal, the Nietzschean lover is wracked by doubt whether the beloved will return her goodwill. The effect of this uncertainty is to intensify the Nietzschean lover's attachment to life. Nietzsche follows the Provençal troubadours in conceiving of a kind of voluptuous suffering that is its own reward. By connecting Nietzsche's anti-Platonism to the tradition of courtly love, this thesis advances our understanding of how Nietzsche's development of a pedagogy of eros directly challenges the Platonic idealist tradition.

This thesis significantly advances our understanding of Nietzsche's relationship with Stoicism. Despite his early praise for Stoic *eudaimonism* as a rival to the morality of

---
[1] GS P 3.

pity,[2] in *The Gay Science* his assessment of Stoicism makes an about-face. Here he accuses the Stoics of evacuating the world of value. The Stoic aspiration to embody universal reason implies the destruction of the passions. By destroying the passions, Nietzsche claims, the Stoics destroy that which gives shade and colour to the world.

In *The Gay Science* Nietzsche is comparatively sympathetic to the figure of Epicurus. He compares the Epicurean's "subtle irritability" [*feine Reizbarkeit*] favourably to the Stoic's hard and insensitive.[3] However, this praise is heavily qualified. Nietzsche's evocative and melancholy portrait in *GS 45* emphasises the modesty of Epicurean hedonism. In *GS 306* Nietzsche brings his implicit criticism of Epicureanism into the foreground, revealing the Epicurean's deep need for analgesics and shelter from the accidents of existence.

Despite their quarrels, the moral schools of antiquity all aim for different forms of tranquillity. This thesis systematises Nietzsche's rejection of tranquillity as an ethical ideal and his claim that this ideal of a symptom of cowardice. Chapter five demonstrates the crucial diagnostic role played by the ancient school's conceptions of eternity. Nietzsche argues that the eternities venerated by Plato, the Stoics, and the Epicureans expose an underlying state of distress: each provide different refractions of a common fear of transience. The three ancient philosophical therapies offer merely palliative treatments. Chapter six develops Nietzsche's own properly therapeutic remedy.

The centrepiece of that remedy is Nietzsche's reconfigured conception of eternity. With the doctrine of the eternal recurrence, Nietzsche directly challenges, and seeks to displace, the ancient ethics of eternity. While the ancient desire for eternity was premised on the denial of the passions, Nietzsche's doctrine entails the affirmation and incorporation of the passionate longing the ancients found so disruptive. It heralds liberation from the debilitating tyranny of reason.

---

[2] D 139.

[3] GS 306.

The eternal recurrence has recently returned to scholarly attention, after long neglect, in the form of Paul Loeb's cosmological reading.[4] This thesis makes sense of the centrality of the doctrine of the eternal recurrence to Nietzsche's philosophical project, not as an extravagant cosmological theory, but as the necessary expression of the healthy soul. If Nietzsche seeks to displace particular ancient ethics of eternity, he nevertheless revives the ancient concern for eternity as a philosophical object. By bringing his conception of eternity to the foreground of his ethics, this thesis raises the question of what role eternity plays in our ethical theories.

The crux of this thesis is the fundamental incompatibility Nietzsche exposes between eros and tranquillity. Nietzsche symbolises this opposition with his use of hydraulic metaphors of the soul. He figures his experimentation with the Hellenistic schools as an "icing up" at the wrong time.[5] In *Assorted Opinions and Maxims* he holds out hope for a "thawing breeze for the frozen will".[6] On the title page of book four of *The Gay Science*, he refers to the blood miracle of St Januarius[7] and attached an poem as epigraph.[8] Nietzsche conceptualises the sudden and unexpected return to health attested in *The Gay Science* as first a melting and then a turbulent surge towards the "highest hope and goal". Nietzsche signals on this title page that *The Gay Science* marks the overcoming of Hellenistic tranquillity in favour of a more elevated post-classical disposition.

---

[4] Paul S. Loeb, *The Death of Nietzsche's Zarathustra* (Cambridge: Cambridge University Press, 2010).

[5] GS P 1.

[6] AOM 349.

[7] "The blood of St Januarius is preserved in a phial in a church in Naples, and on a certain holiday a miracle takes place causing it to liquefy. The people think a great deal of this miracle" (Sigmund Freud, *Psychopathology of Everyday Life*, 2nd ed. [London: Ernest Benn Limited, 1948], 13).

[8] "You who with your lances burning
Melt the ice sheets of my soul
Speed it toward the ocean yearning
For its highest hope and goal:
Ever healthier it rises,
Free in fate most amorous:-
Thus your miracle it prizes
Fairest Januarius!" (Friedrich Nietzsche, *The Gay Science: With a Prelude in German Rhymes and an Appendix of Songs*, ed. Bernard Williams [Cambridge: Cambridge University Press, 2001], 155).

This thesis gives coherence to Nietzsche's diagnoses of past philosophies as forms of sickness, alongside the centrality of eternity, both to these diagnoses and to the prospects of devising a viable therapy. It systematises Nietzsche's striking assertion that passions, hitherto neglected or derided by philosophy, are an essential component of the good life.

Bibliography

Ancient Sources

Augustine. *The City of God against the Pagans*. Translated by George E. McCracken. 7 Vols. Loeb Classical Library. Cambridge, MA and London: Harvard University Press, 1957.

Cicero. *On Ends*. Translated by H. Rackham. Loeb Classical Library. Cambridge, MA and London: Harvard University Press, 1914.

———. *Tusculan Disputations*. Translated by J. E. King. Loeb Classical Library. Cambridge, MA and London: Harvard University Press, 1945.

Cleanthes. *Cleanthes' Hymn to Zeus: Text, Translation, and Commentary*. Edited and translated by Johan C. Thom. Tübingen: Mohr Siebeck, 2005.

Diogenes Laertius. *Lives of Eminent Philosophers*. Translated by R. D. Hicks. 2 Vols. Loeb Classical Library. Cambridge, MA and London: Harvard University Press, 1972.

Epictetus. *Discourses. Fragments. The Enchiridion*. Translated by W. A. Oldfather. 2 Vols. Loeb Classical Library. Cambridge, MA and London: Harvard University Press, 1998.

Epicurus. *The Essential Epicurus: Letters, Principal Doctrines, Vatican Sayings, and Fragments*. Translated by Eugene O'Connor. Buffalo, NY: Prometheus Books, 1993.

Gellius. *Attic Nights*. Translated by John C. Rolfe. 3 Vols. Loeb Classical Library. Cambridge, MA: Harvard University Press, 1927.

Hesiod. *Theogony. Works and Days. Testimonia*. Edited and translated by Glenn W. Most. Loeb Classical Library. Cambridge, MA and London: Harvard University Press, 2007.

Homer. *The Illiad*. Translated by A.T. Murray. 2 Vols. Loeb Classical Library. Cambridge, MA and London: Harvard University Press, 1924.

Homer. *The Odyssey*. Translated by E. V. Rieu. Revised by D. C. H. Rieu in consultation with Peter V. Jones. London: Penguin Books, 1991.

Livy. *History of Rome*. Translated by B. O. Foster, Evan T, Sage, Frank Gardner Moore, Alfred Cary Schlesinger, Julius Obsequens, and J.C. Yardley. 12 Vols. Loeb Classical Library. Cambridge, MA and London: Harvard University Press, 1919–2018.

Long, A. A. and D. N. Sedley. *The Hellenistic Philosophers*. Cambridge and New York: Cambridge University Press, 1989.

Lucretius. *On The Nature of Things*. Translated by W. H. D. Rouse. Revised by Martin Ferguson Smith. Loeb Classical Library. Cambridge, MA and London: Harvard University Press, 1992.

Marcus Aurelius. *Meditations*. Translated with notes by Martin Hammond. London: Penguin Classics, 2006.

Plutarch. *Plutarch's Lives*. Translated by Bernadotte Perrin. 11 Vols. Loeb Classical Library. Cambridge, MA: Harvard University Press, 1916.

Seneca. *Epistles*. Translated by Richard M. Gummere. 3 Vols. Loeb Classical Library. Cambridge, MA and London: Harvard University Press, 1917–25.

———. *Moral Essays*. Translated by John W. Basore. 3 Vols. Loeb Classical Library. Cambridge, MA and London: Harvard University Press, 1928–35.

———. *Natural Questions*. Translated by Thomas H. Corcoran. 2 Vols. Loeb Classical Library. Cambridge, MA and London: Harvard University Press, 1971–2.

Simplicius, of Cilicia. *On Epictetus Handbook*. Translated by Charles Brittain & Tad Brennan. 2 Vols. Ithaca, NY: Cornell University Press, 2002.

Thucydides. *History of the Peloponnesian War*. Translated by Rex Warner. London: Penguin Classics, 1974.

Plato. *Euthyphro. Apology. Crito. Phaedo*. Translated by Harold North Fowler. Loeb Classical Library. Cambridge, MA and London: Harvard University Press, 1914.

Plato. *Parmenides, Philebus, Symposium, Phaedrus*. Translated by Harold N. Fowler. Loeb Classical Library. Cambridge, MA and London: Harvard University Press, 1925.

Plato. *The Republic*. Translated by Paul Shorey. 2 Vols. Loeb Classical Library. Cambridge, MA and London: Harvard University Press, 1963.

Plato. *The Symposium*. Translated by M. C. Howatson. Edited by Frisbee C. C. Sheffield. Cambridge: Cambridge University Press, 2008.

Modern Sources

Annas, Julia. *The Morality of Happiness*. Oxford: Oxford University Press, 1995.

Ansell-Pearson, Keith. "Heroic-Idyllic Philosophizing: Nietzsche and the Epicurean Tradition." *Royal Institute of Philosophy Supplements* 74 (2014): 237–263.

——— ed. "Nietzsche & Epicureanism." Special issue, *The Agonist* 10, no. 2 (2017).

———. "True to the Earth: Nietzsche's Epicurean Care of Self and World." In *Nietzsche's Therapeutic Teaching*, edited by Horst Hutter and Eli Friedland, 97–116. London: Bloomsbury, 2013.

———. "A Melancholy Science?: On Bergson's Appreciation of Lucretius." *Pli* 27 (2015): 83–101.

Arendt, Hannah. *The Human Condition*. Chicago: University of Chicago Press, 1958.

Armstrong, Aurelia. "The Passions, Power, and Practical Philosophy: Spinoza and Nietzsche Contra the Stoics." *Journal of Nietzsche Studies* 44 no. 1, (2013): 6–24.

Auerbach, Erich. "*Passio* as Passion." Translated by Martin Elsky, *Criticism* 43, no. 3 (2001): 288–308.

Berry, Jessica. *Nietzsche and the Ancient Skeptical Tradition*. New York: Oxford University Press, 2011.

Bett, Richard. "Nietzsche, the Greeks, and Happiness (with Special Reference to Aristotle and Epicurus)." *Philosophical Topics* 33, no. 2 (2005): 45–70.

Blumenberg, Hans. *Shipwreck with Spectator: Paradigm of a Metaphor for Existence*. Cambridge, MA: MIT Press, 1997.

Branham, R. Bracht. "Nietzsche's Cynicism: Uppercase or lowercase?" In *Nietzsche and Antiquity: His Reaction and Response to the Classical Tradition*, edited by Paul Bishop, 170–81. Rochester, NY: Camden House, 2004.

Brobjer, Thomas H. "Nietzsche's Reading of Epictetus." *Nietzsche-Studien* 32, no. 1 (2008): 429–52

———. *Nietzsche's Philosophical Context*. Urbana and Chicago: University of Illinois Press, 2008.

Brown, P. Michael, ed. *De Rerum Natura III*. Warminster: Aris & Phillips, 1997.

Brunschwig, Jacques. "The Cradle Argument in Epicureanism and Stoicism." In *The Norms of Nature*, edited by Malcolm Schofield and Gisela Striker, 113–44. Cambridge: Cambridge University Press, 1986.

Came, Daniel. "The Themes of Affirmation and Illusion in *The Birth of Tragedy* and Beyond." In *The Oxford Handbook of Nietzsche*, edited by Ken Gemes and John Richardson, 209–25. Oxford: Oxford University Press, 2013.

Capellanus, Andreas. *De Amore*. edited and translated by P. G. Walsh. London: Duckworth, 1982.

Carson, Anne. *Eros the Bittersweet*. Princeton: Princeton University Press, 1986.

Carvalho, John. "Improvisations, on Nietzsche, on Jazz." In *Nietzsche, Philosophy and the Arts*, edited by Salim Kemal, Ivan Gaskell, and Daniel W. Conway, 187–211. Cambridge: Cambridge University Press, 1998.

Caygill, Howard. "Under the Epicurean Skies." *Angelaki* 11, no. 3 (2006): 107–15.

Clark, Maudemarie. *Nietzsche on Truth and Philosophy*. Cambridge: Cambridge University Press, 1990.

Cooper, Laurence D. *Eros in Plato, Rousseau, and Nietzsche: The politics of infinity*. University Park, Pennsylvania: Pennsylvania State University Press, 2008.

De Rougemont, Denis. *Love in the Western World*. New York: Pantheon, 1956.

Davidson, Arnold I. "Ethics as Ascetics." in *The Cambridge Companion to Foucault*, edited by Gary Gutting, 123–48. Cambridge: Cambridge University Press, 2005.

Elveton, R. O. "Nietzsche's Stoicism: The Depths Are Inside." In *Nietzsche and Antiquity: His Reaction and Response to the Classical Tradition*, edited by Paul Bishop, 192–204. Rochester, NY: Camden House, 2004.

Emden, Christian J. "Toward a Critical Historicism: History and Politics in Nietzsche's Second 'Untimely Meditation'." *Modern Intellectual History* 3, no. 1 (2006):1–31.

Farrington, B. "The Meanings of *voluptas* in Lucretius." *Hermathena*, no. 80 (1952): 26–31.

Faustino, Marta. Review of *Kulturkritik et philosophie thérapeutique chez le jeune Nietzsche*, by Martine Béland. *Journal of Nietzsche Studies* 47, no. 3 (2016): 488-492.

Feinberg, Joel. "Harm to Others," In *The Metaphysics of Death*, edited by John Martin Fischer, 171–91. Stanford: Stanford University Press, 1984.

Foucault, Michel. *The History of Sexuality*. Vol. 3, *The Care of The Self*. New York: Pantheon Books, 1986.

———. *The Courage of Truth*. Translated by Graham Burchall. Basingstoke, UK and New York: Palgrave Macmillan, 2011.

Freud, Sigmund. *Psychopathology of Everyday Life*. 2nd ed. London: Ernest Benn Limited, 1948.

Gemes, Ken. "Freud and Nietzsche on Sublimation." *Journal of Nietzsche Studies* 38 (2009): 38–59.

Gill, Christopher. *The Structured Self in Hellenistic and Roman Thought*. Oxford: Oxford University Press, 2006.

———. "Psychology." In *The Cambridge Companion to Epicureanism*, edited by James Warren, 125–41. Cambridge: Cambridge University Press, 2009.

Hadot, Pierre. *What is Ancient Philosophy?* Translated by Michael Chase. Cambridge, MA: Belknap Press, 2004.

———. *Philosophy as a Way of Life: Spiritual Exercises from Socrates to Foucault*. Translated by Michael Chase. Oxford: Blackwell, 1995.

Halliwell, Stephen. *Greek Laughter: A Study of Cultural Psychology from Homer to Early Christianity*. Cambridge: Cambridge University Press, 2008.

Hatab, Lawrence J. *Nietzsche's Life Sentence*. New York and London: Routledge, 2005.

———. "Nietzsche, Nature, and Life Affirmation." In *Nietzsche and the Becoming of Life*, edited by Vanessa Lemm, 32–48. New York: Fordham University Press, 2015.

Hegel, Georg Wilhelm Friedrich. *The Philosophy of History*. Translated by John Sibree. Mineola, NY: Dover, 1956.

Hobbs, Angela. *Plato and the Hero: Courage, Manliness, and the Impersonal Good*. Cambridge: Cambridge University Press, 2000.

Hutter, Horst and Eli Friedland, eds. *Nietzsche's Therapeutic Teaching: For Individuals and Culture*. London: Bloomsbury, 2013.

Inwood, Brad and Pierluigi Donini. "Stoic Ethics." In *The Cambridge History of Hellenistic Philosophy*, 675–738. Cambridge: Cambridge University Press, 1999.

Inwood, Michael J. "Hartmann, Eduard von (1842–1906)." In *The Oxford Companion to Philosophy*, ed. Ted Honderich, 2nd ed, 361. Oxford: Oxford University Press, 2005.

Janaway, Christopher. "The Gay Science." In *The Oxford Handbook of Nietzsche*, edited by Ken Gemes and John Richardson, 267–9. Oxford: Oxford University Press, 2013.

Jensen, Anthony K. "The Rogue of All Rogues: Nietzsche's Presentation of Eduard von Hartmann's *Philosophie des Unbewussten* and Hartmann's Response to Nietzsche." *Journal of Nietzsche Studies* 32 (2006): 41–61.

Jenkins, Scott. "Life, Injustice, and Recurrence." In *Nietzsche and the Becoming of Life*, edited by Vanessa Lemm, 121–36. New York: Fordham University Press, 2015.

Kaufmann, Walter. *Nietzsche: Philosopher, Psychologist, Antichrist*. Princeton and Oxford: Princeton University Press, 2013.

Kenney, E. J., ed. *De Rerum Natura Book III*. Cambridge: Cambridge University Press, 1971.

Lange, Friedrich Albert. *The History of Materialism*. 3 Vols. London: Routledge & K Paul, 2010.

Loeb, Paul S. "Eternal Recurrence." In *The Oxford Handbook of Nietzsche*, edited by Ken Gemes and John Richardson, 645–671. Oxford: Oxford University Press, 2013.

———. *The Death of Nietzsche's Zarathustra*. Cambridge: Cambridge University Press, 2010.

Magee, Bryan. *Wagner and Philosophy*. London: Penguin, 2001.

Magnus, Bernd. "Nietzsche's Eternalistic Counter-Myth." *The Review of Metaphysics* 26, no. 4 (1973), 604–16.

Montinari, Mazzino. *Reading Nietzsche*. Translated by Greg Whitlock. Urbana: University of Illinois Press, 2003.

Most, Glenn W. "Six Remarks on Platonic Eros." In *Erotikon: Essays on Eros, Ancient and Modern*, edited by Shadi Bartsch and Thomas Bartscherer, 33–47. Chicago: University of Chicago Press, 2005.

Nabais, Nuno. "Nietzsche and Stoicism." Chap 4 in *Nietzsche & the Metaphysics of the Tragic*. London: Continuum, 2006.

Nagel, Thomas. "Death." *Noûs* 4, no. 1 (1970): 73–80.

Nehamas, Alexander. *Nietzsche: Life As Literature*. Cambridge, MA: Harvard University Press, 1985.

Nietzsche, Friedrich. *The Will to Power*. Translated by Walter Kaufmann and R. J. Hollingdale. New York: Vintage Books, 1968.

———. *Philosophy and Truth: Selections from Nietzsche's Notebooks of the early 1870's*. Edited and translated by Daniel Breazeale. New Jersey and London: Humanities Press International, 1990.

———. "On the Relationship of Alcibiades' Speech to the Other Speeches in Plato's Symposium." *Graduate Faculty Philosophy Journal* 15, no. 2 (1991), 3–5.

Nussbaum, Martha C. "Pity and Mercy: Nietzsche's Stoicism." In *Nietzsche, Genealogy, Morality*, edited by Richard Schacht, 139–67. Berkeley: University of California Press, 1994.

———. *The Therapy of Desire: Theory and Practice in Hellenistic Ethics*. Princeton, Princeton University Press, 1994.

———. "The Speech of Alcibiades: A Reading of Plato's Symposium." *Philosophy and Literature* 3, no. 2 (1979): 131–72.

Parsons, Bethany and Andre Okawara, eds. "Self-Cultivation: Ancient and Modern." Special issue, *Pli* (2016).

Pembroke, S. G. "Oikeiôsis." In *Problems in Stoicism*, edited by A. A. Long, 114–149. London and Atlantic Highlands: The Athlone Press, 1971.

Pippin, Robert B. *Nietzsche, Psychology and First Philosophy*. Chicago: University of Chicago Press, 2006.

———. Review of *The Affirmation of Life: Nietzsche on Overcoming Nihilism* by Bernard Reginster. *Philosophy and Phenomenological Research* 77, no. 1 (2008): 281–291.

Porter, James I. "Epicurean Attachments: Life, Pleasure, Beauty, Friendship and Piety." *Cronache Ercolanesi* 33 (2003): 205–27.

Reginster, Bernard. *The Affirmation of Life: Nietzsche on Overcoming Nihilism*. Cambridge, MA: Harvard University Press, 2006.

Reydams-Schils, Gretchen. *The Roman Stoics: Self, Responsibility, and Affection*. Chicago and London: The University of Chicago Press, 2005.

Rosen, Stanley. *The Quarrel between Philosophy and Poetry*. New York and London: Routledge, 1988.

———. *The Mask of Enlightenment: Nietzsche's Zarathustra*. New Haven and London: Yale University Press, 2004.

Rousseau, Jean-Jacques. *Julie, or, The new Heloise*. Hanover, NH: University Press of New England, 1997.

Rutherford, Donald. "Freedom as a Philosophical Ideal: Nietzsche and His Antecedents." *Inquiry* 54, no. 5 (2011): 512–540.

Ryan, Thomas and Michael Ure. "Nietzsche's Post-Classical Therapy." *Pli* 25 (2014): 91–110.

Saul, Nicholas. *The Cambridge Companion to German Romanticism*. Cambridge: Cambridge University Press, 2009.

Schlegel, Friedrich. *Lucinde and the Fragments*. Translated by Peter Firchow. Minneapolis: University of Minneapolis Press, 1971.

Sellars, John. "Marcus Aurelius in Contemporary Philosophy." In *A Companion to Marcus Aurelius*, edited by Marcel van Ackeren, 532–44. Chichester, UK and Malden, MA: Wiley-Blackwell, 2012.

———. *The Art of Living: The Stoics on the Nature and Function of Philosophy*. Aldershot: Ashgate, 2003.

———. *Stoicism*. Chesham: Acumen, 2006.

———. "The Point of View of the Cosmos: Deleuze, Romanticism, Stoicism." *Pli* 8 (1999): 1–24.

———. "An Ethics of the Event: Deleuze's Stoicism." *Angelaki* 11, no. 3 (2006): 157–71.

Shapiro, Gary. *Nietzsche's Earth: Great Events, Great Politics*. Chicago: University of Chicago Press, 2016.

Singer, Irving. *The Nature of Love*. 3 Vols. Cambridge and London: MIT Press, 2009.

Sommer, Andreas Urs. "Nietzsche's Readings on Spinoza: A Contextualist Study, Particularly on the Reception of Kuno Fischer." *Journal of Nietzsche Studies* 43, no. 2 (2012): 156–84.

Sorabji, Richard. *Emotions and Peace of Mind: From Stoic Agitation to Christian Temptation*. Oxford: Oxford University Press, 2000.

Strauss, Leo. *Leo Strauss On Plato's Symposium*. Chicago: University of Chicago Press, 2001.

Taub, Liba. "Cosmology and Meteorology." In *The Cambridge Companion to Epicureanism*, edited by James Warren, 105–124. Cambridge: Cambridge University Press, 2009..

Tsouna, Voula. "Epicurean therapeutic strategies." In *The Cambridge Companion to Epicureanism*, edited by James Warren, 249–65. Cambridge: Cambridge University Press, 2009.

Ure, Michael. *Nietzsche's Therapy: Self-Cultivation in the Middle Works*. Lanham: Lexington Books, 2008.

———. "Nietzsche's Free-Spirit Trilogy and Stoic Therapy." *Journal of Nietzsche Studies* 38 (2009): 60-84.

———. "Sublime Losers: Stoicism in Nineteenth Century German Philosophy." In *The Routledge Handbook of the Stoic Tradition*, edited by John Sellars, 287–302. London: Routledge, 2015.

———. "Senecan Moods: Foucault and Nietzsche on the Art of the Self." *Foucault Studies* 4 (2007): 19-52.

———. "Stoicism in Nineteenth-Century German Philosophy." In *The Routledge Handbook of the Stoic Tradition*, edited by John Sellars, 287–302. London: Routledge, 2015.

Vlastos, Gregory. *Socrates, Ironist and Moral Philosopher*. Ithaca, NY: Cornell University Press, 1991.

Warren, James. "Lucretian Palingenesis Recycled." *The Classical Quarterly* 51, no. 2 (2001): 499–508.

Williams, Bernard, ed. *The Gay Science: With a Prelude in German Rhymes and an Appendix of Songs*. Cambridge: Cambridge University Press, 2001.

———. *Truth and Truthfulness*. Princeton: Princeton University Press, 2002.

Wilson, Catherine. *Epicureanism at the Origins of Modernity*. Cambridge: Cambridge University Press, 2008.

CPSIA information can be obtained
at www.ICGtesting.com
Printed in the USA
BVHW070636130223
658295BV00014B/1366